www.AbneyPark.com, robert@AbneyPark.com

Text set in Times New Roman

Designed by Robert H. Brown

Cover art by Robert H. Brown

RETROGRADE

by
"Captain" Robert Brown

Illustrations by
Juan Pablo Valdecantos Anfuso

CONTENTS

PREFACE

Despite what you might think, one man *can* change the world. You can look at it as it is, decide where you think it doesn't work, or doesn't fit your taste, map out how you would like it to be and what it would take to get the world from where it is now to where you want it to be.

Then you set your plan in motion, making little tweaks here, setting up little systems there, until the whole world is working towards changing itself. If you get enough gears turning, each gear setting others in motion, before long there are things working towards your goals that you know nothing about.

While you are changing the world for the better, saving it from itself, correcting where it has gone astray, it will seem like an impossibly monumental task. But just as you're on the verge of giving up, you'll find you've succeeded! You will have made an entirely new world, just as you imagined it should be.

I have done this.

However, this world might not appreciate your efforts, as it sometimes seems it doesn't appreciate mine. Some will say it wasn't you who changed the world after all. "The world was heading this way with or without you!" they will say. But that doesn't explain the strangely specific way it has conformed to all of your very eclectic and specific tastes and morals. Despite that *In The Beginning There Was Nothing,* and so you decided to make a world in your own image, and in the end, sure enough, there was a world that exactly fit your plans...for some reason they will claim that this was not your doing!

Others will be angry that it *was* you, and you didn't do it exactly how *they* would have liked it done. (I've even had people tell me both that I had not done it AND that I did it in a way they didn't approve of. The world is full of fools who contradict themselves and don't even see it.)

Sure, many will thank you profusely, but those aren't the ones that will stick in your head. For every thousand bits of praise you receive you'll also have one dissenter, and that will eat you up, gnawing at your soul until you can't stand the world or yourself. It's these dissenters who, through jealousy, through boredom, or through a need to make themselves important, incite the crowds to all throw stones, until finally you are running from your new perfect world, as fast as feet will carry you.

Even if you escape the angry throngs of the new Utopia, what then? Do you live in solitude, far away from the perfect world you created? If you do this, you might return to find that the world you created has corrupted into a disgusting manifestation of your vision. Or do you slink back into your world, and await your own execution? For you will be killed. Eventually all worlds kill their creators.

- Victor Hippocrates

Retrograde

A heroine, a deity,
On heroin, or vanity,
To jack their personality
Beyond normal humanity.

A crowd of massed humanity,
Bow and worship diligently.
He's built a loyal following
And they steer him thoroughly.

But jealous man plots from the pews,
No need for valid righteousness.
One slightly truthful word set free,
Will turn the tides quite easily.

Our accusations need not be
What would bury mortal man.
The sins of our own deity
Are tiny, but on these we stand.

So once upon the podium,
A crucifix we then erect,
And nail our hero heartily,
Hands and feet, we bind his neck.

The reasons for our worship fade,
Our Idol drenched in his own blood,
Forgotten are the virtues that we
Valued beyond royalty.

With joy we dig his shallow grave,
Anticipating pains to come.

We watch the wriggling dance of death,
And laugh lighthearted at Death's fun.

We pounded out the joyous light.
Our savior's buried now for years.
A legend now of time gone by,
A martyr of forgotten tears.

- From the song Stigmata Martyr

DEPARTURE

Two thousand feet above the Black Forest hung a pirate ship. Its intricately carved railings, dozens of protruding cannon, white sails, and complex network of rope ladders and rigging could belong to nothing else. Unexpectedly, the masts and crow's nests of this ship hung out of the bottom where you would normally find water. Above the hull, where you would expect the masts to be, was a massive canvas balloon roughly the shape of a fifty-yard-long football holding the vessel aloft.

As beautiful as she was, this was a ship in trouble. The year was 1943, and the world was at war. German fighter planes circled the ship, filling her wooden sides with bullets the size of sticks of butter, and sending many of her Victorian sailors plummeting to their deaths. This pirate ship did not belong in this time, and it was paying the price.

Deep inside the ship was a wispy girl of twenty-two, who

took little notice of the chaos around her. She was angry, bitter at being ignored during all this, and in her anger she decided that now was the time to leave. She threw open the door of her cabin (where she had been pouting angrily over the fact that nobody had noticed she was in her cabin pouting) and pulled a very large suitcase full of very small clothes down the narrow hallway that led to the rear of the ship.

The hallway shuddered, and one of the walls burst open in a series of one-inch round holes. Sunlight streamed in through them, forming beams of light in the now smoky corridor. She didn't pause. She was confident those bullets wouldn't dare touch her, given the mood she was in. Being killed by a stray bullet was beneath her. She was of course right–or this would be a very short chapter–but just how close those bullets had come to popping her open like a piñata she would never know. One actually pulled through the tousled red hair on her pretty little head, and tickled her as it did so. All Lilith was aware of was that her hair was "bothering her", so she pulled a leather flight helmet out and put it on, arranging her red bangs and ponytails to protrude attractively from under it.

At the end of the hall, up a nearly vertical set of stairs, a hatch opened, and threw even more sunlight into the hall, while amplifying the sounds of men yelling and running on deck. A pair of boots came down the stairs, followed by legs, kilt, and finally a man. His scarred face was covered with blood, and he paused when he saw Lilith.

"Tanner," she said impatiently. "Take this." She nodded toward the large suitcase she had been dragging behind her.

"But I've got to find the Doctor–" he began to say, but

11

she interrupted coolly.

"Later. I'm leaving. I've had enough of this ship." She was going to add, *People should be thanking me, not ignoring me–I'm everyone's favorite!* But she realized this made no sense slightly before she said it, and chose to be blunt instead.

Tanner looked towards Doctor Calgori's room, then at the insistent and poisonous look on Lilith's beautiful face. Lilith was far more persuasive to him than an old scientist he could not see, so he took the bag, and hoped Calgori could wait.

He followed her down the hall, and around a corner to a maintenance door. He knew where they were going. He had carried many things here before, all under Lilith's stern orders.

Lilith reached for the door handle, but as she did, an explosion rang out from somewhere far above them, and the ship swung violently, knocking them both into the walls. Tanner's head was thrown against a low rafter and cut open. He dropped the suitcase to wipe the blood out of his eyes.

"Fine," Lilith said, irritated, and she stooped to pick the case up again. She threw open the hatch, and the door swung open to reveal a small basket-shaped gondola suspended between two glass globes. The basket was also tied to a large cloth bundle of parachute fabric she had scavenged weeks before. She threw her suitcase into the basket and climbed in.

He looked at her expectantly. He was waiting for her to invite him to join her. They had never spoken about his going along, but he had assumed all of his help was for "them," not just for her. Assumed...or wished.

This had never occurred to Lilith. From the time she was born, she had been accustomed to people doing things for her because she was beautiful. When she hit puberty women started to become cold to her, but men began to go to comical lengths to find ways to help her. Over the past year, Tanner had her fairly convinced that, with his help, she could have her own ship to captain. Lilith wasn't sure she even wanted that, but she had accepted his help nonetheless.

After months of him helping her prepare, she was ready to leave. Not bothering to say a word, not even bothering to look back over her shoulder, she reached above her and pulled a handle. The handle pulled a rope through a pulley that was attached to the clamp which held the basket in place. The clamp opened, and Lilith was suddenly falling, basket, globes, suitcase and all.

As she fell, the ropes around her straightened, and when they were tight, they pulled the huge bundle of parachute silk from where it was attached to the side of the pirate ship, and it broke free as well. The unraveling ropes tangled around her wrist and arm, pulling her off her feet as they sent the basket spinning. She strained to look up, and saw the parachute above her had ripped, and was not fully inflating. The bottom of the pirate ship was shrinking in the sky above her at an alarming rate.

On the side of the basket, a clockwork was mounted. This had been stolen from the ship's doctor a month prior, and he had never noticed. He had also failed to notice when she had torn a page containing his travel calculations from his notebook. She had used this page to set the clockwork. This was not a simple task, but Lilith was clever and driven, if not modest. Now she strained to reach the throw-switch on the side of it, but she couldn't reach it.

In a panicked moment of desperation, she kicked at the switch with her foot, and managed to knock it into the "on" position.

Instantly the orbs filled with a pink gas the color of clouds just before a lightning storm. As they did, the air around her grew deathly cold and formed a cloud that encompassed her basket.

From far above, Tanner saw the clouds form. He saw the parachute pulled rapidly into them, but he never saw anything come out again. When the clouds finally parted, all they revealed was empty air, and the ground beneath them.

Lilith Tess reappeared, alive. This was a fairly miraculous thing. As you travel through time, your body does not magically stay in the same relationship to the earth that it had when you left. The earth spins on its axis, and the earth whirls around the sun at a frantic rate. Disappearing from one time and reappearing in another, odds are that you will appear in the black of space, with the earth on the other side of its orbit somewhere. Even if you do get close to the correct time and date so that the earth will be in the same position of its rotation as when you left, it is far more likely you will emerge deep inside the planet, rather than in the thin crust of atmosphere that is so comfortable for us living things.

But, unbeknownst to captain or crew, Lilith had been taking classes in time travel from Doctor Calgori, the man who had invented and operated our time travel device. I can't say Lilith mastered the science of this, but clearly she spent enough time pretending to learn this delicate art from the good Doctor to trick him into doing the calculations for her. She was very good at getting men to do things for her.

So she appeared alive, and that's something.

But that was the end of her good luck. When she appeared, she was plummeting toward the earth, arms tangled in the ropes of a parachute that was failing to inflate. She was falling so quickly that her ears couldn't pop fast enough, and they were now bleeding and hurt excruciatingly. Fear overwhelmed her. She could lean her head over enough to see the ground coming at her, and knew she had seconds to live. The last thing she remembered before she hit was seeing the trees give way to glossy blackness.

A horrible impact sent the basket up to crumple her body, shattering her legs under her. She was now icy cold, disoriented, and couldn't breathe. Her body was floating slowly in blackness. As she tried to draw a breath, her lungs burned and she choked. She hoped she would die soon because the pain was too much to bear.

Something tangled her legs, and started to pull them down. Her arms came free of the ropes, but something else wrapped around her wrist and started pulling her in the opposite direction, which shot excruciating pain through her shattered legs. She tried to scream in pain, but her mouth and lungs were full of water, and so she just thrashed about in dizzying agony.

Finally, whatever was tangled on her legs slipped loose, and something slipped under her armpits, and before she knew what was happening, her face was out of the water. She coughed water up from her lungs, and soon she was breathing painfully. She was still alive, and she was grateful enough for that miracle that she didn't notice that she was no longer alone.

Under her, swimming strongly, was a young man of twenty-two. He had seen the parachute falling and run for the lake. In fact, he had jumped in before she hit, and had swum out to meet her.

From his standpoint, this scenario was too good to be true. Victor had been painfully bored and angry on his parents' trip to Germany. He hated being dragged along on these trips almost as much as he hated his parents. At lunch, he had once again found himself in an argument with them over their careers. He had screamed at them for, "buying beautiful land, and stripping it, and killing it, and replacing it with concrete and steel, and shopping malls, and factories, and poisoning the air, skies, and animals that had once lived there!"

His father had stood and yelled back that, "Well you sure as hell don't complain when it pays for all this life you enjoy so goddamn much," and "that school, which costs more than my parents made in their whole life! They grew up in the Depression, and they taught me how to appreciate things!"

This made Victor stand up and yell back that he "didn't need the damn schools to tell him how his own parents were destroying the planet," which was, "worse than genocide! Worse than Nazis!" This made the white-coated, white-gloved, stern German waiters all stop and glare. This made his mother turn red and scream at Victor, which made Victor throw his napkin on the table, and storm off into the pretty little field that led down the pretty little hillside towards the pretty little lake.

Just at the point where he had started to calm down, and was starting to get bored again, and had walked so far from the restaurant that he was wondering how he could get back, he saw what he mistook for a burst hot air balloon. It was falling towards the lake. He assumed someone was inside, and needed rescuing, and *that* was something *interesting* to do.

He was a wonderfully strong swimmer, so he ran to the lake and jumped in. He watched the basket hit from a few yards away while treading water, and then swam into the fray to find whomever needed saving. When he saw the figure twisting and writhing in the ropes of the balloon, he was stunned. This was not some grizzled old German balloonist as he had pictured, but perhaps the most beautiful girl he would ever set eyes on.

This had just become the best day of his young life.

But things became terrifying, fast. The water was turning red with her blood, and her legs were bending in places legs shouldn't bend, as they were pulled deeper, tangled in the basket ropes. All he could do was grab her wrists, and pull, and swim, and hope she slid loose.

Eventually she did, and he put his arms under hers, and kicked, and floated on his back so she could breathe. Once she was breathing air, he confidently swam to shore, and pulled the delicate and crushed beauty into the grass.

Lilith looked up at her angel, this flawless Adonis who had just saved her, and her perspective on the world changed forever. This was not a lesser being to be manipulated, as she had previously seen all men. He was easily her equal in beauty, and he had just saved her life. As she lay crushed and in pain, he was calmly handling things. He was like a prince from a fairy tale: beautifully, confidently, saving her life in a romantic land. The last five minutes had changed so much of Lilith's perspective on the way the world worked, she would have to start over.

As she slipped into unconsciousness, she knew only two things: she was alive, and she was forever in love.

RETROGRADE

AWAKE AT LAST

Victor watched Lilith sleep. As she lay on the grass near the lake, he held her hand. He dried her with his clothes, which he had discarded before he leapt into the water. He took her pulse. He pressed his ear to her breast, and listened to her waterlogged, raspy breathing.

This was not the right thing to do. The right thing to do was to carry her directly to a hospital, but something about the foreignness of the situation made him feel isolated, as if it was his job alone to heal her. But after what felt like hours, Victor began to realize that he was running out of things he could do to help her. That's when she woke.

"Are you okay?" he asked, because there was nothing else to ask, but he immediately felt stupid for doing so. She looked terrified, hideous and beautiful. Her ankles were bent at odd angles, skin bleached white as it stretched over nearly protruding bones. Her legs and arms were bleeding, and her hair was matted with blood. Her eyes pleaded to him for something he couldn't easily grant: reassurance.

This strengthened him, and focused him in a way he had never been strong before. He became falsely confident, seeing that was what this broken beauty needed most from him. He smiled back at her, and when he did, his eyes sparkled and said, *With me here, nothing more can happen to you.* He scooped her up in his arms and carried her.

For miles he carried her, past the lake, through the grassy meadow, and up the hill to the inn where he was staying with his parents. Some part of him knew that if he took her inside, someone else would drive her to the hospital, and he'd never see her again. *She needs me,* he thought to himself, though there was no rationale for this. So instead of taking her inside, he set her on the seat of his father's convertible. He flashed her a look of reassurance, and ran into the large carved wooden entrance of the hotel.

In a moment he was back with the keys he had stolen from his father's nightstand. He started the car, which made poor Lilith jump slightly. She'd never been in a car before, and even the cars she'd seen on the streets of London in 1906 looked and sounded nothing like this 2011 Mercedes. It purred, rather than sputtered, and nothing in it looked like it was made by man. But she was in so much pain from her broken legs she spent no time thinking about it. In fact, her feet were now in a pool of blood on the floor of the car, and she was slowly losing consciousness again.

He drove her to a nearby hospital, skidded to a halt in front of the main entrance, and carried her up the front steps while the car still idled in the drive. By now her clothes and hair were dry of the lake water, but she was soaked with her own blood, and would not be conscious again for days.

The following day, Victor's father noticed his car was gone. Finding his keys missing from his nightstand, he guessed that his son had taken it. In this family, this was not a simple matter of borrowing the car without permission. In this family, this was theft, and it was unforgivable.

After a long evening of pacing and ranting to his wife, red-faced, veins popping on his temples, Victor's father declared, "That spoiled brat of a son has left the nest. So be it. A summer on his own in Europe might teach him something we could not. Let that car be his final support from me. He can sell it, and live off the money until he learns respect, or self reliance, or humility."

Victor's father considered this gift of a car a great charity. A last fatherly gift as his son set out in the world. He had always intended to send his son off with a small savings, from which a wise young man would start his first business.

To Victor's mother, this was all a tragedy beyond measure. Worse than a son dying in war, she was now torn apart from the boy she loved, and had given life to. But she feared her husband too much to defy him. She was not a strong woman.

To Victor, this was simply time forgotten. When he returned to the inn a few days later, he expected a fight. He expected reprimand, and discipline. But instead, he found that his parents had left Germany entirely. This added abandonment to the crimes he saw his parents commit, and this pain fueled him.

Victor sat next to the white hospital bed holding Lilith's hand. The hospital staff assumed they were American newlyweds who had been in an accident on their honeymoon. Unsurprising to them, this cocky young American boy spoke nothing but English. When Victor stammered out something about a burst balloon, and a fall, nurses and doctors concocted a story that was far more believable than the truth, and they were satisfied with the story they invented.

Victor held Lilith's hand for days. Late one night, he woke to find Lilith staring at him. She remembered him from the day of her fall, mostly because she had been dreaming of him every day since. As she looked at him, her pale face barely illuminated by the lights of machines on stands nearby, she seemed to see all the thoughts in his head, and her expression seemed to show she knew more about his sacrifice than he did.

"Thank you," she said.

"You're welcome," he replied. "Are you strong enough to talk? You've been asleep for days."

"I, I think so. I'd like to try," she said. "Honestly, I feel a bit restless."

"What's your name?"

"Lilith. Lilith Tess."

"I'm Victor Ha..." Victor was going to say, "Victor Hackett," his birth name, but in the days he had been sitting here watching Lilith, he had spent a lot of time thinking about the fight with his parents. He was ashamed of his family. So he lied.

"Victor Hippocrates," he said. He had read the last name on a bust in the front hall of the hospital. "Where did you...I mean, how did you come to fall in the lake?"

Lilith had learned when time traveling to never say more than you needed to. Leave things half-said and people will make up their own acceptable versions of the truth. So instead of fully explaining, she said, "My ropes broke, and I dropped." As soon as she finished saying this, she knew that her explanation was not going to be enough.

"I saw that, but how did you come to be in a balloon over Germany? You're English, aren't you? Why travel by balloon? Isn't that just an 'extreme sports' thing?"

"What? I'm not sure I follow you. I was traveling. I left my crew by parachute, but it malfunctioned, and dropped me in the lake."

Victor looked at her questioningly. "So *where* are you from? What brings a..." (he wanted to say *startlingly beautiful*) "...girl like you to a balloon over Germany?" In Victor's experience, beautiful girls never *did* anything. They were in the world to be waited upon, and pampered, and so they were of no interest to him. But not this girl. *This* girl was interesting.

"In your balloon's basket, I saw lots of antique

equipment. I'd never seen anything like this. It was cool, but why would you keep antiques in your balloon?"

"Do you have them?" she asked quickly, her eyes lighting up. "My things?"

"No. I assume they're at the bottom of the lake."

"Can you help me get them?"

"I'm sure we can. What are they?"

Lilith wanted to tell him the truth far more than she wanted to lie. She was tired, she was lonely, and she was tired of being lonely, so she inhaled deeply, and said, "It's a Chrononautilus. Think of it as map, compass, and cart, used for navigating time." These were the words Doctor Calgori had used when he started teaching the Chrononautilus to Lilith.

Now, Victor was a very young man, and Lilith was a beautiful young lady. He would have willingly believed her if she had told him she was a Unicorn. Also, Victor had a gift. He could read people in all sorts of ways. He could tell their skills just by looking at them, and he could see when people were telling the truth. Lilith was not lying.

This of course surprised Lilith, too. She wasn't sure why she didn't lie to him, and she was scared by the fact that he seemed to believe her, so she added, "I'm kidding."

Victor stared back with piercing blue eyes and said, "No, you're not." Then again he repeated, "*Where* are you from?"

"I'm from England. Actually, I was born in Scotland in 1886. I'm now twenty-two." She waited for him to do the math in his head, and call her a liar. When he didn't, she went on. "I stowed away on a tall ship I found in the Port of London, in 1906. It turned out not to be a military ship headed for America, but a scientific experiment. It had been fitted with a clockwork that allowed it to travel through time."

"That's incredible," said Victor in a calm voice, pretending it was only moderately amazing to a worldly man such as himself.

"On our first week out, the captain was killed. After that it was easy to pretend to be a member of the crew. We traveled the world, to different places and times. It was exciting, but I was not appreciated, and I was lonely. So I made friends with the old man who built the Chrononautilus, and from him I was able to learn to set it. Then I stole enough pieces of it to assemble my own, and I stole a spare parachute. I left the ship by parachute, but the chute's ropes tangled and I fell too fast."

"And that's when I found you? Amazing story."

"Yes." She looked at her hands. "All right, your turn. Tell me about who you are, and how you came to be in the lake."

"Well, I'm a student. I was born in 1989, and I'm twenty-two. My parents dragged me along with them on one of their work trips. They're land developers. They purchase beautiful parts of the world from poor families, cover the land with concrete, and build factories on it that pollute the environment and kill millions. Last year they helped hundreds out of their family farms, and replaced them with factory farms. Do you know what those are? Huge buildings that torture and kill animals. Do you know what they do to pigs, and cows, and chickens by the millions in those huge factories of death?"

"No."

"It's horrific! It's terrifying! It's torture! I've been in them, and I've seen. They slaughter animals when they are only a few months old! Still children! Creatures that would have lived nearly as long as people, and they are slaughtered after a few months of life. Slaughtered by the thousands! These animals are *practically* people, better than people in many ways. They deserve the same life as we have! It's the evilest side of man, and that's how mankind stays alive! Feeding on death."

Lilith had never heard animals talked about like this. At first she couldn't tell if he was joking or not. In the place and time she grew up, animals were livestock, food, workers sometimes. No one ever thought of them as people. But she could see the passion and pain in this young man's face, and she wanted to agree with him and comfort him. So she said, "That's terrible. Someone should do something!"

"Hah! What can be done? There are so many people in the world now. Even when I'm most optimistic, I can't imagine turning the entire world to vegetarians, or vegans." Here Lilith looked confused, but Victor didn't notice. "There are just too many people, and nearly all of them eat meat! Once, man hunted the same way that animals hunt. The world was fair, and balanced. We hunted animals, and animals hunted us, and we were part of the food-chain. But now there are too many of us to think hunting will feed us all, and no animals hunt us, so our numbers swell."

Victor continued, "There simply need to be less people. So then what do you do? You can't just kill people. In nature, predators and disease keep animal populations in check, but humans have no predators, and have nearly eliminated disease. I suppose you could stop them from reproducing, but even if you did, we'd still have this massive world full of concrete, and filth, and crowds of billions of people packed shoulder to shoulder as far as the eye can see."

Lilith looked down the row of hospital beds. There were perhaps 30 beds in this small room, filled with the sick, and nurses hurrying silently back and forth. She pictured Victor's description literally, and had a vision in her head that if she could see out her window, she'd see crowds of people in a land of black concrete. She shuddered. This *Future* seemed worse than any past she had been to.

Victor went on, "The world has gotten rich and bloated. Fat people, rolling in money and food, and doing whatever they can to rape the planet for more money and food. Someone has to stop them, before there is nothing left."

"Someone needs to change the world," Lilith said matter-of-factly.

Victor looked exasperated. "But how?"

"It's easy, changing the world. I've done that loads of times." Lilith said it casually.

Victor looked at her.

"Look, all you do is go back in time to before the world went amiss. Find the people, or circumstance, that will cause the world to go wrong, and put a stop to it. It's easy."

"But...the problem is that the world is out of balance! In nature, predators keep everything in balance, by thinning out the herd. Mankind has no predators. How would you keep the world from just becoming overpopulated again?"

WET ASHES

"Just when we thought we'd won
we were back to the start again,
With no wind in our sails
and the doldrums settin' in."
-excerpt from Post Apocalypse Punk

A very long time later, a pirate ship floated in a jade-colored sea. This ship is the same ship from the beginning of the book, none other than the *H.M.S. Ophelia*, and she had had a bad night. To look at her now, you'd think her tale was near an end.

Her balloon had been consumed by fire the night before, and it floated in the sea around her as wet ash. Inside of that balloon, the *Ophelia's* original masts had stood unused for years. You see, the *Ophelia* had been a sailing ship for a short time, and the balloon was added later. Now the masts stood above her decks, smoldering but proud. The ship's rigging crisscrossed the deck, still burning in spots. The ship's railing and decking were blackened, too, and it gave the ship a hardened feel like an old warrior covered with scars yet strong as mahogany.

The crew had collapsed exhausted the night before, and was now beginning to wake. They stirred around the deck, taking count of who still lived.

It was an odd bunch. There was a whiskery, ornery, one-eyed sailor called Mongrel, who never looked before he lunged, and who may or may not have killed the previous captain over the loss of his eye. He wore a faded leather patch over his eye socket, which always itched him.

There was Daniel, my old friend. He was one of the first I met on board the Ophelia, and always by my side to help. He was slim, six foot one with short blondish hair. He was career military, although *whose* military seemed to change from year to year, until he finally ended up amongst our ragtag crew.

There were two huge mountains of men, shirtless, bald and clad in gold bracers: Nieroo and Atoosh. Their skin was blue-black, and the only things deeper than their perfectly matching black eyes were their perfectly matched voices.

When I say their skin was blue-black, I don't mean that literally of course, but when I tell you of another whose skin was copper and brass, I do in fact mean that *literally*. His name was Gyrod, and he was strong, noble, tired, and sick. Gyrod had a four-inch hole in his head, from back to face. On a man, this would have been instantly fatal, but Gyrod was not easily subdued. He also had a broken gear in his chest. When he exerted himself, the gear had the tendency to seize up and stop him mid-stride. Gyrod did not dare pull the old gear out, for fear that it would end him, so he wore its replacement on a chain about his neck.

Also among the crew was a sixty-year-old scientist from another time. He was the man who had built Gyrod and his sister Timony, who was waiting in another part of the world for her brother's return. This old man had hair of mostly white, and his body was frail as he lay unconscious in the cold metal arms of Gyrod.

And there was me. I'm Captain Robert. I caused this whole mess. I had good intentions, but it's my fault nonetheless. I've got issues, it would seem. I need to be a hero, even when no hero is needed. Put a vessel like this under my command, and you can scarcely imagine the damage I can cause. I changed the world through perhaps unneeded heroics by going back and forth through time "rescuing the world" from its natural history. This had the unfortunate side effect of weakening the world, and now I am trapped in the result. I find myself after the fall of mankind (caused by me) in a land where mankind is constantly hunted, or enslaved in the name of "safety".

Let me describe my appearance. It'll help when you try to picture the jackass who set the world up for this fall by trying to be a hero. I'm six foot two, 220 pounds, and built like a football player. I've got pitch-black spiky hair, left over from a life before I was a ship's captain, when I was actually the singer in a band. I used to be a musician, and though that was long ago, I still write songs. Some of my lyrics you'll find strewn through this novel.

At the time of this story, I am around thirty-two, which never really bothered me, because that was about the age Han Solo was during the first Star Wars film. I was born in the 1970's, but that was a long time ago. Actually, well over a hundred and fifty years ago.

Now, if you haven't yet, you really should read the book that I wrote before this one. That book describes how I got the world into this mess. It's called "*The Wrath Of Fate*", and if you read that first, it'll save me a lot of time explaining as things go on.

Go on, read it now, I'll wait.

Finished reading it? See, I told you this was all my fault.

Gyrod, the brass man, had set Doctor Calgori to rest against some crates, and currently stood over a sea chest pulling out yard after yard of white canvas, using it to dry himself before the rust set in.

"Gyrod, what have you got there?" I asked.

"I am not sure," he replied. "Just dry fabric. I need to dry off before I patinate. I once had a sister named Patina..."

"Arr! Dem's da sails!" said the gravelly, cockney voice of Mongrel, almost as if he was doing a cartoon impression of a pirate. He even had an eye patch!

Historically speaking, it's quite possible Mongrel was the source of our caricature of pirates. He grew up in the West Country, in England during the 1880's, which is where the accent comes from. His parents both died in a pub fight (with each other) when he was 4, over his name. His father called him "Dog" in defiance of his mother, who named him Percival.

"Might as well call him Mongrel, since anyone in this pub could be his father!" his father had yelled on his final night. His father was not far off, but factually wrong. His mother, who could not have known for sure that his father was wrong, struck his father in the face with a spittoon, breaking his nose while simultaneous spilling its contents on a group of angry and drunken Irish sailors.

So Mongrel kept the name his father gave him on the day he died, and lived with his aunt until he was 13. After that, he got a job on a ship as a powder-monkey, and rarely set foot on land again.

"Do we have rope for those sails?" I asked Mongrel.

"Rigging? I can bloody well check!" he replied, and headed belowdecks excitedly.

Within an hour, Mongrel, myself, Gyrod, Daniel, Nieroo and Atoosh were hauling sails and rigging up the masts, which were still smoking in some places. This was not easy work. If you've never tried to lift a twenty-foot sail up the equivalent of a giant burning telephone pole, then you can't image the challenge. Couple that with the precarious height, then throw in some tropical sun causing your whole body to be lubricated with sweat, and the result is nerve-wracking and exhausting.

Another problem we were having was that Mongrel was really the only ocean sailor among us, and though he did his best to patiently explain things, it was nearly impossible to understand what he was barking at us.

"NO! The man-sel! Bloody 'ell! Dat's not even scriboard! Take the doo-key, and tick it frew de plankard! NO, NO, NO! Duh udder 'ay. Gah! ...Bloody 'ell," he'd yell at us (although I might be paraphrasing), and we'd all look confused and bumble our way around with rope and sail. At one point he was yelling at me while I tried to *thread the jib on the foremast*, while Nieroo, Atoosh and Gyrod took some initiative on the mainmast. They had hooked a sail to its yardarm, probably wrongly, and had opened it before its rigging had been tied off correctly. Since the sail was so high on the mast, this caused the whole ship to lean suddenly away from the wind, and Mongrel slid across the deck, and went over the missing railing into the warm sea.

When he surfaced, there was a torrential string of incomprehensible swearwords, occasionally interrupted by submersion and sputtering. By the time he climbed back on board, the rest of us stood on deck with our eyes on our feet, looking like whipped puppies. He stomped up to us, dripping and angry, and rubbing a dirty rag under his eye patch.

We all kept a straight face, staring guiltily at our feet, until Daniel asked, "Salt water in the socket?" The resulting laughter interrupted work for another half hour.

By the end of the day, the ship was half rigged correctly, a quarter rigged incorrectly, and patience and strength had left our bodies. So we lay on the deck and enjoyed what was left in the rum barrel as the sun set crimson over the Caribbean sea.

> *"Rocked in the cradle of the deep,*
> *lay me down in peaceful sleep"*
>
> *- old sailor's saying.*

SEA-RATS

My feet were cold. That's what woke me. I wasn't woken by the small delicate fingers that went through my pockets. I wasn't woken by the sound of soft boots scurrying around my sleeping body. I wasn't woken by the cleverly gentle way in which my boots were pulled from my legs. I only woke because my feet were cold.

For a few seconds I lay still, trying to remember where I was. I saw masts and their loosely dangling rigging. I saw millions of stars floating in the blue-black sky, framed in a thin ring of gold; the sun was preparing to rise.

I rolled my head to one side, and I saw a half-dozen figures stooping over the sleeping crew. They were searching gingerly through our pockets, removing articles of clothing that looked valuable, removing swords, knives and pistols. These men were small in stature and build, unshaven, tanned as dark as the wooden deck, and clad in long sleeveless coats. They wore headwraps, large gold earrings, and curled mustaches. One had a fez...and they had long, thin knives tucked into their brightly-colored sashes, or clenched between their teeth.

I held perfectly still, eyes open only a slit, and waited motionless until one got close to me. When I saw a leg near enough, I instantly seized the man, and just as instantly he kicked me in the head with his other leg, and leapt up into the air. I got up, but almost before I could get to my feet the little scavengers were leaping off the ship, some swinging from the rigging, others running silently across the deck and leaping over the rail.

I ran after the nearest man and grabbed his vest from behind, at which point he crouched into a ball in the flick of an eye, sending me tripping and flying over him. Just as quickly, he stepped up onto my prone body and tossed himself up into the rigging. He climbed as easily as you or I would walk across the deck, and was soon out of reach. But I knew where that rope was tied, as I had tied it the day before. So as he climbed, I pulled the pin the rope was tied to, which sent him flailing to the ground.

He landed on his feet, but I grabbed him by the front of his shirt with one hand, preparing to sink my sizable fist into his face. In that instant he looked at me with moist blue eyes, deep and infinitely sad. For a minute I had pity for this small man, trying to do his best to survive in this huge scary world. Doing whatever it took to get by, suffering the life of a scavenger, only to be caught by me. I felt horrible.

During this moment of pity, he brought his knee up into my chin, which set off white hot flashes in my eyes. I staggered back and released him, reeling on the verge of losing consciousness. He laughed merrily and sprang away.

He would have leapt right off the ship, but I grabbed a massive and charred wooden pulley, about the size of a water bucket, and tossed it into the back of his knees, which folded him like a rag doll. Then I strode over, grabbed him by his sleeveless coat and lifted him off the ground. He kicked viciously at me, and then wriggled out of his coat and dropped out of my grip and off the ship.

I looked over the railing and saw a boat in the water. It was much smaller than ours, with three long narrow hulls, a small cabin in the middle, and a series of six seats with bicycle pedals on the outside hulls. These were manned by more of these sea rats (or Jypseas I later learned), who were peddling furiously. Their boat was pulling away from ours at a commendable pace.

I had half a mind to jump for it, but was reminded by my cold feet that I was in no way equipped for a fight, not even against so petite a mob. So I strode quickly back to my still sleeping crew, kicked Mongrel in the shoulder, and said, "Wake up! We've been taken, and you slept through it!"

I know what you're thinking, "Don't you have an automaton on your crew? A mechanical man...*he* was asleep?" Fact is, automatons kind of do sleep. As it was explained to me (in condescending tones by the good Doctor Calgori, who played quite a big part in the fact that there were automatons at all), they expend more energy per day than they can generate. Deep in their chest, each automaton has a generator composed of a ring of magnets that are positioned so that they are all pulling a polarized disk to turn. As this disk spins, it tightens a spiral clock spring. When an automaton does anything, they slowly unwind the spring, just like a clock. Thinking uses by far the most of this energy, but even the task of seeing, and recognizing objects that they see, draws so much power that they would shut off completely after about 20 hours of being "on", if they were doing anything energetic. So if they have been particularly busy, they need to shut down almost all of their systems for hours at a time in order to build up enough reserves to start going again.

Which, the more I think about it, sounds exactly like sleep. So, yes, we were *all* asleep.

Anyway, as the crew jumped up, I headed over to the grappling cannon. This is a huge crossbow mounted on a swivel. It fires a bolt attached to a rope, which is attached to a crank and reel. I aimed and fired, and the bolt stuck cleanly in the small fleeing vessel. I then turned the crank, and found I didn't have the strength to pull that ship back, against all the peddlers, so Nieroo and Atoosh took the cranks. With much straining, the two giants wound up the rope, and pulled the little ship in. Then Gyrod leapt onto their tiny deck, and with one graceful motion he grabbed two men around the neck, and lifted them far above his head.

After a few sword strokes proved useless against the brass man's legs, their diminutive captain spoke, "Alright, vee are at standstill. You 'ave your tings back, ok?" He said it in an accent that sounded at once Turkish, Italian, and Romanian. With the way this world was shaping up, it probably was.

"It would seem I can have anything I want," I said, putting a bare foot up on an overturned crate. "But let's start with my boots."

We brought their captain and a couple of the crew, including the blue-eyed man whom I had fought, back on board the *Ophelia*, as well as the things they had stolen. Then we tied them to the mast. You gotta love the classics.

"Tell me, where are you headed?" I asked.

"Da Flotilla," their captain replied, with a defiant sneer.

"A flotilla?" I asked.

"Da Flotilla. Da floating city? You can probably see it from here, ifs you looks from your crow's nest. But zen, you can't probably geet to zee crow's nest, wiz yours rigging all drooping around your deck like zee pants of a man on a toilet," he said, sneering under his finely curled mustache.

Mongrel decided he was going to take offense at this, and he backhanded the captive across the face, cutting his cheek with one of his rings, and knocking the man's fez to the ground.

"Watch 'ere language when's yer talking about a lady! *Ophelia's* the finest...um..." But Mongrel trailed off, looking at the burnt decking, broken lanterns, and dangling sails.

"Well, she's not lookin' 'er best at the moment."

"Let us hope not!" smirked the Jypsea captain.

Daniel pulled me aside and whispered, "Robert, these guys seem to know a lot more about sailing than we do. A LOT more."

"Good point," I whispered back.

"I'll tell you what," I said, turning back towards the mustachioed captain. "Help us rig this ship correctly, and I'll pay you. We can walk through the hold together, and come to a suitable price. After she's rigged, and sailing, you can be on your way. I think you'll probably end up making more than if you had gotten away with your little raid, and we'll be able to sail."

"Even if we rigs zis boat for yoose, you don't look like you 'ave enough sailors of make it go. Unless you 'ave more below deck who have still not waked up?" He grinned.

"We don't. Have anyone you can spare?"

He frowned for a moment, then smiled, "Yes, I do! My cousin Titus here I would be delighted to get rid of," he said, gesturing to the blue-eyed man. "He's my wife's cousin, and he never stops playing that infernal violin of his, it's pretty much all he does. Take him, and Don Julio, and they will get you going again, and help you get to the floating city to get repaired. I tinks you need a lot of repairs," he ended with a chuckle.

And so that is how Titus and Don Julio joined our crew, and how the *HMS Ophelia* once again became seaworthy. In a few days we were sailing east-by-northeast across a salty emerald ocean towards the great Flotilla, in hopes of finding repairs to our no longer flying airship.

41

CLOCKWORK MERMAIDS
& RUSTY TUBES

When the *Ophelia* was fully rigged, we climbed to the top of one of the crow's nests and saw the *Flotilla*. Far off in the blue distance, it floated like an island. It was a massive series of concentric rings, composed of floating docks, tall ships, barges, and Victorian manors on wide hulls. The entire city was perhaps three miles wide, and from my vantage in the crow's nest I could see the floating city ripple as each large, rolling ocean wave passed under it. These ripples buckled the docks, and made ship masts sway like trees in a storm, but it was all part of life on the Flotilla.

When we came within a few hundred feet, I could see figures in the water, darting along with us, easily matching our speed. At first I mistook these for dolphins, but they turned out to be people. Men and women, who had long segmented mechanical tails pulled over their legs and attached to their waists. Inside each tail was a clockwork, like you would find in automatons, and any motion they gave with their legs was strengthened to a degree that allowed them as much grace as a dolphin. Leaping in our bow wave, they gestured for us to follow. They led us into the spiral labyrinth of the Flotilla's many concentric docks.

This next part is embarrassing, but if I left it out you wouldn't believe this story.

Here goes: I have never sailed. Well, not on water.

I had been captain and pilot of an airship for years, and although it had comparable elements to sailing a ship, (sails, for one thing) there are few major differences. The most important being that I had two huge propellers I could use to turn, or reverse the ship as needed. Without propellers, it will come as no surprise to you that I made a horrible mess of the delicate job of sliding a massive sailing ship into a small slip.

As we threaded our way between docks and ships into this constantly drifting marina, I ran down to the bow bridge. (the *Ophelia* had three separate bridges:

43

bow, captain's-quarters, and poop deck. Stop giggling, the "poop deck" is the elevated deck in the back of a ship.) From the bow, I could see the narrow slip that the semi-mechanical mermaids were pointing to, and I internalized a bit of anxiety at what I knew was not going to be graceful docking. The slip appeared only *just* big enough for the *Ophelia*, assuming I could pilot her in flawlessly, and the mermaids did in fact assume this.

"Capt'n," Mongrel said warily, "are you sure you got this?"

"Of course. I've been piloting the Ophelia for years!" I was over explaining.

Daniel flashed a look at Mongrel that he assumed I didn't see, but then turned to Don Julio and Titus and said, "You two go below deck and bring up the...um...bring up the cofferdam."

"Da what?'

"Cofferdam. Surely you know what a cofferdam is, don't you?"

"Of course!" said Don Julio with pride, and Titus followed him, looking confused. After they left I asked Daniel, "Um, what is a cofferdam?"

"It's something to do so that proper sailors don't watch you botch the docking," he said. I frowned.

Turning the wheel, the ship slowly began to respond, but as it did, our bowsprit caught the railing of one of our neighbors. There was a tremendous "*CRACK*!" which sent a ten-foot section of railing off into the sea. After that, I was on course for a bit, and we straightened out and slid into the slip.

But now we were moving too fast, so I instinctively reached for the propeller throttle, to reverse and therefore slow us. Of course moving it did nothing. Our aerial props sat motionless at the aft, and we headed towards the far dock at too great of a speed. There was no way I knew of to slow down the ship.

On our right, I heard voices coming from the dock, and Mongrel shouting, "Toss 'em the mooring lines!" as he struggled with huge coils of rope at our starboard. Soon a half-dozen men on the docks were pulling on the lines, which slowed and turned her, but not enough.

We crashed into the dock ahead of us, sending splinters of ship and dock into the air, and dragging longshoremen off their feet and into the warm sea.

Titus and Don Julio ran up from below deck. "What was that?"

Daniel said, "Did you get the cofferdam on deck?" and they turned and went back below again. Truth be told, a cofferdam is a real part of a ship, sort of. It's the narrow space between bulkheads. It's possible that Titus and Don Julio would have heard the term before, but it was not possible to bring one on deck.

Once the ship was moored, Daniel, Mongral, Titus, and I strode down *Ophelia's* gangplank, and onto the floating wooden dock. Doctor Calgori, Don Julio, Gyrod, Nieroo and Atoosh stayed onboard to start planning repairs.

Each dock segment was about as long as a city block, floating on large barnacle-encrusted barrels. Ours was filled with a hustle and bustle of sailors loading, or unloading, or calling out to passersby about the various things they were selling, or services they had to offer. This was as nautical a bunch as you could hope for. Blousy linen shirts, with knee-high boots over striped pants, or under kilts or baggy short pants. Skin tanned as dark as leather. Braided beards and eye patches, and even a tricorn or two. Somewhere in the distance a single concertina droned a tune that I swore was, "*Yo, Ho, Ho, and a Bottle of Rum.*"

At this point, a lady one could only describe as a "wench" swaggered over to us, bursting out of her corset, makeup painted on thick and skirt tied high up her thigh. Without a pause, she kissed Mongrel straight on the mouth.

"Pleased to meet ye!" he said to her with surprise, then turned to us with a lipstick-smeared mouth, adding, "This is my kind o' port! Captain, please tell me we plan to stay on a bit." Then he turned back to the wench and asked, "Where is the nearest tavern? We need a drink, and a bit o' news."

She led us a short way down the dock, and soon we stood in front of a small, moldering cottage that sat on its own barge. It was roofed with both thatch and rusty aluminum, and had walls of old cedar planking, bamboo, and wicker, all in a haphazard patchwork.

We crossed its swinging bridge to a round, red painted doorway that could have come from a Chinese monastery. Once inside, I could hear the sound of glasses clinking, and a staticky radio crooning some 1930's ballad, wherein the singer advised the listener:

You've got to fix the boat,

Or get out and swim.

Don't sit there bitching, sinking,

Clean up that mess you're in!"

The inside was lit by numerous hatches in the roof that were thrown open, sending streams of light to the tables below. Several shady customers sat on barrel chairs around tables made of old rigging spools, while two pretty Asian waitresses in tight silk dresses, each with a pink flower behind one ear, brought drinks around on trays.

I walked up to the bar, and asked a pair of sailors what was good.

"The stuff in the coconuts is a bit sweet, but will have you pleasantly asleep in no time!"

"Hum, I might need to pass on that for now, then. I need to hire a crew," I said. "We need at least a dozen sailors."

"Oi, whatcha do with the last crew?" he snarled, and I tried not to frown, thinking of the number of men I'd lost over the last few weeks.

Both the crusty sailors then chuckled. "Well, never mind that," the first one went on. "I don't rightly care, as long as there is pay in it. Air or sea?"

"Currently sea, but with any luck, we'll take to the air again soon."

"Hah, got yourself a sick duck, then?" They laughed again. *Sick duck* seemed to be a term for an airship that was stuck in the water. This made me feel a little better, since it meant I was not the only captain to suffer this.

"Where will your ship be headed?" he asked.

"Isla Aether," I said.

Mongrel shuffled his feet, then cleared his throat."Well, cap'n, it's actually High Tortuga."

Dan stepped forward authoritatively, "No, I specifically told them Isla Aether."

"Aye, I know that was the plan," said Mongrel defensively, "but Tanner mentioned some stuff that he needed to be doin' first in High Tortuga. And I heard him myself, tellin' the pilot of the hired vessel he wanted to head there."

"Well, that's just great," said Daniel.

"I asked him about it, and he said you guys were okay with it. He said he'd take them to Isla Aether after a few weeks." Mongrel frowned.

I sighed. "I'm not sure Timony will be excited about heading back there," I said, then I turned back to the sailor at the bar. "I guess we are headed to High Tortuga."

At this, the sailor groaned. "Oh, pity. I'm afraid that'll be hard to do," he said in a hushed tone.

A shiver raced up my spine. "Why is that?"

"High Tortuga isn't there anymore. As least, it's not in the sky. What's left of it is burning on the ground, spread over twenty miles of prairie!"

"What!?" I was horrified.

"Yea, 'tis a pity," the other sailor said. "When the Emperor died, the Grand Admiral took command, and he's not one for doing things halfway! The navy stopped turning their heads as much as they used to, and seems hell-bent on killing everybody outside the cities that doesn't come quietly back! They burnt High Tortuga and she fell to the ground."

"My god!" I exclaimed. "How long ago did this happen?"

"Dunno, maybe half a week? Not long."

My head raced. I had left my family in that city. Kristina and the girls might have been killed! I had to get to them and try to find out what happened to them. Perhaps they had left the city before it fell. Perhaps the city was only partly ruined, and they had survived.

But my airship was stuck in the sea, and would be for some time. She needed extensive repairs, if she was ever going to fly again.

So I asked, "Can you tell me the fastest way to get to where the city used to be?"

"I'd say charter a plane. Airships are nice, but that will take you a couple of days. A good airplane should have you there in a few hours. But your gonna need to wipe that look off your face. No pilot's gonna take you, with you looking all fearful like that. They'll know they're in for trouble!"

I walked quickly back to my group, and said, "Look, something has happened to High Tortuga. I don't know if the news is exaggerated or not, but they're saying the whole city has been burned. We need to get there, and find out what's happened to the rest of the crew, and to my family!" I choked up here, and my eyes were moist, but I went on.

"Mongrel, I want you to stay here with the *Ophelia*. I'm putting you in charge of the crew. Get her flying, if you can. Do whatever Doctor Calgori needs done."

"Daniel, Titus, and myself will see if we can find another way to get to High Tortuga."

Following the advice of a couple of pirates, we headed down to a less crowded part of town than the one where we were docked.

There, floating in the water next to a dock, was a large

seaplane. It looked like a giant chrome bullet, freckled with rusted rivets, bobbing sadly up and down, and creaking with each passing wave. Its chrome glimmered in a few places, but it was so rusted that in others that you could see right through the fuselage. It slumped in the water in a way that reminded me of a nearly defeated boxer hanging from the ropes between rounds.

This might be our fastest way to travel, or it might be the fastest way to come to a crashing end.

Gyrod spoke, "This plane does not look to be very healthy."

"Yeah, I agree," I said. "We might need to make do, though. We are kind of in a pinch."

"We are always in a pinch," Daniel said.

Leaning in the doorway was a man with a braided black beard, a curled mustache, long hair covering many piercings, and a mischievous grin on his face. He held a bottle under one tattooed arm, and watched us examining the plane.

After watching us for a few minutes as we assessed the plane's state of dilapidation, he said, "So, what you're going to do is–" he paused for effect, "–*get in the tube.*"

"Excuse me?" Daniel asked.

"You're gonna get in the tube," and here he patted the side of his plane, "and I'm gonna fly the tube. It's going to be great." He smiled mischievously.

"Maybe. But how do we know it's not going to just drop out of the sky?" Daniel asked.

"Only one way to find out," he grinned.

"Uh, can we take a look around first?" I asked.

"Sure, come on in!" he said, and he stepped back into the shadow of the plane's interior.

Daniel hopped in, then me, and as our eyes became accustomed to the dark, I could smell a blend of cumin and cooking meat, along with gasoline. The floor was covered in old beer cans, pieces of paper, and feathers that once belonged to one of the several chickens that clucked indignantly if we walked too close to them.

"You're in my tube," he chuckled, and led us through a series of small cluttered rooms, up an aluminum ladder, and into a kitchen, where he paused to stir some bubbling stew in a pot. "So, where are we headed?"

Daniel answered. "*We*," he paused, "are headed inland. To High Tortuga."

"Then I hope you have a time machine," he smiled, "because High Tortuga isn't there anymore." He set down his spatula and led us into another room.

I raised an eyebrow to Dan, and then followed. This pilot could not have known the full implications of his joke, but it did make me a bit nervous.

We walked into a cramped navigation room littered with old maps, and then into the cockpit. Here our host was sitting at the controls. Various postcards, and old black & white photos were taped around the cockpit, and a small hand-cranked record player was spinning slowly, thinly reproducing a complex and moody gypsy guitar.

There were more beer cans, a couple of small pipes, and a familiar smoky pungent smell that I recalled from the green rooms of the rock concerts I played in another life.

The pilot opened a window and said, "I'm Josh, by the way. Welcome aboard the Eustace Xanther, finest seaplane that..." he paused, "well, that *I* own, anyway!" He smiled again. "So, since your destination is no longer in the present tense, where would you like to go?"

Burning and Falling
(Three Days Prior)

High above the prairies of North America was the

city of High Tortuga. An aerial port of a hundred docks, suspended on hundreds of balloons, keeping its population safe from the predator-filled wastelands below. The city was composed of a series of concentric rings, that were both streets to the hundreds who lived and worked in the city, and docks for the multitude of airships that converged there daily. The balloons that held the town aloft soared high above the city like a canopy of massive jungle trees, and they threw broken shadows on the streets below, so that you were always walking either into or out of the sunlight.

Between the streets hung houses, bars, workshops, markets, helium^2 tanks, warehouses, brothels...all the things it takes to make a bustling, swashbuckling town of free people. When I say people, I mean outlaws, for when freedom is outlawed, only outlaws are free, and although these were not the only free people left in the world, these were the ones most hated by a government that thought it was better for the world to keep people caged and working every hour they were awake.

Before our airship, the *Ophelia*, had fallen into the ocean, we had sent my young wife Kristina, my two adopted daughters Chloe and Isabella, and a few of my crew to look after them. There they waited for us, with much of the *Ophelia's* cargo (things we had stolen from various times we had visited). The cargo was left as currency, as they waited to see what had become of Doctor Calgori and myself, and hoped for our return.

With them was Tanner, who had stuck with our crew after Lilith had abandoned him carelessly, so long ago. He stayed with us, quietly making his own plans, and all the while putting up a cheerful, but not very believable, front. I noticed his mood change after that day above the Black Forest, and I suspected what must have happened. Although I did everything to try to make him feel welcome without mentioning what I assumed, it was no use. Once you betray your crew, you will always feel like an outsider, even after they forgive you.

Another with them was Timony, who looked like a beautiful eighteen-year-old girl, but was actually an elaborate clockwork bedroom toy. She wore toe shoes, a tutu, and a look of fragile determination. She had escaped a life of servitude and prostitution, only to end up back here in the city where we had first met her. She was delicate, complicated, and very breakable.

Our castaway crew had rented rooms in a little inn that hung under the city, and spent their time wandering the sun-bleached hanging wooden streets of High Tortuga.

This was a city of sailors trading their goods, spending their hard-earned cash on much needed supplies, or simply trying to rest after far too many weeks aloft, cooped up on a small airship.

It was also a city of refugees from the Change Cage. Self-freed slaves, staggering onto the docks half-dead, bearing starvation, sickness, poverty, fear...and bearing their dead families, the unfortunate majority who could not endure the transition from slave to freeman. Most who escape from the Cage stumble out into the filth around the cities, lost and alone. They are hunted by the beasts of the field, and they watch their friends and family killed off as they struggle to survive. Those who are lucky meet up with Neobedouin tribes, nomadic ground-dwellers who have learned to fight back against the harshness of the natural world. If the newcomers are accepted, they will live in the wagon-trains of the Neobedouins, in gorgeously ornate Gypsy Hauls, and they will herd animals and raise crops, but they will forever be on the run.

Other refugees will find their way to the sea, and some lucky ones had found their way here, to High Tortuga.

As days stretched into weeks in this city in the clouds, the girls saw less and less of Tanner. First he was "going out" in the evenings. Then he had plans during the days as well, until finally it had been a week or more since they had seen him at all.

This day, Kristina, Chloe, Isabella and Timony were on one of their many long drives on the sunny roads of High Tortuga. They took our *Bandersnatch*–that's what we named our little motorcycle and sidecar–to some unexplored section of town, little girls in the sidecar, and Timony perched on the seat, arms wrapped around Kristina's waist.

They arrived at a nearly deserted section on the edge of town, and saw the midday sun illuminating white puffy clouds just out of reach beyond a long empty dock. As they clambered off of the old motorbike, the kids were drawn to a cluster of the many birds that flocked to the city. These were gulls and pigeons, mostly, but joined by an occasional budgie or parrot. They pulled out little brown bags of crumbs torn from crusts of bread, as they followed Kristina and Timony down the dock.

Here they came across a pitiful thing. Hanging incredibly in the air was perhaps one of the most rundown and ill-designed airships they had ever seen. The gondola was scarcely forty feet long, and must have at one point been a sailboat, as there were still barnacles clinging white and sun-dried to the now useless keel.

This dilapidated gondola hung under a cluster of old weather balloons that were tied with a series of fishing nets. Together the balloons barely provided enough lift to keep this thing afloat, but gave the impression that at any moment the nets could burst, and the balloons would drift up and away while the sailboat plummeted to the ground below.

Between the balloons were yardarms, and from them hung sails, now tightly wrapped. This ship appeared only to be wind-powered, with nothing but a small pivoting rear prop to change heading or altitude. It was little more than a makeshift hot air balloon with sails, and it was covered in birds who had relieved themselves so much on it that the deck now looked white and lumpy.

As they walked past this sad ship, Kristina noticed that a new name had been given to it. In fresh paint, hand brushed on the side of the bow, it read "The Tanner".

"That's...odd," Kristina began to say, when she saw a notice on a pole a few feet away. Stepping over to it, she read:

Crew needed for newly acquired ship, The Tanner. Three good sailors required. Captain Tanner of The Tanner will lead you on a great adventure, I'm sure, as we together decide our own destinations! No experience necessary.

Kristina put her head in her hand, embarrassed on his behalf.

"This? This is what all the sneaking and hiding has been about?" she said to Timony. "He wanted to captain his own ship? Why even bother hiding it? Why would we care? It's not like we needed him for anything. He could have done this with our blessing...or our help, for that matter! I just don't understand," she said, but part of her felt betrayed. They had stuck by him for years, silently forgiving his betrayal in the hopes of reforging a friendship they once shared. All while he silently planned to sneak off.

Timony said nothing. She didn't understand how human loyalty worked. Automatons like herself treated each other as family. All automatons were brothers, or sisters, or cousins, or aunties, or uncles to each other. Whereas humans hardly treated their family as family. She couldn't respect this, but instead of getting angry about it, she chose to just be confused.

"Fire-gurks!" interrupted little Isabella excitedly, looking off across the city. Kristina looked off across town. Over the short, hanging buildings and the hundreds of ropes that held the city to its balloons, she saw bursts of fire.

"Imperial Navy!" said Timony, her voice quivering slightly. "That's back towards our inn..." But as she spoke, a shadow fell across them, blocking the midday sun and setting the birds around them to flight.

A massive black airship, emblazoned with the imperial navy's crest of an eagle crushing a human skull, was pulling up to the dock. Huge doors were open in the side of its gondola, and within them waited dozens of imperial marines, with rifles in hand.

An amplified voice boomed out, "You are in violation of Population Control and Confinement Law. Any persons found outside the Grand Admiral's cities will be subject to immediate incarceration. Those found resisting incarceration will be executed."

"The Grand Admiral's city?" Timony said. "Not the Emperor's city?"

Kristina said, "Come to me, Chloe," barely concealing the fear in her voice, while picking up Isabella, and starting down the dock towards their motorcycle.

The Zeppelin collided with the dock, and as it did, marines leapt. The first to find footing lifted their rifles to their shoulders, and fired at the running girls.

One of the horrible differences between movies and real life is that in movies, bad guys never seem to hit the good guys. Not the good guys you really like, anyway. But this is not a movie, at least not yet, and none of these four marines missed.

Three of the four bullets ripped open the delicate skin of young Timony, and she spun to the ground, sparking, twitching, and oozing fluid. An assortment of delicate brass parts glimmered on the ground around her, and she shuddered as she tried to stand back up and failed.

The fourth bullet hit Kristina. It slid effortlessly into her back, shattered her scapula, nicked her left lung, and exited her chest. It then ripped into Isabella's blouse, entering the tender pink flesh under her little arm and popping out the other side. Isabella didn't cry, but screamed at the unfairness of her unexpected pain, shocked and angry at an undeserved punishment.

Kristina, suddenly weakened and breathless, fell to her knees. She coughed, and blood speckled Isabella's hair and face. Kristina stood back up, still holding Bella. "Ruuu–" she started, paused, then inhaled with a gurgling sound. "Ru...ru...*Run!*" she struggled to say to Chloe, and then stumbled forward into a trot.

Timony watched Kristina running. She then turned her head and watched the marines leaping from the airship and running towards her. She wanted to run after Kristina and escape together. Somewhere in her clockwork head, she even thought, "If I could just run faster than Kristina...and surely I could, in her condition...then I could escape". But she hated herself for that thought, so instead she stood up and turned toward the approaching marines.

Timony had spent her whole life trying to escape slavery. Shortly after she did gain her freedom, she had taken up with this crew, and now a few weeks later she found herself confronting either servitude or execution. She wanted to run, more than even you or I would want to run, but instead of running, the ballerina took first position; heels together, arms gently curved in front.

As they advanced, the soldiers saw her take fifth position, arching her arms gracefully above her head. This confused them, but they took it for a sign of surrender and advanced on her.

A quick sweep of her hand wiped the rainbow-brown hydraulic blood from her face, and a little push of her foot started her pirouette. She spun, slowly and sensually at first, commanding all the marines' attention as Kristina and the children stumbled down the dock behind her. But as the men came to seize her, she kicked harder, and went into a spin that a living human prima ballerina could not have maintained. At this point, the marines were nearly upon her, and her tutu flared up until it was parallel to the ground. The speed of her spin exposed razors embedded in her skirt. They extended a mere two inches, but at that speed, they sliced deeply into the legs of several shocked marines, who stumbled backward, gushing blood.

Then she paused and wiped away more hydraulic blood from her face. When the next wave of marines moved in to grab her, she spun again, and again they fell bleeding. They didn't see that down the dock Kristina was doing something with one of the vertical ropes that held the city, while the girls climbed into the motorcycle and sidecar.

Timony spun again, but instead of reaching out for her, a marine thrust his rifle butt into her spinning head. She grabbed the gun, not even slowing down, and released it, sending it soaring into the clouds.

Out of the zeppelin then strode a grey-haired but powerful-looking officer. His eyes were the color of steel, naturally ringed like a raccoon's, and his mouth was pursed and perpetually annoyed. He strode impatiently down the gangplank, lifted a large but decorative pistol into the air, and shot Timony straight in the forehead.

Timony fell to the ground like a marionette whose strings had been cut.

From far across the city, hundreds of cries could be heard. If Kristina had had a higher vantage point, she would have seen thousands of ropes burning, and snapping, releasing the massive balloons and sending whole city blocks plummeting thousands of feet to their destruction. Some streets and blocks dangled vertically from where they were attached, while their inhabitants struggled to climb to safety, or fell into the clouds below.

The city was burning and falling.

Out of the assaulting airships and across the city's streets came the harpies. These lighter-than-air automaton hunters were designed from the ground up to strike terror into their prey. The predators looked like the torso of a vaguely human creature, brass bones and sinew exposed, and they hung suspended from armored balloons. They each had two oversized arms with large claws that could clasp the waists or the necks of the people running and screaming through the streets. Once caught, they would lift them high enough that they would stop struggling, and drop them into the massive basket of a prison ship. Then the flying paddy-wagons would take their cargo of barely-alive men and women back to the Change Cage for "processing".

A few brave citizens fought back against the harpies, thrusting swords or firing pistols, but it was no use. Bullets and blades glanced off the automatons' fortified brass. Meanwhile, the claws of the harpies were unforgiving in design: if they made an inaccurate grab at your neck, they might scrape open a vein, and you might lose too much blood to survive your trip back to the Cage. Children often slipped right through their grip, which resulted in either a temporary escape, or a fall of 2,000 feet to the prairies below.

And these weren't the only metallic hunters unleashed on the floating city. Huge copper centipedes unrolled like pill bugs on the docks, and clattered their way through crowds. These mechapedes were fifteen feet long, and three feet thick, and instead of heads they had huge pincers that could snip a man in two. They were not collecting, they were exterminating. Simply being outside the Change Cage cities merited the punishment of death. Due to their length, and countless legs, they could easily descend a vertically dangling city street, and free hangers-on of their hold.

But none of this could be seen from the isolated dock where the girls ran. The dozen marines turned their attention away from the fallen Timony, back to Kristina. Kristina was now pushing the motorbike with the girls on it. The marines started to jog, or reloaded their rifles, but as they passed *The Tanner*, they got a surprise! Out jumped Tanner himself, sword in hand, with a half-dozen misfit pirates. They engaged the marines, and as they did, Kristina straddled the motorcycle.

Kristina looked back towards Timony, and saw her lying face down in a pool of parts and fluid. No one could survive the loss of blood Timony had suffered. There was no point in Kristina risking the little girls' lives going back for her body, so Kristina pushed the small bike and girls off the edge of the dock and into the sky.

The girls and motorcycle fell only a moment, before being jerked to a stop. When the marines had been distracted, Kristina had tied to the bike several smaller balloons that held the dock aloft, and the bike now dangled under them.

But as soon at the weight of the bike pulled the ropes tight, several balloons came undone. Now, the weight of the motorcycle, Kristina and the girls was too much for the remaining balloon, and they began to fall again.

They fell far too fast. If they hit the ground at this speed, they would surely all die. Now only one large balloon barely held on as they raced towards the ground from 2,000 feet aloft.

Kristina could feel her ears popping from the dreadful descent. Her chest was wet with blood, and she was becoming both nauseated and drowsy. If the bike hit the ground at this speed, they would all certainly be crushed. If she managed to live through the collision, she would surely die of blood loss in the wastelands below due to the bullet wound in her chest.

Kristina looked at the horrified expressions on the small girls' faces, and she looked at the city disappearing above her. She looked for something to throw off the bike, to decrease the weight of it, and hopefully slow its terrifying fall, but she saw nothing to throw off.

With nothing else to do to save the little girls, she took a deep breath, and threw herself.

DRIFTING

"Got shotgun shells and twelve cans of beans,
And an old stuffed doll coming 'part at her seams
Your little lace dress you've worn for too far
As you watch the apocalypse from Daddy's sidecar"
- From the song To The Apocalypse In Daddy's Sidecar

A gentle wind was blowing, and it pushed the balloon that held a small motorcycle and sidecar aloft above the prairie wastelands. It drifted about for hours, catching different air pockets that lifted it, or dropped it.

The two little girls had screamed at first, clinging desperately to the sidecar, terrified of falling. When it became apparent that they were not falling fast, they cried that they had lost their mommy. Finally, after they had no more energy or emotion left, they just stared.

Yellow grassy fields covered the ground below them, and stretched off far into the distance, where they turned into blue hills, dotted with trees. The sky about them was blue, with white feathers of cloud.

"Those are *serious* clouds," Isabella said. "That's what the feather ones are called."

"*Cirrus* clouds, Bella," Chloe corrected.

Down on the plains, they could see animals in herds. Mostly these looked no more than little specks, but sometimes they were so close, Isabella could see their little legs. She would then close one eye, and reach out her fingers in front of her and pretend they were tiny toys she could almost pick up.

After a few hours, the terrain changed to little green-black speckles of dry bushes on dry yellow dirt. The bike was getting lower to the ground now, only a few dozen feet.

"It looks like we're dissenting," Isabella said, watching the ground getting closer.

"Descending," Chloe corrected, and she wondered if it would be a good idea to leap out when the bike got low enough. But just as she stood up to get a better look, the balloon dropped them a little more, and the wheels bounced creakily on the ground.

This made the ropes that held them go momentarily limp, which caused the balloon to leap up, which caused the ropes to snap tight and lift the bike once more into the air. A wind was picking up now, and so this "jump" carried them a good forty feet before the wheels touched down again.

At the highest point of this jump, Chloe could see in the direction they were headed. About a hundred feet from them, the ground disappeared. They seemed to be headed towards a canyon or cliff of some sort. Although she didn't know it, they were in fact coming to the edge of the Grand Canyon. Chloe looked up at the balloon as it pulled them up again, and caught more wind and more speed. She looked at the ropes, and where they were tied to the frame of the motorcycle. If they remained tied to the balloon they would be pulled out over the edge of the canyon.

"Help me! Bella!" she said, and pulled desperately at the loops of rope. Soon both the girls' tiny fingers were pulling hopelessly at the thick knots, trying to untie them.

The bike touched down again, and was dragged sideways. Because of the sound of the bike wheels dragging against the dry dirt and through the small bushes, the girls could not hear a distant, frantic braying coming toward them. The balloon again lifted them into the air, and as it did, a herd of mountain goats darted beneath them. Fifteen goats ran sprinting past, and in pursuit behind them were several large cats, each about twice the size of an adult tiger.

Just under the bike, a cat leapt on a mountain goat, and crushed its neck easily in its jaws. Before it could sit down to feast, its eyes were caught by the sight of the large balloon slowly lifting a motorcycle into the air twenty-five feet above it. The cat had hunted beasts of this size before, and found them to be far more filling than the small mountain goats. It dropped the goat, crouched for a second, gave its rear a little wiggle, and then leapt twenty-five feet into the air. It caught hold of the bike with its massive front paws and hung. The girls screamed.

The cat was now dangling under the bike, and the added weight of the cat pulled the bike swiftly to the ground. When it reached the ground, the cat landed with the bike on top. Even a small bike like this one weighs at least 600 pounds, and for a moment the full weight of the motorcycle was pressed onto the massive cat's belly. It screamed in pain and let go. The balloon then lifted the bike back up into the air above the cat.

In an instant, the cat was on its feet again, and it crouched for another jump. Another brief wiggle, and the beast was in the air. The girls watched in horror as it flew up towards them, but as it leapt, the ground opened up below it, dropping down 3,000 feet to the river below. Again the cat grabbed the bike, but it only held on an instant before its grip gave way, and it fell out of sight.

In another hour, the girls had drifted to the far side and caught in the branches of an uncooperative tree that stood in the high desert near the edge of the canyon. That tree had stood there for two hundred years, enduring wind and drought, and it would be damned if any floating motorcycle was going to pull its branches off. Their ropes tangled on it, leaving the bike more or less upright, and about two feet from the ground.

"I'm hungry," said Isabella when the motorcycle had stopped swinging. "Let's play house, and cook some food."

Bella climbed out of the sidecar, hung from it, and dropped from the bike. She then proceeded to pull some small logs around the end of a larger fallen tree, in order to make a picnic table.

Chloe turned around so that she was kneeling on the seat of the sidecar and opened the small rear trunk to look for food. She pulled out and tossed to the ground: one old green plaid blanket, a flashlight, a box of shotgun shells, a very heavy and annoying to remove shotgun, a large knife in a leather sheath, and finally a knapsack full of canned foods. She then hung and dropped out of the bike.

Seeing Isabella had set up her rag doll at the makeshift table, Chloe looked around for her own doll. It was in the knapsack, so she pulled it out, carried it over and set it across the table from Isabella's doll.

"It's good for you to have come to dinner," Isabella said for her doll, to Chloe's. "Oh, I'm very hungry," she then responded in a slightly different voice for Chloe's doll.

Chloe walked back over to the knapsack. She pulled out a can of beans, and looked about on the ground for the knife, to see if she could slice it open the way she had seen daddy cut it. She doubted she could, but she was hungry enough to try. The knife had bounced behind a tree root, and as she picked it up, she heard over her shoulder a rattling sound. It sounded like a milk jug half full of gravel being shaken, and she wondered what Isabella had found to play with.

Then Isabella screamed.

The table her dolls sat around had lifted four feet into the air, and had opened its jaws and bared its fangs at her. The dusty body of the massive snake was as round as a tree trunk, and it flicked its coils around her in an instant to block her escape. It rattled its tail menacingly.

The snake cocked its head slightly as it contemplated the width of this bite, and then opened its jaws wide enough to consume the small child without chewing. Just before Isabella's head entered the snake's mouth, there was a loud crack, and the snake's head disappeared in a cloud of red vapor. Its body went limp and fell heavily to the ground around Isabella.

"NO MORE MONSTERS!" yelled Chloe angrily as she stood back up. The shotgun had left a huge blue-black bruise in her shoulder when it threw her backward. "I am so sick of monsters ruining our fun!" she went on. "They never eat us, anyway. They always try, but they never have, and I'm DONE WITH THEM!" And with that, the nine-year-old girl slid six more shells into the gun, and stomped back towards the bike.

Isabella looked down at the headless snake, and in a quivering voice said, "That was uninspected!"

Chloe liked string. She liked rope, and ribbon, and knots and bows. Often, the cabin they grew up in had looked like a spider lived there, so many threads were blocking doorways, or windows, or tying around bed posts, until the children's clockwork guardian would stumble in, exhale in a tired way, and then silently go about the task of untying it all. Because of this love, Chloe always had several balls of yarn, or twine, or string or rope about her.

After the girls cut the motorcycle down from the tree (this took the better part of an hour, and so much sawing that even taking turns left all four hands aching), Chloe set about the task of tying the shotgun to the sidecar.

Her thought was this: if you held it as you had been told, up against one shoulder, and pulled the trigger, the gun would hit you so hard as to leave you lying on the ground and bruised. But if you looped string around it, through the finger guard, and over the barrel, over and over; the gun would just stay in place. After she tied it, Chloe and Isabella sat in the sidecar, and pulled the trigger. The gun made a terrific noise, but it stayed in place, and neither girl was hurt. Since it was only tied in its center, Isabella could even pivot it around a bit to aim at different things: a bush, an old stump, the headless body of the forty-foot snake.

After they were bored of that, Isabella asked, "Where will we go?"

"We need to find Daddy," Chloe replied.

"Where is Daddy?"

"I don't know."

"How will we find him? I miss Mommy," Isabella said, and she began to cry softly. Chloe would have cried too, but she knew she had to be the mommy, and the daddy, if there was no mommy and daddy about, so she hardened herself as best she could.

"Maybe we should go back to the cabin. Daddy might look for us there." Chloe had a vague understanding that the world was very big, and it would be unlikely that Daddy could find them out here. The only other place they had been together was the cabin, so it was certainly more likely than staying out in the wastelands. Also, Chloe was beginning to think perhaps they didn't have enough food, and it was the only place she had seen a store of food.

She knew the general direction of home, but she had no idea that there were 1,500 miles between them and that cabin in the swamps.

She sat up on the motorcycle, and clutched the handlebars. They were very far apart for her, and she had to lean forward to reach them both. There was a key in the headlight, and she turned it. That made the light turn on, and the speedometer wiggle a little, and that seemed a good sign.

"You have to jump on the thing," Isabella said. "Jump on the thing, while squeezing in the hand-thing, there."

"This?" Chloe said, pulling in the clutch.

"Yes, now jump on the thing." Isabella got out of the sidecar, and walked around to the far side of the bike. With some straining, she pushed the kick-starter into place. "Jump on that while squeezing the thing."

Chloe jumped, but instead of starting the engine, the bike rolled forward an inch.

"You have to squeeze the thing harder," Isabella said, and she grabbed it too.

"I can't get the kick-step thing to go down!" Chloe said. "I'm too light!"

So without letting go of the clutch, Isabella climbed onto the kick-starter. Now both girls stood on it, and jumped together.

The engine turned over, sputtered a bit, and stopped. They did it again, and again it sputtered and stopped. Isabella reached past the seat to the throttle on the other side of the bike, and twisted it twice. "Daddy does that," she said.

They jumped again, and the bike rumbled and sputtered to life.

In a flash, Isabella ran back to the sidecar, and jumped in. Chloe slowly released the clutch, and the bike lurched forward, and nearly died, but Chloe turned the throttle and away they went.

They rattled down the road, and as they got going a little faster, the bike whined, and whinnied for the gear to be changed. Chloe knew to do this she had to squeeze the clutch, and then stomp on a pedal with her right foot. After a bit of experimentation, she was able to shift gears, and they continued on their way.

CAUGHT

"I fear what they'd do if they finally catch me.

I fear they'd take my home if they find I roam, find I'm free.

They want you to think it's possible to live a life without their chains,

But if you go too far, you'll find they're pulling on your reins"

- *From the song Fight or Flight*

Kristina leapt from the motorcycle, but she did not fall. Although she had not seen it at the time, a harpy, one of the lighter-than-air automatons of the Grand Admiral, had been in close pursuit of the falling motorcycle. When Kristina unexpectedly turned and leapt off of it, the machine methodically and deftly snatched her out of the air, and then turned in a regimented manner towards the city.

It held her about the waist in a massive brass claw that was crafted to look like a sinewy skeletal hand. As it passed under the burning city, it dodged falling bodies and burning wood. It passed through vertical rivers of smoke, and over slowly falling airships that were losing their ability to stay aloft.

When it had finally carried her to the other side of the city, Kristina saw its destination. The vessel had two large cigar-shaped balloons, and between them was a fifty-foot-long basket. It was fifteen feet deep, with smooth steel sides and a mesh bottom. In the marginally more peaceful days of Emperor Victor, this vehicle had been used to relocate large beasts. Now the basket was filled with people. Men, women, and children, some alive, and some dying.

The harpy released its claw over the basket, and for a second Kristina held on to its arm. Then she noticed it wasn't stopping. It was turning around and heading back to the battle. If she didn't let go now, she'd likely lose her grip over the wastelands, and die in the fall. So she let go, and dropped into the basket.

She landed on her back with such force that her head hit the thick steel mesh, and she saw no more for many hours.

When her eyes opened again, there was a dark-haired lady kneeling over her, doing something painful to her chest. Stabbing, cutting pains dug into her, and she screamed and thrashed about. The lady then yelled to someone Kristina couldn't see, and put her knee on Kristina's arm to hold her down.

"I think the bullet must have come cleanly out the other side," the dark-haired lady said, "I can't find any part of it."

Then another sharp pulling pain made her kick, but the effort was too much for her. Kristina swooned and again fainted.

Several hours later she woke again, and the sky was blue-black. The first few stars were appearing like the sinister eyes of unknown monsters in a child's nightmare. There was a foul sewage smell in the air. She turned her head to one side, and could look down through the mesh in the basket. The ground was black and nearly featureless here, but she saw railroad tracks, an oily river, and then finally a wall.

The wall was massive, a hundred feet tall, and it was topped with train tracks and searchlights. Their airship crossed over the wall, and she could see a grid of city blocks, each surrounded by more walls. Each block was packed with tenements, or factories, or work yards filled with little figures in lines like ants. There were no yards, or parks, or playgrounds between the buildings.

In the center of the city was a massive tower, which served as a prison for any citizens who attempted to live outside of the very strictly enforced social structure of the city. This tower was called the Change Cage, or simply the Cage by people who lived in the cities, and all feared what might be waiting for them inside it.

The airship pulled alongside the building, and a cage door opened in the side of the basket. Through this door stepped an uninterested-looking man in a sinister black military uniform, and several tall and evil-looking automatons of the exact same make as Gyrod. The automatons held large steel rods in one hand, the ends of which were glowing red-hot.

As the man spoke into a megaphone, the automatons grabbed the prisoners and branded their ankles with a black mark. "You are being branded, so that you can be retrieved later when your fate has been decided. You will be assigned residences and work as you wait for your case to be tried in court," he said.

Kristina heard the screaming of a child. She tried to stand, but as she did, a huge brass fist grabbed her leg and hoisted her high. There was a searing pain in her ankle, and she smelled her flesh burning before she was dropped again.

She was then marched with the other prisoners into the massive structure. They were shoved down dark metal halls, past numerous doors with barred windows, inside of which wailing and crying could often be heard. Then she was shoved into a large freight elevator, so big it could hold all twenty prisoners, plus the automatons that drove them.

The elevator dropped a dozen floors or more, and opened onto a huge black room. It was poorly lit by flickering and sputtering electric lightbulbs that were so dim you could easily make out the orange coils inside their burnt glass bulbs.

On the far side of the room was a tall and forbidding desk, and behind it sat an old man in a powdered wig and black robes. In front of his desk stood two more automaton shepherds, and a grey-haired, but important-looking officer. His eyes were the color of steel, naturally ringed like a raccoon's, and his mouth was pursed and perpetually annoyed. Kristina immediately recognized him from the docks where she had last seen her girls. This was the man who had shot Timony.

Kristina was the first to be thrown forward.

"Approach the bench," said the judge, bored. "What are the charges?"

"Your honor," said the steel-eyed man in a voice of mild outrage. "This woman was found outside of the City. Her charges are trespassing, consorting with a known progressor...an obviously self-aware automaton." As he said this, Kristina thought she might have seen one of the automaton shepherds break its blank forward stare and glance nervously at the prosecutor. "...and resisting arrest. Due to the extent of her crimes, and the dangerous nature of her obvious lack of Victorian principles, I recommend a judgement of death."

The judge sighed. "Yes, you do, don't you? Regularly," he said with tired distaste. "Does the accused have any family outside the City?"

"No, your honor. They were all killed while resisting." Kristina's face went hot, and her chest grew tight, and her vision became blurred with tears. *Killed*? Her brain whirled in panic. She had hoped that somehow they had survived. She had hoped the girls had been seized shortly after she herself had been seized. Had they fallen to their deaths, slipped from the careless claws of a harpy?

The judge looked at Kristina over half-moon spectacles, and then exhaled. "Let her be returned to the populace to await sentencing."

The steel-eyed man look outraged, "Your honor!" he said in a barely constrained tone. "Surely punishment or confinement is warranted, considering her crimes!"

"Yes, undoubtedly," said the judge in a tired voice. "But these are volatile times. I will not stick my neck out for a dead emperor until I know his successor is like-minded." He shuffled some papers nervously on his desk, then proclaimed in a louder voice, "I stay verdict for two months."

CAPTIVITY

She's got a terrible affliction,
It's got her spinning around like a top.
But it is a common addiction,
She follows the rules and can't stop.

She doesn't care what they're there for,
She doesn't know what they mean.
To stray from the norm she does abhor,
She thinks questioning rules is obscene.

- From the song Stigmata Martyr

Kristina woke because her ankle hurt, a dull burning that had kept her from ever fully falling asleep, without ever fully being awake. Her breathing rattled, but the scar in her chest did not hurt. It was stitched up inelegantly, and there was a green clay pressed over it that looked like dried guacamole. She touched her wound, and found her chest was numb.

The room was not lit, and while her eyes became used to the dark she tried to remember where she was. She lay on some sort of thin, lumpy mattress, and there was a blanket over her, coarse and scratchy. She was wearing a very elaborate and ill-fitting nightgown. She could hear many other people sleeping around her, breathing deeply and slowly. There were several heavy ticking sounds.

She had lain in this bed for days uncounted. Her gunshot

wound was so severe that she had been nearly always asleep and unaware of where she was, or what she was doing. This was the first morning she had really become conscious of her surroundings.

She thought about the last thing she remembered before going to sleep. She had been taken in handcuffs to a train which traveled on tracks on top of the walls that surrounded each city block.

Police officers, dressed like characters from a Sherlock Holmes novel, had mercilessly dragged her under gas streetlamps into a neighborhood of high tenement buildings. She remembered stumbling on wet cobblestones, and many glowing eyes peering at her from the dark alleys they passed.

They knocked on the doors of one, and were greeted by a sleepy but surprised and nervous man in nightclothes. He brought her inside, and several women undressed Kristina and put her to bed. All the while they grumbled about why they should carry the burden of someone else's lack of work-ethic. Kristina was too tired and wounded to try to understand this.

Now in the dark, as she sat in bed trying to remember all this, an angry-sounding bell went off in the room. As the mechanical alarm clock mercilessly rattled, the dark silent room was transformed.

Many people were waking in the small room. Gas lamps were lit, and in their light, Kristina saw many beds crammed into a narrow room that looked more like a short hallway than a bedroom. The floor was bare wood, with one small, handmade and very worn carpet. On the walls hung many small framed drawings of a large family, silhouettes of children, teens, parents and grandparents.

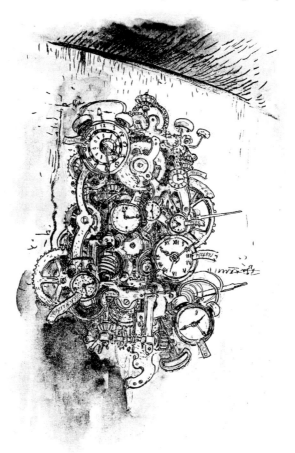

There was a cluster of several alarm clocks built into one rather chaotic-looking device, exposed gears turning. The clock had several faces, and handwritten on them were people's names. Fredric, Raphy, Martha, Bethany, Victoria, and so on.

There were also many bunk beds crammed together in

this small room, and on each bunk several children had slept. Two adult-sized beds sat at the opposite end, each holding a married couple, with another child at their feet. All these people were rising, and dressing, shaving around long mustaches and sideburns, brushing teeth, or helping children get dressed.

One scrawny grey cat stretched, and then dodged under a bed to avoid being trodden on in the commotion.

The eldest woman, who looked around sixty-eight, but was actually in her mid-fifties, approached Kristina. She wore a look of both disapproval and false sympathy. She said, "Alright young lady, you too. You're back to the real world now, you can't sleep until noon any longer. I'm Ms. Ellen, but you can call me Martha." And she briefly pressed her thin lips together in what was meant to be a smile, but only truly conveyed distaste.

Kristina swung her feet to the floor and looked around for her clothes. Her head was spinning from exhaustion, and lack of sleep, and blood loss. She noticed the rest of the family putting on nearly matching clothes: long dark dresses with lacy white collars and aprons for the women and little girls. Shabby, threadbare suits and thin ties for the men.

"You can't wear that inappropriate attire to work, as I'm sure you should know," said Martha, in falsely pleasant tones, as she tied her apron. "I assume you haven't forgotten how to dress for work?"

From the top of one of the bunks came two small girls, and a short but buxom young lady in her early twenties. She had big lips, and bright red hair, and as she helped the younger kids down from the bunk she said, "She can borrow from me, Mother."

She pulled her red hair into a ponytail, stooped and pulled two tidily-folded outfits out of a chest at the foot of the bed. Then she turned to Kristina with a sleepy but well-meaning smile and said, "I'm Jenny. You'll be coming to work with me today, and I'll get you set up with the administrator..."

"Well, you'd better hurry then, or you'll be late yourself. Jenny, you can't expect to leave at the same time as you usually leave and make it to the administrator's office and your job on time."

"I know, Mother," Jenny said.

From the kitchen, another woman called, "Breakfast! Come soon, we've all got to leave in twenty minutes!"

Kristina quickly put on one of Jenny's uniforms, but on her much longer body it looked more like a 'naughty maid' outfit from a tacky halloween costume shop, than any formal work wear. As she walked into the small but crowded kitchen, Martha Ellen flashed her another disapproving look. "That is *highly* inappropriate. But I'm sure you've lost track of right and wrong lately, haven't you, sweetie? You could get fired in that outfit! ...and on your first day back, too. You know it's illegal to be unemployed, or don't you remember?"

"Mother, it's all we have," said Jenny.

"Well, I guess you have no choice, then. Your actions have repercussions, don't they, angel?" Martha said condescendingly.

One of the girls, a tiny child maybe six years old, with brown curly hair and big brown eyes, beamed at Kristina over her large but mostly empty porridge bowl. "I think she's beautiful," she said.

"Aw, thank you!" said Kristina.

"Oh I'm sure it's fine in *some* lines of work," said Martha, cheerfully ladling porridge into bowls. "But you're not pretty enough for *that* type of work any longer, are you, dear? With that scar?" Here she nodded at the freshly treated bullet wound in Kristina's chest.

"Mother!" Jenny snapped.

"Oh Jenny, you're so sensitive. Always making a drama out of everything. I'm just being realistic. Our choices have repercussions, and her bad choices are having repercussions on our family."

Kristina ignored this, and smiled back at the small girl. "What is your name?"

"Victoria."

"That's a very pretty name! Are you in school?"

"Yes," the child beamed back.

"What are you learning in school? Have you started your multiplication tables yet?" Kristina asked, trying to avoid more conversation with Martha. The table went quiet.

"Go on Victoria, tell our guest what you've been doing in school," said the child's mother, a tired-looking woman in her mid-thirties, who looked closer to her late forties.

"I push the scrap cart past the tables!" the small girl beamed proudly. "Then I load them into the chopper-upper-choppers."

"What's that?" Kristina asked, confused.

"Carter," her mother declared.

"I push the scrap cart past the tables. The other kids empty their peel bowls into the cart, and I push into the bins, and I tip the cart into the chopper-upper-choppers. That's what I call them." She was obviously proud of her work.

"Math and reading and such like that are extra-curricular, if ya want 'em. But in my grade we push the scrap carts."

Seeing the confused look on Kristina's face, Jenny spoke. "They are in Kitchen school. Victoria is practicing Kitchen Lines this year. Next year, she'll be a peeler like her sisters."

Martha interrupted, "Jenny, I'm sure our guest knows all about schools. She obviously spent at least as much time in school as you have."

"Actually," said Kristina, "schools where I'm from are much different than here. We spent our time with books, and pencils, and playgrounds. What you're describing sounds more like work than school," Kristina said, and was going to go on before she was interrupted.

"Oh, nonsense!" Martha snapped. "You're from the City like everybody else, and you probably went to the same school district as these kids. You're just confused, and I don't want you confusing the children. For heaven's sake!" And as she washed some dishes, she mumbled something about "freelander's disease," and "delusional!"

"Experience Training," said a confident man behind a newspaper. He was skinny and awkward-looking, with a comically large mustache and sideburns. Without looking up from his newspaper, he went on, "It's never too early to learn a work-skill. When she's an adult, she'll be prepared for work-life, and make her mommy and daddy proud." He then looked over the top of his paper with a fatherly smile and glanced around at the kids one after the other. "Maybe when you lot get bigger, the family can make enough to move to a fancy apartment, eh? Separate rooms for boys and girls? Maybe even one bedroom just for the parents?"

"I'm going to be a ballerina when I grow up," said little Victoria cheerfully.

"Don't be silly, Victoria," Martha said in a singsongy condescending tone. "That's not a job, that's a hobby. You can do that in your spare time after work."

"But who has time for a hobby?" said the father with a chuckle, still in his paper. "Better to not get your hopes up."

Kristina kept to herself for the rest of the meal, and in a few minutes, another clock rang, and set the family in motion once again. Long coats were thrown on, backpacks were placed on children, mothers nagged their kids about not eating enough.

As the family was leaving, four teenaged boys trudged in. They exhaustedly dropped ancient-looking briefcases on the ground, hung their coats on the coatrack, and headed straight for bed.

"You boys need to bathe before you get into my bed!" Martha yelled. "I don't want to smell you on my sheets all night long!" Martha yelled at them, as she led three of the small girls down the hall and out of the apartment.

CONSUMPTION POINTS

From where she stood on the street, Kristina could see cobblestones blackened by the unending marching of boots, and filthy brick walls that seemed barely able to hold up the smoggy ceiling.

Gas lamps strained to cut through the coal-stained fog with their hissing and sputtering light. These gas lamps were chosen more for effect than function: electric lighting had been invented over two hundred years ago, but everything about this city was designed to recreate an environment of a time long gone.

This was the paranoid fear of the world government Victor had created. It feared mankind would overwhelm their police and their walls, if left unchecked. So they had removed all but minimal technology. The less tech, the less comfort, and the less free time to pursue rebellion. The harder life is kept, the more time people are forced to work, attending to daily survival, forced to ignore the unrest, oppression, and depression that is part of their daily lives.

Jenny pulled Kristina through the crowd, which angrily pushed back into them, bumping shoulders, glaring. It seemed there were no emotions in the street other than anger, exhaustion, irritation and disappointment. Many coughed raspily as they stumbled along to work.

Kristina's head was spinning from the wound in her chest and her loss of blood. As she stumbled along, Jenny led her though a series of consecutively darker and smokier streets. She was following directions on a scrap of paper she had pulled from the pocket of her shabby grey maid's dress.

Wherever they walked, a dark presence followed them. In the deep blue-black sky above them was a tower of steel and rusted rivets. The tower was so tall it reached the clouds, and completely disappeared from sight in them. Looking at the few barred windows, Kristina imagined she could hear screams from some poor soul imprisoned inside.

"I've never been here before," Jenny said, glancing at her scrap of paper. "It's a jewelry shop my employer remembers from years ago."

"Who's your employer?" Kristina asked.

"Well, I guess she's *our* employer now. The letter they left with you said you would be working for the Lady alongside of me. We'll mostly be doing house chores, like setting the table, or washing dishes. The Lady doesn't want clockworks to handle her fine china. She says the plates will slip through their metal fingers, which is ridiculous, but there is no arguing with a Lady. I honestly think the truth is it's cheaper to employ the likes of us, than to purchase more clockwork servants. Anyway, we'll also dress the Lady and her husband, who is old and frail beyond belief. I think *he* would be a kind employer if she wasn't around, but he's not strong enough to stand up to her."

"The Lady isn't a kind employer?"

"Well, few are! But no, she has a bit of a reputation, and it's well earned. Fired three girls this month already."

"I'd be happier being fired by her, rather than work for a cruel employer," Kristina grumbled.

Jenny stopped, and looked sternly at Kristina. "No, you wouldn't! How long have you been outside the city?"

"I've never been in the city before."

"Don't be ridicu…" Jenny began to say, but the sincerity in Kristina's eyes told her she wasn't lying, and that confused Jenny. She had been raised to believe that nobody could survive long outside the city's protective walls. Anybody who escaped would be promptly returned to the city. She had heard of a few criminals who told stories about living outside the city for years, but they were quickly diagnosed with *freelander's disease*, and taken to the Cage.

Jenny wondered if that's what was wrong with Kristina. She certainly looked sick.

"Well...if you lose your job, you go into the lottery for another job, but at a lesser level. Less pay can lower your living conditions, and working conditions, and quality of food you eat, etc. The other problem is there aren't as many jobs as people looking for jobs. You work for the right to live in an apartment with us, and pay for your food. If you remain unemployed for too long, you accumulate debt, and by the end of the month, the police will come and take you to debtor's prison." Here she glanced darkly at the gargantuan black tower in the sky.

"Okay, so I'll avoid being fired."

"Yes, you will. Aw, here it is," Jenny said, coming to a small shop in the side of a shabby building. The storefront was dark, and a look into the soot-blackened windows showed that most of the shelves in the shop were empty.

Jenny turned the doorknob, and the door pushed open with an irritating grating sound. "Jeez, it's like this door is rusted shut!"

The shop inside was covered in a layer of dust, undisturbed for years. There was a notice pinned to the cash register. It read:

The Occupants of 11463, 423rd street,
block 616 have been relocated to
the Change Cage, as a result of
failure to adhere to Ordinance #1366

"Oh god!" Jenny exclaimed. "Thirteen-Sixty-Six is basically not being Victorian enough. This is not just bad for this poor shopkeeper–I know the Lady will somehow find this is my fault. Anytime something doesn't go according to her plans, she blames the person she asked to execute her plans. That's how the last three girls were fired."

"That's horrible!" Kristina said. "Well, what did she send you to get? Maybe we can find something here that will satisfy her."

"I doubt it, but we might as well try," Jenny said. "Napkin rings, silver napkin rings to go with her new candlesticks."

"Alright, well, this room is empty. Let's see if he had something in the other room," Kristina said, and she pushed through a dusty curtain into a dim back workroom.

In the center of the room was an old wooden worktable. On it lay many black rubber metal molds, a smelting pot, cast iron tongs, and other metalworking tools. Behind the table stood a perfectly still automaton, one arm frozen midway through pouring brass into a mold, and the brass had hardened all over the molds and table. In the other arm was the skeleton of a newborn baby, swaddled in a once soft pink blanket. The clockwork had the face of a tired and very worn old lady. Its eyes were dim and rusted.

On the floor around its legs, and on shelves around the shop, and in boxes and buckets and barrels, and all over the floor, were bees. Brass bee pendants, thousands of them, filling every corner of the shop, and spilling out of the room.

Jenny screamed, then fell to her knees and covered her

face. "God, it's horrible!"

"I...I don't understand," Kristina stammered, trying to sound sympathetic, though she couldn't grasp the scene she was seeing.

"She...she died...well, she obviously..." Jenny sobbed while trying to pick her words carefully. "It's obvious the shopkeeper gave her orders to start making these brass bee pins while holding the baby, but he must not have instructed her when to stop making them. When he was taken, she just kept going until her joints locked up, and she...stopped. The baby must have starved in her arms."

"Oh, god!" Kristina said, finally understanding .

Jenny went on, "This child must have been an illegal. If you don't earn enough, they can take your children, so some poor people will hide children they know they can't pay the taxes on. The shopkeeper must have been hiding this child in the arms of this automaton while he dealt with the police. Without being told to stop, the automaton just kept making pins."

"There must be thousands of them. She couldn't stop without his permission?"

"Don't you see? If she stopped, she would be admitting she was self-aware. Admitting she was too advanced for the Emperor's laws! Unless someone came back here, and told her to stop, she couldn't! If she would have been caught, she would have been crushed."

"Couldn't she have just...I don't know, lied? And what about the child, don't automatons care about people?" Kristina asked, starting to feel a little desperately irritated. There seemed far too much obedience in this city, considering what they got in return for it.

"Maybe, I don't know how that works," Jenny said. "Come on, let's get out of here."

Jenny left the shop empty-handed, but for whatever reason, Kristina found herself now fingering a brass bee as she stumbled down the streets towards their place of work.

When they arrived at the elegant, though claustrophobic house of the Lady, Jenny was a bit relieved. Whatever fate was to befall her when her wicked employer learned of the jewelry shop had been postponed. The lady of the house had not come home from a party the night before, and had sent word that she would not be home today, so *please don't bother making anything too elegant* for her husband. The Lady was much younger than her decrepit husband, and would often stay out late at parties, only to return several days later.

They spent the day washing, polishing, dusting, folding, ironing, sweeping, and dusting again. Kristina swooned several times from the exertion on top of her recent wounds, and when she did, Jenny would stand by the door and keep a watch, so Kristina could sit down while working.

It was a very long day, well over eleven hours, and when they had finished, Kristina was practically collapsing. When they had been dismissed, they started the trudge home.

Kristina noticed at the end of the day that Jenny looked ten years older than she had at the beginning.

The walk home was long, so they took a cramped underground train for several miles, and then climbed the filthy and packed stairs out of the station onto the street where they lived.

The sky was again black when they emerged from the underground. They had been inside working during every hour of daylight, and missed the day completely.

Up the stairs of their tenement they trudged, and headed down a dark and stale-smelling hall to a set of elevators. Jenny, with some effort, pulled open the iron gate of one of the ancient elevators, and led Kristina in. She slid a gauge to her floor number, and pulled down on a chain handle which began their lurching and noisy ascent.

As soon as the elevator came to a stop, and its rattling mechanism had silenced, they heard crying.

"Oh, no," Jenny said softly but with foreboding, and her eyes grew moist. She quickly rattled open the gate, and half jogged down the hall, towards where their apartment door stood open.

Just inside the doorway was a man in a dark grey military suit, holding a pen and clipboard. He wore small round glasses, and the flat official-looking hat of an officer. On his left and right were burly police, and standing in the hall was one massive crouching automaton, of the same make and model as Gyrod, yet with a duller and more vicious look in his eye.

The family's father, who had been so confident in the morning, now stood with his back to the wall, his face hidden in his hands. The mother was on her knees, clutching a small child tightly in her arms, crying loudly. It had been her that they had heard from the elevator.

The child's face was pressed against her mother's chest.

The officer spoke with a tone of condescension. "Of course, we can always relocate one of the older boys, instead of the child. Let's see…" He did some math on his paper, and said, "Oh dear, I'm afraid that would change things for the worse. You see, your sons are all producing in excess of what they consume. The child is producing less than it consumes. So if you were to lose a son from this household, you'd actually be at a larger debt-to-income ratio."

"But, surely there is another option!" the mother said desperately.

"No. I'm afraid not. The deficit of this household is simply too high. You've simply more people consuming than you do producing. I'm afraid little Victoria is going to have to go," and at this he motioned, and the two police officers strode across the room. One picked up the child by the collar, while the other drew his pistol and held it to his side.

"Mother!" Jenny exclaimed, running to her. "Mother, what is happening?" she said, throwing her arms around the crying woman.

"What did you think would happen?" said Martha from

the doorway to the kitchen. "Each month they fall a little more behind. What did you think would happen? Victoria and Bethany together didn't earn enough to cover one of their Consumption Points! Whereas the older kids were all earning more than their CP's."

"What?!" Kristina asked, talking fast, trying to understand the situation. "What does 'relocate' mean?"

"It means they take my child, and I never see her again!" the mother burst out.

Kristina was disgusted with the weakness of this child's mother. She was exhausted from her daily excursion, but the anger shot to her face like boiling water poured onto a red hot stove. Rage, plus exhaustion, often equals violence. This was no exception.

"Bullshit it does," she said darkly, and in the blink of an eye she reached into the holster of the officer in the doorway, pulled his small elegant pistol from it, and held it to his temple. "Put - Victoria - down," she demanded in a slow, confident voice.

The officer with the drawn gun stepped forward to within a couple feet of Kristina, and tried to point it at her face. But before he had even completely raised the gun, Kristina kicked it from his hand with one long leg, and then kicked him in the throat.

He staggered back while she mumbled, "Idiot". She was thinking of all the battles she'd been in over the last few years. It was almost insulting to her that this officer couldn't see that he was no match for her. *What does a girl have to go through to be worthy of respect?*

"No!" Victoria's father and mother gasped, as if this was

the worst possible thing that could happen. "No Kristina, put the gun down! This isn't going to help!"

"Ya know, fuck this town." Kristina swore. "I have not fought battles through time, for years and years, only to end up here. Enduring this...this injustice!" Her voice was filled with wrath. "This is not going to happen!"

But before she had time to pull the trigger, she felt a cold steel hand wrap around the base of her neck, and lift her from the ground. Her head was jammed into the ceiling, and she saw no more.

When Kristina woke, Jenny was crying with Victoria's mother. She could hear the father repeating softly, almost as if he were singing to himself, "Victoria, come back to me. I should have never believed."

Now, I know what you are thinking right now, as you sit there reading this on your sofa, or on the bus to work, or in the crowded subway car. You are thinking, "This is just a pulp science-fiction novel. Don't let it get to you. This kind of thing doesn't happen in *real life*." I was thinking the same thing as I typed this. I thought, "This book I'm writing will be too unbelievable with its walled cities, political executions, genocide. This is just unrealistic."

But then I remembered a trip to Berlin. I saw the remains of the Wall. The Berlin Wall reminded me of the walled city of Kowloon I visited as a teenager. Not walls to keep the people safe, but to keep the people held in. I went to the Stasi museums, and I saw "The Cage". *But this is ancient history!* I reassured myself. *All kinds of terrible things happened in history.* But no, this argument didn't hold either. I was in high school when the Berlin Wall fell. Kowloon City still stood when my band Abney Park started gigging. And those are just the places I've visited.

And parents give up their children for debt all the time, a debt they would never have voluntarily entered into if they had understood how it worked. Families torn apart by systems they never wanted in the first place.

These things happen. They happen in far off countries. They happen in your country. They happened a hundred years ago, they happened thirty years ago, and they happen today.

Why is it that when a bear attacks a family, the father and mother would gladly lay down their lives for there children, but when a governmental system threatens to take a child away, people hide? Cowering in their own poverty, suffering a complete lack of freedom, they remain in the system that oppresses them. This has happened for thousands of years, and as far as I can see, it will keep happening.

When freedom is outlawed, only the outlaws are free.

WHAT BECAME OF THE LITTLE GLASS GIRL?

Lilith Tess had grown up in a glass shop. Her father, a respected and handsome young glass smith, had inherited the shop and career from his father, and so at a fairly young age, Mr. Tess became a valued member of the community.

But his life was tragic. He watched Lilith's mother die in childbirth, and this sadness nearly killed him. Before Lilith was old enough to be aware of this, he realized it was his duty to hide his sorrow from her. All his tears he hid from little Lilith, and instead he showered her with hugs, kisses, exaggerated chivalry, and eventually tutelage. This made her feel like a princess, but deep inside she sensed she was never enough for him. So while he was always trying to please her, she was always trying to do more to make him happy.

She spent her long days adored by him in his workshop behind the store. She watched him craft the most amazing things out of glass, and from this she inherited his cleverness. Electric lights were becoming all the rage in London, so a glass smith had to be familiar with electricity. Lilith and her father knew all there was to know about electricity and glass in 1906, and she never forgot it.

Her love for her father became a love of making things, and it was because of her love and skill at making things that Doctor Calgori had taken her under his wing. He liked to have a pretty young girl around him, and interested in him. This was not for romantic reasons–he was an old man. This was because it was flattering companionship. Her energy kept him energetic and feeling young, and her attentive need to learn helped him to feel valued. Lilith felt at home in the Doctor's workshop, working side by side as she did with her father.

But now Lilith was in a strange time. When she and Victor pulled her balloon from the lake, they used a truck that looked nothing like the machines of her day. It was massive, and square, and powerful beyond anything she knew. When they drove it down the road, it was nearly silent, and the view out of its windows was strange and foreign and ugly. Roads were rivers of shiny metal cars. There were no horses, no carriages, and almost nobody walking. Buildings were huge, and gray, and unadorned, and they lined the roads like oppressive walls. Signs glowed angrily from the side of the road, advertising things she didn't understand. People dressed in strange and unflattering clothes, of seemingly intentional shabbiness.

To Lilith, this was what 2011 looked like. It was foreign and uncomfortable for her, and it scared her more than anything she had yet seen.

So you can imagine her relief when Victor rented a very old and isolated workshop far outside of town, and the two set out to repair her Chrononautilus.

The walls were of wood, and they looked "right" to her. There was always a fire going in the wood stove, and it reminded her of her father's furnace. Victor wore an apron like her father did, and he was constantly moving about the shop, making plans, fixing things, asking her to fix things, or to explain how they should be fixed. He also spent many long nights reading books of history and farming techniques, and creating a vast and enterprising plan that little Lilith only partly understood.

Having spent many years on the *Ophelia*, she knew the Chrononautilus, the time device. The most challenging part of the repairs would be replacing the massive glass globes that generated the chronofield. Each one was the size of a bathtub, but completely round, and they had to be perfectly airtight so they could hold in their special aethers.

It was Lilith who constructed the new globes, not out of solid glass like the originals, which would have been beyond her skill, but out of stained glass and lead, like a church window in a cathedral. Perhaps she put more artistry into this design than was functionally necessary, but isn't that the joy of creating? She wove artwork into the designs–hearts and flowers, the names "Victor" and "Lilith," and in one spot that she hoped would not be seen, a baby in a crib, a little girl in a white lace bonnet.

Victor took many trips into town. This had something to do with what Victor called a "Wi-Fi hotspot," and though she didn't know what this was, she was more than content to stay in the workshop, and away from the ugly and confusing world outside it.

When Victor talked about changing the world, Lilith had no problem in sympathizing with his rationale. This world obviously needed saving, and this was a concept she was familiar with.

Late one summer night, after nearly a year and a half of preparation, Lilith and Victor drove to the grassy field where they first met. They unloaded their gondola together, and tied it to their collapsed balloon. They inflated the huge balloon with a noisy gas-powered fan, while Lilith loaded the gondola with books, clothes, and a Chronofax.

This device was Doctor Calgori's first effort with chronofields. It was the size of a small typewriter, but it had a little screen, and on it you could type yourself a note and send that note to a specific time, either before or after the time you were writing it. That note would then appear on the screen at that time, and in this way you could hold a conversation with yourself. So far there hadn't been much use for this, since of course they had just acquired it.

Somewhere in the back of Lilith's head she thought she would one day be able to have a conversation with her father, but since he had never owned it, she had not yet figured out how to do this. Sometimes, when Victor was asleep, she would send messages to herself ten years into the future, telling herself how much she loved him, and never to let him go. She never got a response.

As Lilith was packing the balloon, Victor tied the gondola to a large covered object they had brought on the back of a very large trailer.

Soon the balloon was rigid in the sky above them, confidently lifting their gondola, and starting to lift their heavy cargo. With the tug of a cord, they released themselves from the ground, and balloon, basket and cargo leapt into the air.

Lilith had not been aloft since her great fall, and it made her nervous. But having Victor there, excitedly talking to her about all of his great and seemingly impossible schemes, comforted her. She saw in him her father, and she was happy to be a part of his plans.

THE WIZARD OF OK
OKLAHOMA, 1934

There was an ocean of dust clouds 100,000 acres wide covering most of Oklahoma and much of the states around it. A huge sepia sea, churning, and frothing, and fuming.

Had you been on the ground, you would have had a scarf tied across your face, just so you could breathe, and you would hardly have been able to see your hands in front of you.

Farmers sat inside their homes, windows shut, towels stuffed under doors, yet still the dust got in and clouded the air of their small kitchens, settling on tables and food and in their water.

These farmers were beyond hope. The dust covered their crops, eroded their soil, and made working nearly impossible, so they huddled inside their little farmhouses, fearing for their livelihoods, and waiting until the storm passed so they could go outside and survey the damage.

A mile above this storm, however, the skies were blue and peaceful. The sun shone, and the air was crisp and cool and clean.

One particular patch of sky was growing dense. The air was falling in on itself, and soon a small pink cloud began to form and swirl. It was the color of the sky just before a storm. There was a loud crack as all the air in the cloud instantly doubled, and the cloud exploded outward, then gently dissipated. As the pink mists turned grey and faded, they revealed a large hot air balloon, striped like a circus tent. The balloon swung angrily, and leapt upward, which knocked Victor and Lilith to their knees.

Lilith grabbed Victor's hand and looked up at the ropes above them, hoping she would not see a frayed line, or ripped fabric, or a cracked basket. She could not control the wave of panic that rushed over her, and she could not stop replaying her fall in her mind.

Victor squeezed her hand tightly, just enough to get her attention, and he looked into her face with a calming smile. "We're good. We've made it," he said, with a reassuring display of confidence. He stood up, and leaned his head out over the basket, looking down. A huge parcel hung below them, wrapped like a gift in colored fabric. It was considerably bigger than any tractor, and it took many ropes to hold it up.

Victor smiled when he saw that it was safely suspended, and he said to Lilith, "We are going to blow these people's minds."

They stayed aloft all that night, and when the sun rose the next day the dust storm was gone. The ground below them was bleak. The dust had half-swallowed buildings, cars, and wagons, and left everything a dreary grey-brown. A color photo would have hardly looked different than a faded sepia one.

There was a city about a mile south of them, and as fate would have it, the winds were blowing in that direction. Victor glanced at the BTU gauge, and then turned the red painted handles of his gas tank. This extinguished the burners that were heating the air inside the airbag, and after a bit, the balloon began to slowly drop.

In the town square, dirty and tired citizens were gathering around a stage, and on the stage paced William J. Gault. He was a man in his late fifties, in a pin-striped suit with a tight white collar, and a massive handlebar mustache. He had been mayor for eleven years, and he was running again for a reelection. But the people of this town were becoming poor, and hungry, and angry. They stood before him impatiently waiting for a solution, while he stood nervously trying to figure out how to get their minds off of their troubles.

"Now, now. Settle down everybody," he said. "We are all in this together, and through hard work and integrity, the strength of our backs, and the sweat of our brows, we will persevere!"

But this was not a solution, and the people knew it. Unmoved, the crowd rumbled with noises of discontent. They grumbled things like, "That's no kinda answer!" and "Slick Willie done run outta ideas!"

"Mister Gault, I haven't had any work this week! How'm I supposed to look after my wife and little boy?" said a dusty man of thirty, in equally dusty overalls. "I've gone from farm to farm, but none of thems a-hirin'!" There was a tired sadness in his eyes, but also anger. To him, it was great selfishness that caused the farmers not to hire him.

"I am willing to work, and work damn hard. Isn't it my god-given right to be allowed to work for my family?"

"Jim," said an older man. "How can I afford to hire farmhands, when I can barely afford to feed my own family? After last night's storm, I'll be surprised if I have any crop left to bring in. I can't afford to hire on, even if it is your god-given right to work."

"We'll work for food!" some yelled.

"I ain't got none to spare!" yelled others.

Things were heating up, and the two policemen at either side of the stage looked nervously at each other.

Suddenly a shadow fell across the crowd, and all looked up in awe to see a huge balloon descending on the square.

"Greetings, friends!" Victor yelled from his gondola. He had a confident smile in his voice, and projected an aura of friendly trustworthiness.

The younger members of the crowd were enthralled by the balloon. Some of the older, wiser townspeople glanced up at the mayor and wondered if this was some distraction he had arranged for, but the mayor had an undeniable look of shock on his face.

The massive parcel under the gondola touched ground first, and it rocked a moment with the sound of creaking springs. This held the balloon in place like an anchor, and Victor tossed a rope ladder over the side of the basket.

Then he placed a brand-new beautiful grey top hat on his head, winked at Lilith, and whispered, "Let's change the world," before swinging out of the gondola.

As he climbed down the ladder, he addressed the throng. "Ladies and gentlemen, I come to you in your hour of despair, but I bring with me the instrument of your salvation! I humbly ask your attention for a bit, and I will set all of your minds to rest, and fill your hearts with hope!" He might have been laying this on a bit thick, but in order to get a feel for the speech of this time he had been listening to old recordings. Most of the recordings were sermons.

"I see before me a distraught people. Your farms are dying, the soil is drying, and the winds are blowing it away. With no crops to harvest, people are out of work, people are hungry, and tired. That's right, you've got troubles." He walked across the square with a rope in his hand, and tied it to an oak that stood by the podium.

"But I have brought you a miracle, when nothing short of a miracle will do," he said, climbing onstage next to the mayor. Victor's blue eyes were sparkling. "I bring you a miracle," he paused for effect, "of Science!" He threw his arms into the air, and as he yelled out the word "Science" ,Lilith pulled a cord up in her basket that released the parcel, but not its covering. The balloon rose another 20 feet, lifting the brightly colored cloth to reveal a brand-new cherry-red combine harvester.

It glowed in the morning sun, and it was modern beyond anything these people had ever seen. In fact, if not for Victor, the world would see nothing like this for another 70 years.

"What is it?" asked Jim skeptically, to the crowd.

"It's a harvester. It'll reap, thresh and winnow your wheat faster that you can walk from one side of your field to another," Victor said, and many in the crowd gasped.

"Do I have your attention, fine people?" he went on. "Because this is not the only gift I bring. I'm an inventor. A scientist. And not only have I made you this fine machine, I have also devised a solution to every one of your other problems. Listen, your problem is the dust and the winds, and the lack of water. This fine machine will help you to bring in your crops, but there will be no more crops if you don't change the way you've been farming. You need to rotate your crops, you need cover crops, soil terracing, and wind-breaking trees need to be planted. No one of these things will end your problems, but all of them together will turn things around, and lead us back into a time of prosperity! Can I help you to do that?"

The crowd cheered. William J. Gault decided on the spot that perhaps it was time to retire. Later that month, a mayoral election was held, and it was not even close. Within a year, Victor had combine harvesters being built, perhaps not to the quality of the one he had brought with him, but based on that, they were able to create similar machines. People were busy building combines, re-planting farms, or making a thousand other changes Victor had brought back with him. Soon neighboring communities began to follow suit, and word of Victor's revolutionary ideas spread fast. The rest of the country wanted him to do for them what he had done for Oklahoma.

All through this, Lilith held his hand, and wondered where her place in this new life was. He would set plans, and effect them. He would rant about how much better the world was at this time when everything had not yet become so crowded. She would listen to his rants about pollution, and animal rights, and how it all came down to overpopulation. She would nod agreement, though she never really felt or understood why he was so angry.

She often thought of herself, alone up in her balloon, watching Victor change the world from afar. She had dreams that he was supposed to hold her anchor line while he was working, but that he had forgotten her, and she just drifted away.

WARNING SIGNS
NAPLES, 1946

"I don't want to look forward,
Or even look ahead.
I don't want the future,
For the future is dead."
- From the song Bad Things Coming

Twelve years later, Victor stood in the warm night air on a white marble balcony overlooking the Mediterranean. In his flawless pin-striped suit, he was at once powerfully confident and charismatic. His appearance defied age. He could have been in his thirties, or in his fifties, as far as anyone could tell, and he had looked that way for the decade he had been in office. He was rereading a few pages he had typed the week before, while pacing back and forth in the warm summer night air.

As he did this, a beautiful young lady of twenty-two walked up to him. Her eyes were like emeralds and her hair like yellow silk. Her name was Floriana Futino, and she wore a white ball gown, the cut of which would have been shocking in the US. But here in Naples, it was acceptable attire for a political function of this stature. As she entered, the warm light of the doorway fell behind her and turned her dress nearly transparent.

"Mr. President," she said in silky tones, "your audience iz assembled". Her voice hinted at an Italian upper-class upbringing, and contained an equal mix of competence and sensuality. She had been raised in the mansions and villas of Milan, and was currently employed in the consulate, primarily for the purpose of meeting the very powerful.

Victor looked slowly up from his papers, his eyes tracing the contour of her inner thighs through the translucent dress' fabric. Though her feet were together, at no point from ankle to hip did her legs touch, and this sent a little shiver up his spine.

"Thank you," he said, quickly returning his eyes to his papers, hoping she hadn't noticed, but she had. In fact, she was aware of every aspect of her appearance as well as his reaction to it. Her graceful step, her flawless figure, and the translucency of the backlit dress were all deliberate. She had planned her entrance carefully.

Victor always avoided eye contact with Floriana. Especially when around his wife, Lilith. He loved Lilith dearly, but Floriana had intended to catch his eye, and she was very skilled at this.

Over the last ten years, Victor's success had made him and Lilith rich. They pampered themselves in every conceivable way, and soon became bored with the houses and furniture, the art and the servants. I'm sorry to say that, even though Victor's love of Lilith had not waned, he occasionally thought of new, more taboo luxuries. Luxuries that involved other women. *Didn't the man that saved the world deserve this?* he would think, before pushing the thoughts back out of his mind again, feeling guilty. Here on the balcony, those thoughts were returning, but he once again subdued his desire to use his confident nature and deep blue eyes in the fashion for which they were designed.

Floriana turned, then, and he let his eyes discreetly follow her as she left the room. *Flawless*, he thought, before forcing his attention back to his speech.

Shortly afterwards, Victor walked briskly onto a massive white marble stage. He set his papers onto a beautifully ornate wooden podium, and took a sip of water from a carved crystal goblet. Behind him was a vast wall of red velvet curtains, and in front of him were hundreds of distinguished guests.

Kings, queens, presidents, prime ministers, maharajas, sultans, sheiks, chieftains, and elders from all the nations of the world awaited him. For a decade, they had heard unbelievable stories about the young inventor who had created a legendary fortune in very few years. Any obstacle he met, he easily overcame. Where he encountered sickness, he invented medicines. Drought he cured with irrigation techniques that were decades ahead of their time. Infestations he met with pesticides, hunger with advanced farming techniques, homelessness with low-cost housing and work programs. Any problem he saw, he fixed with tools that he invented. Tools whose very manufacture seemed beyond the skills of the day.

In the decade that followed Victor's arrival, the leaders of the world heard breath-taking stories of this young man. He became president to a desperate and grateful nation. He applied his seemingly inexhaustible knowledge and innovation towards the troubles of the country, and seemed to take even the greatest tasks in stride. Often he predicted solutions no one could have guessed, in a way that seemed almost unbelievable.

His rule was so successful that the rules of leadership were changed to allow him more power. When no one stood in his way, he was always successful beyond anyone's hopes, so laws were quickly established to prevent any branches of the government from standing in his way.

When his term as president came to an end, a grateful nation voted to remove term limitations. No one could bear the thought of going back to the hard times before Victor Hippocrates. He healed the nation, just as his namesake had healed the sick.

In ten years, he transformed a country in its deepest depression into a garden of prosperity. Rich farmlands and parks now spanned what was once dry, barren desolation. As the other leaders of the world struggled hopelessly against wars, and starvation, and disease, and poverty, Victor strode confidently forward, effortlessly building his Eden.

For this reason, the rulers of the world waited with bated breath to hear this young leader speak, hoping to glean something from his great wisdom. Leading a nation is a great burden, and the nation's woes are great pains to its rulers. Any help they could get from Victor Hippocrates was welcome.

Victor fixed his eye on the assembly. He held a look of confident power, but also of concern. He spoke with strength and urgency. "Esteemed members of the League of Nations, I stand before you on the brink of the worst catastrophe in the history of the world. It is with the greatest urgency that I have called you all together, and I hope that my reputation will strengthen your confidence that what I set before you is of the utmost importance."

"As many of you know, I started my career as an inventor. I have created many things that the world had never seen before, many of which accomplished things previously thought impossible. One of these inventions I have not yet revealed, and it has shown me an impending doom that will befall us all if drastic action is not taken by you, the world's caretakers."

He took another sip from the goblet. His eyes flashed to Lilith, who sat in the front row. She nodded to him reassuringly.

"The invention of which I speak I call a Chrononautilus. It's a vehicle, but it does not travel only from location to location, but also through time. With this conveyance I have seen a future dark and terrible!" The crowd began to stir, hundreds of hushed voices making disapproving and angry whispers. Some thought this young ruler had cracked. Had they been summoned from their thrones and palaces to hear the ravings of a madman?

Others remained confident. Those who have accomplished great things do not find it hard to picture others doing great things, and this explanation, though unique, did explain Victor's successes perfectly.

Before discontent could fester, Victor went on in a stronger tone. "You don't have to take my word about the future I have seen, for it is my plan to show it to you." And with a sweeping gesture of his arm, lights were dimmed and red curtains were pulled back revealing a massive movie screen. In the center of the black screen was a small blue dot that grew slowly. Gesturing to this dot, he said, "This is our home. The planet earth, as seen from the perspective of the stars. In a few short decades, the inventions of mankind will have us traveling so high in the skies that looking downward will show us this view of the earth, and from that vantage man seems like an infinitesimally small population on this world, like a rash, like a virus on the face of a planet. But a virus, no matter how small, can kill the organism which it infects." Here he pounded his fist on the podium, and his face was growing passionate as he raised his voice.

"Over the next hundred years, our numbers will swell! The famines of our grandfathers' times are being eliminated, the diseases cured, and our predators hunted to extinction! This seems to us good, but that vision is shortsighted! Because of our accomplishments, all of the things that keep the human population in check are being eliminated, and the result will be catastrophic!" He was nearly yelling now, and swinging his fist with every point he made. As he spoke, the screen began to show scenes from the future. Hospitals filled with the sick, cities growing rapidly over many years to fill the beautiful nature around them. The audience had seen science-fiction films before, but they were jerky black-and-white things, and obviously fictional. This film was fluid, and in perfect color, and something about those facts helped confirm that these images were in fact from the future.

"You have all seen the filth that our largest cities produce. It has been a problem for hundreds of years. The disposal of this can become an insurmountable task, even now. But imagine a future where all cities are as large as our largest metropolises, and the number of cities is so great that there are no spaces between them! City borders city, from coast to coast! Where then will the filth go? And when the filth pours into our waters, and fills the streets around the endless buildings, piled high against the schools of our children, and the hospitals of our sick and dying parents, what then is to become of our nations?"

"I know in our present time, this seems millennia away, but the images you're seeing are just 70 years in our future! Many of you will live to see this day. You will live to see your children suffer, trapped in a hell on earth by your complacency! If we as the world's leaders don't make a grand unified action, this *will* come to pass." Most of the images he showed were in fact from the 1990's, chosen to represent the very worst conditions. Camera angles showed vast cities, but not the countrysides around them. Dumps and polluted seas appeared, but not the clean and pristine lakes and seas of the day. The result of his edits showed a world on the brink of death, and it was horrible.

It's possible that this is how Victor remembered his time. I'm sure he truly believed this would eventually come to pass. Who can say that it wouldn't? And because of this, Victor spoke with confidence and certainty.

"If we don't create a unified front against the growth of mankind, we will in a short time be confronted with the horrible responsibility of reducing the world's population, or watching the human race choke itself and the entire planet into extinction." The crowd watched the screen with moist eyes, and bated breath as Victor's tirade went unchecked.

He was a marvelous speaker, and had they known it, his style resembled Adolf Hitler more than any other speaker. But they could not have known this, for none of them had ever heard of Hitler. For by this time, young Adolf had been kidnapped as a baby and raised in a nunnery. Eventually he became a not completely unknown painter. It's amazing how a little love and nurturing can change the world.

Victor went on, "I propose we unify the governments of the world, in an effort to create a more integrated system for handling these problems. Instead of wars fighting for resources, let's create a unified government with a single agenda for dealing with this impending doom. Not a hundred individual governments each fighting for what their nation needs, but one government, fairly providing for all. One ruling party. One father to see to it that all of his children are treated fairly. One father to embrace the entire world, men, women, children, animals, and plants, all taken care of, and equally respected."

Its was a brilliant speech, in that it first showed indisputable proof that all of the world's leaders were about to fail, and then at the last second, it gave them a way out. A way to take these responsibilities and hand them to someone else.

If you knew for a fact that you would ruin the lives of your children if you were left in charge, wouldn't you be willing to turn things over to someone who wouldn't?

In the months that followed this speech, Victor was approached by various nations of the world. Nations that suffered poverty or famine were the first to join. They were promised independent rule on most issues, and were promised that they would be provided resources equal to the more fortunate nations of the world. Of course this was easily granted. It doesn't take a lot of resources to show massive improvements in the poorest nations.

As the decade progressed, other nations saw evidence that Victor's predictions were coming to fruition. Even the most rich and powerful countries eventually had a population that could imagine their impending doom. Many wealthy and comfortable cities saw riots, as people feared not being a part of Victor's plans.

In the end, the world begged to give itself to Victor. And Victor was courteous enough to accept.

SEDUCTION
NAPLES, 1946

But this had not yet come to pass for Victor, and after his speech, Lilith found him backstage. He was surrounded by White House aides. Dashing men in suits and fedoras, and beautiful young women in ball gowns all congratulated him and toasted him. This was a celebration. Champagne and egos were all flowing to excess.

His speech had been flawless, and it was obvious that the rulers of the world had been affected in exactly the ways that Victor had predicted. Many of his aides knew his long-term plan was to unite all the nations under his own unique ethics and leadership. To them, they had just made a huge step toward this goal, and the small crowd was excited to be a part of such an historic undertaking. The first step towards a single world government.

This worried no one. The sirens that go off in *your* head when you hear the words "world domination" did not alarm them. This reminded no one of dictators of the past who sought to rule the world, because there had never been the level of dictators in the past that you now remember. The misguided heroics of the crew of the *H.M.S. Ophelia* had seen to that.

History books rarely mention an airship full of pirates appearing and vanquishing the villains of the past, because one does not become a "History Book Villain" if one never has success in the first place.

Lilith tried to force her way into the crowd of supporters surrounding Victor, but after getting jarred by one large and a bit too jovial young writer, she decided to put her attention to a bottle of sparkling wine.

Lilith had been growing nervous lately. The more Victor accomplished, the more his accomplishments were the only thing that interested him. His thrills were no longer in Lilith, but in his own plans and successes, and this made her increasingly uneasy. She feared he was growing away from her. She worried she was no longer stimulating for him. She worried she was no longer a pretty young girl, as she now saw herself an *"old wife of thirty-four"*. This was, of course, silly, but Lilith had always equated youth with beauty, and no amount of consolation from Victor would change her mind. In her insecurity, she turned toward anything that would dull her sense of anxiety, which mostly came out of a bottle.

After the first bottle had been emptied, a handsome young aide opened another for her. He poured her a glass, while standing inappropriately close to Lilith, not recognizing she was Victor's wife. Lilith had always been very beautiful, and she still was, but she was completely in denial about this now. The aide found her exciting and beautiful, but not seeing this, Lilith found the young man simply annoying and intrusive, not flattering and flirtatious. This was probably a good thing, since Lilith hungered to be exciting and beautiful to someone.

By the time the second bottle was gone, so was the handsome man, as well as most of the partiers. So Lilith grabbed a third bottle, and went to find Victor. She felt painfully lonely and abandoned.

He was no longer in the party room, but a mousey brunette in a blue chiffon dress pointed her toward the balcony. She wove her way through the remains of the crowd, trying not to reveal how much her head was spinning from the champagne.

It was dark on the veranda. But the cool night air, the stars, and the quiet all held a sense of magic. Somewhere beyond the balcony, the Mediterranean could be heard gently slapping the smooth sandy beach.

Standing at the rail, hands nearly touching, were Victor and Floriana. Their eyes were locked, and she was talking to him about something. It looked flirtatious, but not completely conspiratorial. Often either Lilith or Victor would use their good looks to gain leverage over someone important, so there was an assumption between them that this closeness could be interpreted as a part of their work. Typically, however, their attention was not on someone as attractive as Floriana, which made this seem more like a crime than usual.

Lilith walked clumsily up to them, meaning to, at the very least, flash Victor an accusing look, but Floriana turned immediately to Lilith, and took her by her hands.

"Lilith, my dear! Congratulations! You two 'ave accomplished an amazing zing tonight!" And she pulled her close and kissed each cheek, as Italians do. Lilith found Floriana's checks smooth, and warm, and she lingered a little too long on them, as she thought, *is this how my cheeks feel to Victor?*

Floriana went on, "I am zo excited for you both. Victor, you are zo lucky to have accomplished zo much, and yet have such a beautiful wife as Lilith." And as she said this she turned towards Victor, but left one arm around Lilith's waist. "Tell me about how much you love Lilith, Victor," she said, taking his hand.

This was of course an awkward question, and Victor indeed felt awkward. But Victor did love Lilith dearly, and Lilith, in her condition, looked up at him with need in her eyes. She was drunk and insecure. He knew she needed reassurance.

"Lilith is everything to me," he said sincerely. "She is my motivation, and my inspiration. She is the instrument of my success, and the reward for it!" And as he said this, he took Lilith's hand, but Floriana did not release his other hand.

"Lilith, you know I could have accomplished none of this without you. You are all of my dreams come true, for none of my dreams could have come true without you." He was right, of course, but I wonder if he believed it when he said it.

Lilith's eyes were growing moist, but she retorted, "Your dreams of me were fulfilled years ago."

"But I don't dream *of* you Lilith, I dream *with* you. Isn't that so much better?"

"Maybe, but…"

But before Lilith could finish, Floriana was changing the subject. "Beautiful girl, you are chilled to ze bone! Come sit with me under your husband's fine coat, and ve will warm each other." Floriana pulled Victor's greatcoat over herself and Lilith and they sat on a marble bench surrounded by potted flowers.

To Lilith, Floriana was soft warm silk. She had an arm around Floriana under the coat, and Floriana felt slender and smooth. This thrilled Lilith, though she didn't understand why it should.

"If I were a man," Floriana said to Lilith, "I would be very jealous of Victor to have a wife zo beautiful as you. No man should be zo lucky as to keep a jewel such as this for only himself." And as she said this, Lilith's eyes were locked on Floriana's. Lilith longed for this attention, these compliments that were once so common in her life, but went away after the world knew her to be married.

Victor pulled up a white painted cast iron chair, and sat near the two girls under the coat. He had also been drinking and so his typically quick mind was in a hazy glow. Something was happening here between these two beauties. Something forbidden and exciting. It felt like a long-sought luxury, and he was growing excited.

Under the coat, Floriana had one arm around Lilith's waist. She placed her other hand onto Lilith's thigh, and said, "Since you are in Europe, and ve are celebrating, let's celebrate ze way ve Europeans do." And with that, she kissed Lilith on the lips. Softly, slowly, Floriana's lips parted, and her tongue flicked inside Lilith's mouth. Lilith's whole body thrilled and shivered. When they parted, Lilith giggled. This was as exciting as her first kiss, an excitement she hadn't felt in years, and she was tingly and warm from it.

Then she thought of Victor, and looked to see if he was angry. Instead of anger, she saw surprise and excitement on Victor's face. He had pulled himself surprisingly close, now, and he had one hand on each girl's shoulder.

Seeing approval, Lilith turned back toward Floriana, and kissed her again, this time long and passionate and deep.

To Victor, it reminded him of watching Lilith eating ripe fruit, slowly biting, sucking, and savoring. He had always loved to give her things, and watch her enjoy them. Pampering her was one of his greatest joys, and watching her excited like this made his chest tighten and swell with pride and love as much as if he had given her a beautiful gem. Much more so, since material things couldn't bring much pleasure when you already had all you could want.

To Lilith, it was decadent, and taboo...and she had Victor's complete attention for the first time in years.

Floriana said, "Now, Lilith, you kiss Victor. Ve don't want such a handsome man to feel left out."

And so Lilith kissed Victor, and found she was more excited to do so than she had been in years. Having Floriana there in the same embrace as she kissed Victor made the kiss infinitely more taboo and exciting. As she kissed him, Floriana leaned in and nibbled her earlobe.

SICKNESS AND REMEDIES
WASHINGTON, DC, ONE YEAR LATER

Floriana Futino slipped silently from Lilith's sleeping embrace, and as quietly as she could, she slid out of bed. Every square inch of her body felt nauseous, and she ran to the bathroom, hoping to reach the toilet before it was too late. On her knees in front of a seat that had held a hundred presidential asses, she realized she had knelt here the last five mornings. She thought, *did I eat something that made me sick?* That would not explain being sick every morning for a week. *Could it be the flu?* No, there were no other symptoms, no fever, no congestion. *Could I be pregnant?*

With that thought, she heaved the contents of her stomach into the toilet. She shut the bathroom door with her foot so no one would hear.

At the same time, the door to the bedroom swung open and slammed into the opposite wall. Victor strode angrily in.

"Egotistical bastards!" he shouted. "What gives them the right! All mankind can be dammed, for all I care!" he said as he threw his coat and briefcase on the sofa.

Lilith was awake in a flash. She knew this mood of Victor's well, and before she asked him what had angered him today, she slipped quietly to the door and shut it. She didn't want the White House staff to hear his lack of control.

"Cats!" he said. "Did you know that the cities are filled with feral cats?"

"Is that bad, my dear?" she asked.

"No! It's good!" he yelled, not meaning to yell at her, but in his passion he did. "We build our cities and cover all the wild! They are running out of places to live. Any animal that can survive in our waste and filth should be allowed to at least try!"

"Alright," said Lilith, waiting for him to come to the point.

"But there is a group, the *Humane Society!* They are rounding up all the free animals, and poisoning them! They say it's unsafe for people, and they imply that allowing the cats to be free is somehow cruel to the cats. It is a goddamn holocaust! It's genocide! An *Inhumane* Society, if you ask me!"

"They've been doing this since my time," Lilith said.

"Yes, and they hadn't given up the practice over 100 years later, in my time!" Victor growled. "If this is not stopped, it will continue for decades, maybe centuries!"

Floriana stepped out of the bathroom, a towel barely covering her slender, flawless body. "What are you zo excited about on zis fine morning?" she said in silky tones, successfully hiding the fact that she had been sick moments ago.

"Feral cats" said Lilith.

"Ugh, filthy things!" Floriana exclaimed. "They kill all the songbirds!"

Victor groaned under his breath. He was angry, and filled with passion for his cause, and he did not enjoy Floriana's company when he was in this mood. Lilith would listen to him, and support his opinions, all while calming him down. Floriana would be condescending toward him, and kiss him, and he would be distracted, and lose his focus.

"I have to go," he said, and by this he meant time travel. "I have to do something about this." He threw a suitcase on the bed. "Mankind's population is still growing, and their self-righteous destruction is growing faster! We spread into the animals' habitats, and the gentler breeds die immediately. Now we are killing animals for no more reason than that they are trying to survive amongst us. There is now talk of reducing the wild horse populations! Killing off the last of the free beasts, to make more room... for what?! For more filth and more men?"

"But my beautiful darling!" Floriana said, "You only just got here! Me and Lilith were having zo much fun while you were away. Come to bed. You should join us. I miss you!"

Lilith ignored Floriana, and said, "Can't you simply send some memos? Have the group abolished?"

Victor wouldn't look at her. "I will not sit idly by and watch this world turn into the world I left. A world I left in anger!"

"The 'Butterfly Effect' is completely backward," Victor growled under his breath. "Every change I make slowly undoes itself, as the world tries to go back to its old broken self. It needs constant force to stay in the direction I need, and by staying in one time I can't apply enough force.

"Well, if I can't make changes here fast enough to stop the spread, to stop this infection, then I will visit a hundred times! I'm tired of waiting here, and watching. My plans are taking too long. I will grow old here before I ever see my plans completed. I need to jump ahead, and start the next step. And if things are still not changing fast enough, I will hit them harder. If the tweezers won't bend the metal, the sledgehammer will!"

"But Victor! I have barely seen you! Please don't go now. Stay a few days. I need time with you." Lilith's eyes were glossy, now, and she felt a sense of panic. He had been traveling more and more without her, and she was constantly afraid he'd get so caught up in his plans that he'd forget to return to her.

"I can't sit by!" Victor said, throwing a change of clothes into the suitcase. He missed Lilith, too, and although he enjoyed their times with Floriana, Floriana was becoming a nuisance. Her mind was only focused on how the three could pamper themselves. She treated his goals as if they were some addiction that was getting in the way of their true happiness. And since Floriana was always with Lilith, it was easier for him to simply leave the two girls when he wanted to work.

"I will travel to 30 years from now, when my plans are more complete. I have left detailed instructions. All I need to do is order them into effect. I need to balance the population. We need a natural, permanent way to control human population, and it's taking too long."

"Take me with you, Victor. I can help! I can! I helped get us this far, didn't I?" Lilith was pleading, and desperate. "I understand the chrononautical equations better than you. If I come, we can make more moves. Have a greater effect!"

"But darling, I have worked this hard partially to save you from all this work. You've seen how it's aged me. If I spend five years in another time, I return to you five years older. You should not have to suffer this fate!"

"I don't care. I want to be by your side. We can grow old together. That's how we started this. Side by side."

Floriana came to Lilith now. She stood partially behind her, with both arms sensually around her, and let her towel slip to the floor. Lilith could feel Floriana's smooth skin through her silk gown. Her breasts pressed to Lilith's back.

"Surely you two would be 'appier to 'ave a few days with me before you go?" she said.

Lilith pulled away from Floriana and went to get her own suitcase. "It's not that we don't love you, Flora, but this is something we have to do," she said.

133

Floriana was going to become indignant at being brushed aside like this. She was going to pout, or protest, or even threaten. But then she felt a wave of nausea come over her again, and she thought, *I must be pregnant.*

So instead of protesting, she said, "Go, then. I want for you whatever makes you happy. Come back in a year." And her eyes watered up with the next wave of nausea.

Misjudging this, and feeling pity for her, Victor walked over to Floriana.

"Flora, darling," he said, gently resting his hands on her naked shoulders. "You are so good to us. You give everything of yourself, and ask for nothing in return." He didn't hear Lilith's grunt of disagreement with this. "I will make sure you are well cared for. We will return in a year, and at that time, I will have a little gift for you. I have been setting something up for us all. A permanent home for the three of us. A castle, on a tropical beach, in a time after all this work is done. You can live there with us in luxury, away from all these efforts that you hate."And with that, he kissed her, and walked with Lilith out of the room.

As soon as the door had shut, Floriana ran back to the bathroom.

Victor and Lilith strode out across the foggy front lawn of the White House, to where the balloon was tied and waiting. He had dictated many pages of instructions to dark-suited aides, and told them he would be traveling abroad on diplomatic missions for most of the next year. He left in their keeping a device called a Chronofax, with which they could contact him on any issues that might come up.

As they walked, Lilith was excited as a schoolgirl, and she took his hand. This was to be an adventure like they used to have, and she was ready for it. She needed to escape.

Lilith both loved and hated Floriana. She loved her attention. She loved the way that touching Floriana felt like she was touching herself, feeling herself from another perspective. But she hated her when Victor was there. She hated comparing herself to Floriana's beauty, as Victor must be doing. She hated when Victor touched Floriana, and above all she hated watching them kiss. Lilith desperately needed to get away with just Victor, even if that meant giving up her obsession with Floriana.

But she hoped Floriana would still be waiting for them when they returned.

Lilith and Victor climbed into the gondola. White House staff handed them several baskets packed with space-efficient but luxurious foods. Then, with a presidential wave, Victor pulled the mooring pins that released their balloon, and the two soared up into the sky.

Since it was a foggy day, they were out of sight almost immediately. This strategy had been in Victor's mind all morning, and it's partly what drove his urgency. He needed to get up and out of sight before the fog lifted.

Once out of the fog, they looked out across a sea of clouds. The only thing protruding was the spire of the

Washington Monument. All the hustle and bustle of the city was obscured from sight, and the world seemed empty and serene. Lilith was reminded of her years on the *H.M.S. Ophelia*, while Victor thought how beautiful the world looked if you could cover up the things of man.

When they reached a sufficient altitude, Victor grinned at Lilith. "Are you ready for another rocky ride?" he asked mischievously.

She grabbed a pair of handles on the walls of the now elegantly-crafted basket to brace herself.

"Let's!" she said with excitement. She thought to herself, *no matter how this turns out, whether we live through this next jump, or die during it, this is what I want. Me and Victor...alone.*

But then she immediately missed Floriana, and felt guilty.

Victor adjusted the dials of the Chrononautilus's control box, and pulled the lever. The two stained-glass orbs filled with a pink gas, the color of the sky just before a storm. As they did, a wind hit the balloon and clouds formed around them. In less than a second, it was raining. Lilith felt her ears pop painfully, just before...CRACK!

The balloon vanished from the sky.

The Royal Vivarium
Washington DC: 1977

There was a second *CRACK!* And the balloon appeared again, swinging violently around on its ropes. The clouds dissipated as fast as they had formed, and soon the balloon calmed its swinging. It was a warmer day now than the one they had left thirty years before, and so the balloon began to drop.

The city of Washington DC was stretched out below them, but it had changed quite a bit in the three decades they'd been gone. Much of the city that they knew had been abandoned, and much had been torn down and replanted.

To the south of the city, they saw large ranches that had not been there before, and huge glass buildings constructed like massive Victorian greenhouses. Large beasts of many kinds could be seen through the glass.

These reminded Lilith of an enormous building she had visited in London with her father when she was a child. It was made of glass and metal, and so big it practically had its own weather. It was built in an extraordinarily short time in order to house an exhibit of science and progress. Her father had taken her there to show her all that could be done with glass, but most of the time they spent inside he was grumbling about the glass shortage the building's construction had caused.

These new glass buildings, called the Vivariums, were used for breeding. Many of the instructions Victor had left behind involved reestablishing habitats and breeding populations of endangered or even extinct species. There was now a large branch of the government dedicated to the repopulating of animals.

Since Victor's plan had been so exuberant, this branch had often been overzealous in the way it executed his instructions. The program now had funding that surpassed the military during wartime, and it had been operational for over 30 years.

When your focus is on "bringing back endangered or extinct species," one of the first questions you ask yourself must be, "species that became extinct at what time?" Dodos were brought back based on DNA from a single specimen found in the basement of the Natural History Museum in London. That seemed fair enough, as mankind had single-handedly caused their extinction. This is what Victor had intended.

But this branch of the government had been given an obscene amount of power, and the size of their budget was based on how many species they were trying to restore at any given time. So after the Dodo was so successful, they turned their enthusiasm towards other species. Bison, camelops, saiga antelope, giant condor, hyaenodon, indrikkus, mastodon... the list was seemingly endless.

Lilith and Victor in their balloon had no idea yet of what had been happening. All Victor knew as he navigated altitude was that the Vivariums had been assigned to undo the damage of mankind. After thirty years of nearly unlimited budget, they had accomplished a good deal more than that.

With a little effort, Victor was able to set the balloon back down on the now greatly expanded White House lawn. They were greeted by presidential aides in clothes of a fashion not much different than when they had left– perhaps even more old fashioned. These aides had a look of startled reverence on their faces that was so intense it actually unnerved Victor. He was used to respect, but these people greeted him with awe.

"Your Majesty," one said, bowing slightly as he said it.

Victor raised an eyebrow, "I hardly think that's an appropriate way to address the president of the United..." but Lilith kicked him in the shin, and flashed him a look all wives have mastered since the dawn of time. A look that said, *shut up!*

"Sir?" asked the aide, confused.

Victor deflected the question. "Do you have my

reports?"

"Yes, Your Majesty," the aide said, fumbling in a dark leather briefcase and pulling out a stack of papers. Victor took them and said, "Lilith and I will walk to the house from here. Thank you, your company will not be necessary." At this the staff looked concerned, but they unquestioningly obeyed him.

Victor walked and read. Lilith walked silently next to him. Occasionally he gave a little "Ah!" of excitement, or a "Hum…" of disapproval, as he read reports of all the progress that had been made by his staff in the last 30 years.

Before they reached the White House, they came to a garden, huge and wonderful, full of peacocks and topiary, bordered by very old and beautiful trees. Under one tree they found a lovely white painted bench. They sat on this bench and Victor continued reading, handing pages to Lilith when he finished them. The day was sunny and warm, and there were more birds singing than Lilith had heard in a very long time.

"It looks like things have been going well!" Lilith said.

"Somewhat," Victor said. "But slower than I had hoped. There are still many species on the brink, this endangered list is eight pages long! There must have been more species than we knew about, half of these are animals I've never heard of."

"Yes, but look at the maps of national parks! These are huge! It looks like more parks than human-populated areas!"

"Yes, yes, that is good, but let's see," Victor skipped to the last few pages of the document. "Oh!" he exclaimed. "This is terrible! Human populations are still rising. Possibly faster than ever! How can this be? We've decreased the human habitat!"

Lilith handed him a sheet. "It looks like the parks have been growing steadily over the years as you requested, but human populations have also been increasing. The result is that the urban areas have been getting more and more crowded, and there have been protests and even rioting from groups demanding to be allowed to settle in the parks. There are even some terrorist groups that have left the cities and set up little moving camps inside the national parks. These terrorist groups constantly relocate, and so far have been impossible to find and remove. They call themselves the 'New Bedouins', and they are really causing trouble. They hunt the protected species, and attack government outposts."

Victor stood, agitated. He looked into the leaves of the trees above them, and Lilith wondered if she had ever seen lines of concern so deep on his face.

Victor mumbled to himself, working something out as he did. "How does nature keep a population at bay? What keeps one species out of the areas of another…" But as he thought out loud, he was interrupted by an abrasive and inhuman cry. It was coming from the center of the garden, shrieking and howling, soon followed by more shrieking and finally growls.

Lilith stood up, and Victor stood on the bench to get a better look. He could see a commotion in amongst the tall flowering bushes, but he could not see what it was.

Suddenly five peacocks shot out of the garden, and ran past their bench in fear, followed by three large panthers.

These were jet black, with glossy fur stretched over rippling muscles. The cats were of exaggerated proportions, larger than any tiger Victor had ever seen, and when the cats saw the two people standing on the bench, they hunched down and stared hungrily at Victor and Lilith.

Lilith glanced above her, and in an instant gave a little jump and pulled herself into the tree. This triggered the nearest cat to leap at Victor, who ducked, allowing the cat to miss him, colliding with the tree behind him, but then landing directly upon Victor.

The cat was disoriented for a second, and the two rolled to the ground. It pinned Victor with a huge claw, but before it could sink its teeth into his throat, Victor blocked by sticking his arm into the panther's mouth.

Lilith screamed from her tree branch, and would have leapt to the ground to help, if not for the other two beasts that circled her tree growling. She knew she would never make it to Victor.

Victor's cat was now shaking him like a rag doll and his blood was covering the cat's face, as well as most of himself. The cat stopped shaking him for a second, and Victor tried in vain to kick the cat's face. This had no effect other than to make the beast thrash him about even more vigorously, and both Lilith and Victor heard his arm snap in the beast's jaws.

Lilith cried out at this, but as she did, one of the other two cats leapt straight into the air, and clambered onto Lilith's branch. Crouching on the branch, and began slowly creeping toward, its bright yellow eyes locked with hers.

There was a loud rifle-shot, followed by several more,

and the cat holding Victor released him. It walked in a circle slowly, lay down, and died.

Below Lilith's tree she saw another panther's head erupt in blood and it fell instantly limp. The panther on the branch next to Lilith received a shot in the hip and turned angrily toward the house before it was shot several more times and fell from the tree.

For a second, all was quiet. No birds sang. Then several men ran up to Victor. They were wearing black uniforms, with silver emblems on their sleeves depicting a bald eagle angrily gripping an American flag. They had huge rifles on their backs.

One of them began, "Don't move, Your Highness. Wait for the doctors to..." But before he could finish, Victor was on his feet. Taking a rifle from the guard, he struck him viciously in the face with it, the stock of the gun slashing the young man's face from forehead to cheek, and cutting his left eye.

Victor was in a rage, and he said, "You fucking ass! You just shot them! How dare you! What gives you the right to take the life of a beast hunting for its own survival?"

Lilith ran to Victor and took the rifle away. "I'm so sorry," she said, handing the rifle to the man. Turning to Victor she whispered, "Victor, he just saved your life!"

Victor swooned and sat down. Blood was running freely from his chest, and his arm was bent at a grotesque angle. He was ferociously angry, but for the moment his injuries were conquering his rage.

The guard Victor had hit was a very attractive man about thirty years old, with a trim blond beard, blue eyes, and white-blond hair. His name was Horatio. As he wiped the blood from his face, he looked angry and bitter, but controlled. This was a man who had spent much of his life angry and bitter. His left eye was closed now, and it would never fully open again, but he showed little sign of the injury.

Horatio had been abandoned by his mother when he was very young, and raised by one of the White House housekeepers. He was an illegitimate child, and had been instructed to hide who his mother and father were, though he kept his mother's last name. His father did not know about him.

As a young man, Horatio had made a career of following orders that often didn't make sense to him, and bitterly suffering the repercussions of them. Being struck by a "superior" just after saving his life was something this man was not surprised by, but it was getting harder and harder for him to endure this treatment.

The only way out of this cycle was to rise in the ranks, so instead of protesting he said, "Sir, I beg your pardon. I must have misunderstood the circumstances. Perhaps, through my dedicated service to you, I can make amends for this thoughtless action."

Victor ignored him, but Lilith thanked him, after which one of the other guards pulled Horatio aside, and whispered, "The nurses have arrived, Captain Futino."

THE BEASTS HAVE ESCAPED
YEAR: 1977

Victor Hippocrates sat on a beautiful white rattan settee, his arm in a sling and his chest wrapped in slightly bloody bandages. He was on a verandah of the White House that had a view of the gardens and the Vivarium breeding houses beyond. For the last week he had sat here in the warm quiet sun, reading about *The Riots*.

As people had been forced out of more and more of the "natural habitats" of the endangered species, there had been an increasing number of protests. Originally, laws stated that men and women could visit the National Parks, which now covered the majority of North America. But people were looking for a permanent way out of the crowded and ugly urban areas. When more and more dangerous species were added to the National Parks, it became clear that people should not be allowed to visit at all. People were not safe in the parks, and this was the reason they built The Wall. The Wall was a massive concrete and steel construction that circled the parks, keeping beasts in and people out. As the national parks grew to cover the majority of the continent, it soon felt more like the people were being locked in while the animals where being set free.

In the shadow of The Wall the lives of the common man became dreary and bleak. Some of these people had a very clear memory of what nature was like; in their dark and dismal jobs, they thought of fields, flowers and birds, and they wanted to live amongst them. Victor, who had no problem thinking generations into the future, viewed this as a temporary setback. In a generation, people would not remember nature, and not miss it.

Hundreds of protests had broken out over the last five years, and as the police tried to subdue the mobs, many protests turned into riots. Now some parts of the urban areas, especially those in the shadow of The Wall, remained in a perpetual state of protest and unrest.

Victor saw all of this as an inevitable side-effect of overpopulation. To Victor, there were simply too many humans for their habitats. Despite all of his efforts, man's population continued to grow, even as he decreased the area they were allowed to dwell in. This angered him, and he had been brooding for days, which greatly worried Lilith. As she sat near him on the verandah, she tried to think of some way to pull Victor out of his depression.

"Victor, I know it's not what you had hoped for, but

perhaps this is simply the next step towards your goals."

"But we came forward so we could avoid these 'steps'! Good god, it's been decades, Lilith. How long is this going to take?" Victor's voice was both angry and desperate.

Victor's raised voice put Lilith on edge. "I'm still on your side, Victor. You need to know that."

"Yes, I know Lilith, but don't condescend! I'm not a child."

Victor stared out the window, while Lilith looked at her hands on her knees and sighed.

Breaking the silence, Horatio Futino strode confidently into the room, his black patent leather boots shining flawlessly in the morning sun.

"Mr. President," he began, in a voice that reminded Lilith of Victor's, though more gravelly and abrasive. "I have a duty today that I think you would very much enjoy accompanying me on. I am overseeing the release of 10 new species to the Park. It will be my duty to protect the release from any New Bedouin terrorist activities. You should join us. From my platform, you will have a wonderful view of the release.

"Oh, Victor," said Lilith. "I think that is exactly what you need! Spend the day watching your success. Don't focus on the–" She was going to say, "failures" but thought better of it, and said, "–bad news."

Victor set down his papers, and stood. "I think you are right. I could profit from setting my eyes on some of my successes, instead of brooding over these numbers. How soon until we leave, Horatio?"

Within a few hours, Victor and Lilith stood next to Horatio on the deck of a vehicle called an aeroflet. It was a hunting platform, fifteen feet by twenty feet, that hung underneath two cigar-shaped balloons. In each corner of the platform was a swiveling propeller in a cage that could be aimed to steer and move the platform about.

With them on the deck were a dozen officers in black, each wearing darkened sunglasses that covered their eyes like goggles, and each holding a long-barreled rifle with a powerful scope. They paced about, staring over the edge of the aeroflet as the craft buzzed its way over crowded city streets towards The Wall.

The craft was one of four similar crafts that kept pace with a long train on the ground. The train was black, pulling at least a hundred black iron cages. It left the Vivarium, and trudged through progressively more and more crowded town, and cities. As the train neared The Wall, it began to slow.

There was a huge crowd assembled at the gates ahead of the train. Thousands of protestors stood with signs, yelling at the train, and up at Victor's aeroflet. Signs read, "Release the people from *their* cages!", "The absentee king hates his own kind!" "Don't choose animals over Man!", and "Give us back our world!"

"Idiots," Victor said under his breath, and to Lilith he said, "I have seen what they would do with *their* world. I'm trying to save it from their destruction."

Lilith could not help but think, *but this doesn't seem*

better than the world I saw when I was in his time. And as she thought this, she saw a group of protestors with torches. They used these to ignite words that had been written in gasoline on the ground, clearly intended to be seen by Victor's aeroflet. "Release Man. Cage Victor!"

Victor saw this, and growled, "How did they even know I would be here?" Victor had visited so many times, and seen so many fluctuating histories that he was beginning to lose touch with where he was, and what time he was seeing.

"Word travels fast," said Horatio. "I'm sure they heard about this on the radio or television news. All eyes are on you, your Highness."

"Well, if this is the result of those technologies becoming so commonly available, then perhaps they should not be allowed those privileges! Technology will consume this planet one day, if man is left to progress unchecked. They protest only because they have heard about something that would have otherwise not affected their lives."

He walked back to Lilith, and put an arm around her. He was feeling increasingly angry and agitated, seeing the filth of the city, and the anger of his people. Looking at Lilith made him think of another, simpler, cleaner time. She had told him countless stories of her Victorian England, and it sounded wonderful. *Perhaps*, thought Victor, *Victorian times were the perfect balance. Man had enough to live comfortably, and yet had not started their massive population boom. If only Man could be frozen in time, and live forever at that perfect balance. I must see to this, and perhaps after my next trip forward in time we will have cured all of this discontent.*

Lilith, however, was looking nervously at the protestors.

She had watched Victor change the world at a rapid pace, and she was growing nervous to see what the next changes would bring. She looked at the oppressive city around them, at the sky scrapers, and at the huge black wall. It seemed horrible to her, and it made her long to run away and hide.

But then Lilith and Victor saw Eden. Their aeroflet buzzed over the massive wall, and everything changed. On the other side of the wall they saw a land of green grass, bushy trees, and sparkling blue rivers. Flocks of birds by the thousands soared and swooped happily over herds of nimble and timid beasts that Victor had never seen. They looked like miniature deer.

"What are those?" Victor asked.

"Dik-dik," Horatio said. "Tiny little buggers. Kinda remind me of a cross between a deer and a Chihuahua. And those over there are saiga," he said, referring to a group of slightly thicker, taller creatures, with antelope horns and short stubby trunks.

"My word!" Lilith exclaimed. "Are those dinosaurs?" She was looking at heads protruding from the top of a cluster of trees. These heads were on long thick necks which were attached to husky bodies perhaps five times the size of an elephant's.

"No, no, nothing quite as exotic as that. Those are just indrikkus. Indricotherium. They are mammals," Horatio said defensively. "They originally lived *millions* of years after dinosaurs. Dumb as a cow, but friendly as a dog. I once came across a band of terrorists who had trained a couple of those, and were riding them!"

"Hmph," Victor grunted. He did not like people in his

Eden. He would never have admitted how excited he was at the thought of riding such a beast.

Behind them, the train was starting to emerge slowly from the wall. Much slower than it should have been. The engineer and gate staff had the riots to contend with. As Victor and Lilith drifted blissfully over this new Eden, the train fully emerged, and the gates were shut behind it. The train continued on another half-mile, then began to stop at a series of small buildings and unloading platforms.

After a few moments, the first six cage cars opened, steel cage doors crashing noisily on the concrete loading platforms. There was an anticipatory pause, and then out leapt perhaps a hundred large hyaenadons. These were foul jungle cats, with ragged manes and striped haunches, each ten feet long and weighing least a thousand pounds. Several of these darted straight into a heard of dik-dik, and the miniature deer scattered like flies.

"We release them hungry," Horatio said. "These cats haven't eaten in days. By releasing them hungry, they learn to fend for themselves almost instantly."

The train then pulled forward, stopped again, and opened the next six cars. All was quiet for a moment, until a few heads started to appear from the cage doors. Lynx with their furry pointed ears, bearded chins, and thick paws slinked out on the platform. These were larger and healthier than anything you would have found in nature, each one as large as a Shetland pony. Men in padded suits with large prods came out and chased them from the platforms, before the train advanced again.

Then a whistle blew, and the men on the platforms all jogged into little double-walled buildings and shut the doors.

Again the train pulled forward, and again the cage doors opened. There was no motion for a full minute, until finally one massive cat stepped out. It was as thick as a grizzly bear, dark orange like a lion, fourteen feet long, and its canine teeth were nearly two-foot-long tusks.

"Machairodontinae. Sabertooth tiger," said Horatio, with a slight sense of reverential excitement. "Lions aren't king of the jungle anymore," he said, smiling.

Victor was concerned now. He had only intended his Vivarium to bring back species that had gone extinct as the result of man's overpopulation. Bringing back species that had died out for natural reasons was never his intent. But at the same time, this was incredibly exciting to him. These were beautiful animals. Surely they deserved to live.

After the first massive cat stepped off the platform, others emerged, perhaps thirty in total, and they stood confidently surveying their new surroundings.

The wardens remained in their double-walled houses. They planned to remain there until the beasts left the platform of their own accord.

Suddenly a noise reached the aeroflet, a huge and distant crash. Victor turned towards the sound. It was too far to fully make out what was happening. He could see a massive cloud growing near The Wall where the train had entered the park from the city.

"Pilot!" commanded Horatio, pointing toward the sound. The pilot throttled up his engines, and the Aeroflot nimbly pivoted around towards the growing cloud of dust.

In a few minutes they saw what was happening. There

were men and women riding a dozen motorcycles, or mounted on beasts like camelops, or ten-foot-tall giant kangaroos. They were riding in a circle around several massive indrikkus. The riders, many dressed like traditional Native Americans (some of which were in fact Sioux Nation, Cherokee, or Black Foot), were brandishing rifles. They did this to protect a dozen massive indrikkus, each with a rider and each tethered to The Wall. As they watched, the indrikkus' riders urged the twenty-ton beasts forward, pulling a section of wall until it folded and crumbled.

"Dammit!" yelled Victor. "Why would they do this? That wall is for their protection!"

"Did you say those cats haven't eaten in days?" Lilith asked in a panic.

"God damned terrorists!" yelled Horatio. "On point!" he said to his marksmen, and then to Victor he said, "We are going to need to stop this quickly. We can't let the beasts get a taste of Man."

Over the rubble of the walls, the urban protestors climbed. Men, women, and many teens, angry with their lives of captivity. They looked into Eden with wide eyes, the sun dazzling them no more than the sight of grass and trees and rivers. They saw the beautiful nature they longed for, and instantly felt a sense of validation as the dust from the fallen wall dissipated to reveal paradise.

But as the people savored the sun and the beauty of nature, the hyaenadons and sabertooth tigers circled the cloud of dust and crouched quietly in the tall grass. As the people of the city walked out into the fields, the cats pulled in closer, many within a single leap of the unsuspecting citizens.

"You are not in control of this situation!" Victor said angrily to Horatio as he watched a small group of five college-aged boys and girls run ahead of the crowd of people leaving the city. From their vantage, the aeroflet could see what the kids could not. They were heading into a field of tall grass where at least a dozen hyaenadons hid.

"I will be," Horatio growled back, as he took a rifle from one of the sharp shooters, and used its long scope to view the students. He then traced the path to the hyaenadons, and as he did so, one sprang.

The foul cat leapt 20 feet in a flash, and landed right in the middle of the students, knocking three off their feet. In the blink of an eye, it ripped the throat from a beautiful girl of eighteen, and her body writhed in vain, kicking for a few last seconds before finally relaxing. Her perfect blonde hair was now matted with blood and dirt.

At this point one of the New Bedouins, a stoic, dark-skinned woman in her mid-thirties, leapt from her motorcycle, and even before her bike had slid to a stop she had taken aim at the cat.

Horatio glanced at Victor, and saw it was not the lady whom he was concerned for, but the cat. Finding a new target, Horatio exhaled and pulled the trigger.

The .50-caliber bullet left the barrel of his rifle, crossed the distance of sky between the aeroflet and the New Bedouin woman in a blink, and entered the top of the her skull. The woman went instantly limp, and crumpled to the grown.

Lilith turned quickly away, so she could not see any more, and so no one could see her moist eyes. This was horrible.

Below the aeroflet, thirty massive hungry predators leapt into a crowd of a thousand people. People screamed and ran backwards. The cats followed them into the city.

Late that night, Victor was in a rage. He passed back and forth down the center isle of a Vivarium, between cages of fearful herd beasts. His agitation was so great that the saiga antelope in nearby cages huddled against the opposing walls, anxious to be as far from him as possible.

He was alone, but he spoke to himself incoherently, shouting things like, "I *gave* them that! Yet *still* they break it!" or growling a low, "That can be taken away, too. If they can't behave, that can also be taken away!"

Two steel doors at the far end of the hall opened, and a silhouette appeared in the light of the room beyond. The figure strode urgently towards Victor.

"Horatio," Victor said. "Things are a mess. Not everything, mind you. The reserves are just as I instructed, perhaps more than I could have hoped for by this time, but the populace! My god, Horatio, the human population is just unacceptable! They are filthy, and violent, and ignorant of all I am doing for the world. They are their own Judas Cows, leading themselves to death and destruction. *Their* filth ruins their lives, yet they blame me for trying to contain it! Their selfishness tears apart the world, usurping the beauty of nature, yet they riot for more!"

"I fully agree, Your Highness."

"Ugh, don't call me that, Horatio. It makes me feel like a tyrant. I'm hated enough in this time. Did you see the

155

rioters' signs? Did you see them? '*Uncage Man!*' I saw! Do they not understand the horrible irony? They have no vision! They can't see how I've saved the world, they only see that they want more of it!"

"Verily."

"People mistake my role in all this," Victor went on. "I'm not here to protect *the people*. I could give a shit about the people! I'm here to protect *the world!* Mankind never needed protecting, and they already have far too big a share of the world. To protect the world...to balance the world, it's time that man gave back to nature. Give up the land. Give up the resources they are consuming. Give up the way they strangle all!"

"But how?" Horatio asked, in a dark and serious tone.

"Horatio, where I am from, people once thought they could simply live more efficiently. 'We consume 18% less fossil fuels, and waste 11% less food!' they'd brag. But every year the population grew faster and faster! Three times the people, consuming 11% less each, still means a massive increase in consumption! All their efficiency wasn't going to slow the rate of consumption when there was no limit to the growth of the population. One can only live so efficiently. There is a limit to the conservation of energy, Horatio, and all those bodies will always consume resources at this limit."

Victor looked disgusted. "Idiotic kine. Too afraid to address the only thing that would stop the world's destruction. Humankind is like an obese man, eating himself to death, Horatio. It will be our gluttony that kills us, and we will consume everything before we die of it. That is why I have done what I have done. Why I do what

I must do."

He went on, "There are *still* too many men. We have bred the beasts back, but breeding beasts didn't create balance. It just created more population. Now we have overpopulation of both men and beasts."

"Something *more* must be done," Horatio said, putting ominous emphasis on "more".

"I know, Horatio! I know!" Victor yelled, wild-eyed. But then he added in a calmer tone, "Yes, Horatio, I know." And he collapsed forward leaning against the cage of the fearful saiga.

He stood quietly in thought. "How did the people know about the terrorist attack? How did the people in the cities know that the...the…"

"The New Bedouins?" Horatio offered.

"The *terrorists*. How did the people in the city know the terrorists were going to collapse the wall?"

"I'm not sure. Radio perhaps? Telephone?"

"TECHNOLOGY! Humanity has been misusing technology for centuries. When they have something new, they turn it to evil. Well, if these people, these *fucking kine,* can't behave with technology, perhaps they don't deserve to have it! We give them these things, you know. I gave them these things. I can take them away!" Victor said.

"Truly."

"Horatio, are you a family man?"

"Excuse me?" Horatio looked surprised. Perhaps a touch nervous.

"Are you close to your family?" Victor looked Horatio dead in the eye.

"Not in any significant way, it would seem." Horatio answered darkly, but Victor did not detect the tone.

"Good. Good. Do you consider yourself dedicated to your work? Are you completely loyal to our cause?"

"More so than anything else. I have given my life to your cause, and your cause has given me a life," Horatio said.

"Good, good." Victor said, walking in to the saiga corral.

"Horatio, I think you might be the man I need. I need someone who can lead in my absence. I need someone who can think like I think, and make decisions as I would. I need someone who can pull the trigger when it needs pulling."

"I can do this," Horatio said quietly.

"I know you can. I have seen you pull the trigger, and that is why I called you here. My next task is not pleasant, and I am too high-profile for it. If the people see a face, and hear a name, they make that name a villain. I need an unseen hand to move under my control. Can you be that hand?"

"I can."

"Good, Horatio, good. Then I have something for you." Victor walked back out of the cage, and towards a small table a few yards away. "I'm going away. Out of sight for a few years. Lilith...well, Lilith is not happy with me, or how things are going. I'm going to take her to...to stay with our friend, where they will be happy."

He approached the table, and put his hands on top of a black leather box that sat on it. "I have a lot of traveling to do, so I will leave Lilith to rest. She's no longer cut out for the work we have to do, and it is better if she doesn't see it. I'll be back in a year or so, and there will be much that needs to be done by you in my absence."

Here Victor pulled the top off the black leather box, and revealed a Chronofax. "With this device, we can stay in touch. You will send me reports, and I will send you feedback and new orders."

Victor looked seriously at Horatio now. "This is a secret. My absence is a secret. Do you understand?"

"Yes, Victor."

"Good. There are many painful changes that need to be made, before the world will reach equilibrium. I have tried to be patient. I have tried to be peaceful. But you can't change the world by doing nothing, and what is violence if it is not change?"

"I fully understand, Victor. You have chosen right in trusting this to me. I want these things you want. Possibly more than you do, and if you grant me the power to do so, I will effect your change by any means at my disposal."

"Then I will make sure all means are at your disposal. But this is no light deed I rest on your shoulders. I fear what history will make of this, and I fear your fate when this task has been completed."

"Then, sir, if I should be so bold as to make a request?"

"Please!" Victor said sincerely.

"That when I have made your changes, when I have pulled your trigger, that you will take me past this time."

Victor shook Horatio's hand, and said, "Yes, I can

take you to the future. That's where I take my Lilith and Floriana." And as Victor said this, Horatio's eyes flashed with fire, and his handshake turned to cold steel.

Then the doors at the end of the hall swung open, and interrupted this stare. Lilith strode through the doorway, not seeing Victor and Horatio in the dark hallway. As she walked she hugged herself, and glanced about, looking for Victor with fear in her eyes. Horatio recoiled when he saw her, and stepped into the shadow behind one of the corral walls.

"Victor?" Lilith called nervously.

"I'm here," said Victor, and while he was still obscured from Lilith's view, he put the cover back over the Chronofax and stepped away from it.

"I'm here, my dear, but what are you doing out of bed?"

"I can't sleep, Victor. Today was horrible. I need to talk with you about it."

"Was it?" Victor said, and something in his voice was like a wall, defiant and cold.

"Yes," Lilith said, and she sensed Victor's resistance and added cautiously, "It was, Victor."

"Growing pains! That's all it was. Growing pains. I'm making the world grow up, and the world is not ready for it. Luckily, those fools don't need to be ready for it!"

Victor's reply was needlessly harsh, and it set Lilith off instantly. "Growing pains? Victor, we shot innocent people!"

"Did we, Lilith? Did you shoot someone when I wasn't looking?! Did I shoot someone I'm unaware of?" Victor said it in a raised and condescending tone.

"You don't need to pull a trigger to kill, Victor. That's beneath you," Lilith said sarcastically. She had stood by him for years, and watched him change into something else. Victor's innocent ideology, that had once been charming and implausible, had now turned into a horrible success. Lilith longed for the Victor she had met by the lake, but she feared this new Victor.

Victor now spoke with a touch of shame in his voice. "Lilith, I didn't expect things to unfold the way they did. It was a matter of choices. Some living thing was going to die, and it would have been counterproductive to kill the animals after all we've done to try to return their population."

"I don't care!" Lilith shouted. "I don't care anymore! When we first started our travels, I thought we were going to do good! When I traveled on board the *Ophelia*, we were saving lives, changing history for the better! With Captain Robert we were doing good deeds."

Victor's stare turned black. "We have been doing far greater deeds than he ever could have! He stopped petty criminals of history, but the blackness of history remained unchanged, and the world had still destroyed itself! Only I have changed the history of the world in a significant way!"

Victor was yelling, and Lilith thought she heard jealousy in his voice. Lilith had once made the mistake of mentioning that for a brief time she had had a bit of a crush on her old captain.

Lilith said, "Victor, we shot young girls! Girls the age I was when we met! Innocent people!"

"Innocent people!? Since when has mankind been innocent?"

"STOP! I'm not listening to this any more. To hell with your ideology, Victor. To hell with your egotistical agenda!"

"Egotistical!? How does ego even factor into this? What part of this is about me? What I do, I do for the world. What do I do for myself?"

"Oh, bullshit. What you do, you do for you. You do it to feel better about your parents. You do it to feel better about yourself. You could give a shit about the world!" Lilith shouted, but afterwards she could not make eye contact with Victor, and Victor stared into the shadows of a corral, not looking at Lilith.

After a moment, Lilith went on in a lower tone, "I can't do this with you anymore, Victor. I love you. I will always love you. But I can't do this anymore, and you shouldn't either."

"Lilith, please. Listen to me." Victor took Lilith by the shoulders, and tried to look in her eyes, but she refused to meet his eyes. Victor went on, "You don't have to, my angel. You don't have to do this with me. I will work, you should relax, and enjoy our success. I have a new home for us. I procured it on our travels. It's a castle, on a tropical beach. You and Flora can relax there. Do nothing together."

"I can't watch the world go through this anymore, Victor! I can't!"

"You don't have to, my angel. I will take you both far into the future. You can live there in peace, long after all the changes have been made. Long after the growing pains have ended. Doesn't that sound good?"

Lilith wanted to disagree, but it did sound good. Floriana didn't care about Victor's politics or agenda. In fact, Floriana refused to talk about them. A private home on the beach, far away from all of this, with someone who loved her, all sounded like heaven.

"I suppose I have nowhere else to go," Lilith said, and she slumped and leaned against the wall. "I will go to Flora. How soon until I can leave?" she asked, and in the shadows, a tear rolled unseen down her cheek.

"I am setting things up now. We can leave in a few days," Victor said.

"Fine," Lilith said, her voice cracking slightly. "I'm going back to the house." And she turned and walked slowly out of the hall.

When Horatio finally stepped from the shadows, his eyes were red and his cheeks were moist. He remembered being a small boy, being told by his nurse that his mommy had gone to a castle on a beach. He dreamed that she would return for him, and take him to his father on that beach, where the three would be a happy family.

But his mommy never came back for him.

RETROGRADE

THE FIRST RELEASE
YEAR 1997

Horatio Futino stood on the balcony of a royal corsair airship, his short white beard whipping in the night air. He was now a man of 50 years, no longer young and beautiful. He was now old, and bitter and scarred. The scar that Victor had left on his face was a deep wide crevasse that started on his forehead under the brim of his general's hat, ran down through his dead left eye, and continued down his cheek.

Horatio had been instructed by Victor to decrease the size of mankind until it was of similar size to that of any other species. How he was to do this was left to Horatio. In 25 years, Victor would return for Horatio, and if he had been successful in his task, Victor would take him at least another 140 years into the future, where he could enjoy the benefits of his labor, and the enjoy the title of Grand Admiral, a position of power second only to Victor himself.

Over the last 20 years Horatio had ordered the construction of a small navy of airships. Corsairs, clippers, and aeroflets had all been constructed because of their ability to stay out of reach of not only the hungry predators of the national parks, but also the angry mobs of the cities.

In addition to the airship armada, Horatio had also ordered massive increases to the size of the national parks. This is how it would happen. Signs would appear in a neighborhood near the Wall, saying "For the good of the people, this neighborhood is being condemned, pending reconstruction. All occupants are to relocate immediately."

After the people vacated the area (often by force), scaffolding would be built around the neighborhood, and draped with large canvas to block the view of any construction behind it. Then another large section of wall would be built immediately behind the scaffolding. The condemned neighborhood and outer wall would then be demolished, thus shrinking the size of the city.

This had been going on now for 20 years, and the result was that urban areas were now much smaller than the national parks, and grossly overpopulated. Disease, starvation, and civil unrest were all at a historic pinnacle.

In Victor's absence, Horatio had met with the scientists

at the Royal Vivarium Society about population control, and spoke with them about how mankind had handled population problems with animals. The scientists then made suggestions, like culling and sterilization, unaware of the fact that Horatio planned to apply their science to human populations.

Horatio ruled out sterilization. It would take generations to have the desired effect, which would allow the population many years to revolt. The outcome of this would be unpredictable.

A massive culling would be nothing more than a declaration of war against the people, and although the people were not as well-equipped as the Royal Navy, citizens vastly outnumbered soldiers. So the outcome of a culling would be unpredictable as well.

Horatio had even considered starting a war between neighboring cities. War would be easy to start, since Horatio controlled the media, and there was so much civil unrest. It is fairly easy to get an angry people to fight with just about anyone, assuming you completely control all their news sources. But again, this option was both messy and uncontrollable. Who could say who would be in power after a war?

An armed population is counterproductive to the control of the population, so Horatio outlawed guns under the guise of public safety. Now only police and soldiers were allowed to bear arms. Unarmed people can not fight back against an armed government.

Horatio decided the best way to remove excess population was to do so quietly, and immediately. The people needed to be relocated when they didn't expect it, and they needed to have no further contact with remaining populations.

Horatio's corsair slowed now and began to descend to a brick rooftop in a crowded and impoverished ghetto. As it did, Horatio could see several lines of soldiers emerging from trucks on all sides of the neighborhood. Black-clad soldiers, with tall black boots and long rifles, ran from trucks and quickly formed phalanxes, blocking each road out of the neighborhood, except one.

Officers in patent leather hats strode down the streets with megaphones, repeating "This neighborhood has been condemned by order of the Royal Navy. All occupants to report immediately to Brazov Train Station for immediate relocation. Bring no belongings with you, your personal things will be brought to you at your new location."

Apartment building after apartment building, soldiers would storm into the front doors. After a moment, they would escort their bewildered occupants out of the buildings.

Horatio walked down the gangplank of his corsair, and strode to the edge of the building. Looking to the street below, he could see a small but tough and angry grandmother waving a finger at one of the officers. She was yelling, and he was angrily pointing towards the train station. She then spat on the officer's boot, so he folded his arms on his chest and turned away. Then the old lady kicked him, hitting him the the back of the knee. This was so unexpected that he fell to the ground, and cut his hands on broken glass. Rubbing the dust out of his eyes, he inadvertently smeared his face with blood.

Several soldiers ran up at this point and saw his face smeared with blood, and the lady still yelling and kicking him. Before he could say his injuries were not serious, she was shot three times.

Horatio grunted disapproval, not at the lady's death but that the soldiers had let things get this out of hand. He pivoted on his heels, lit his pipe, and said to his guards, "Tell those soldiers to leave the the old lady where she lies. That will keep the people more orderly. And tell the pilot to follow the train. I'm through here."

Again the corsair was aloft, and Horatio now watched the line of people trudging bewildered and fearful towards the train station. Here they waited in lines for hours. While in line, they were ordered to remove their shoes for "security reasons" and place them in huge bins. They were then ushered into specially constructed train cars. The outside of each train car looked luxurious and decorative. They gave you the impression that the insides must contain beautiful accommodations, and perhaps even a jovial gathering of people. But once inside you found it was nothing but a sparse steel box. In-between decorative window panes were surprisingly thick steel bars, and there were no seats of any kind, just poles to hold on to. These poles proved unnecessary, as each car was packed so tightly with people that there was no place to fall but into one another as the train began to lurch out of the station.

Instead of heading deeper into the city, the train turned on newly constructed tracks, and headed towards a large gate in the outer wall. Those citizens by the windows were shocked and confused as they the saw train pass through the wall, and into the absolutely blackness of the wilderness beyond.

It clattered along its tracks for hours, and just before dawn the train began to slow. As the sky turned crimson, illuminating the deserted prairies around, the train squealed to a stop.

David was a teenage boy. He stood, nearly crushed, by a window in the frontmost train car, and he peered out the windows at the blood-red morning. As he did, he saw a small aeroflet descend on the train's engine, and remove the engineer and two soldiers, who were the engineer's guard.

In a panic, David said to the people in the car behind him, "The engineer and another man are climbing a ladder to some sort of flying platform! They are abandoning us here, in the middle of nowhere!"

"I'm sure it's nothing," said a condescending middle-aged woman, holding the arm of her frail and elderly father. "Maybe it's his break time. I'm sure a new train engineer will be brought in shortly. They must be moving us to another city."

One of the weaknesses of mankind is that they will go

to great lengths to create a fiction to convince themselves that nothing is happening. When confronted with change, or threat, they will first create a story to tell themselves there is nothing to worry about. That's when their fate will hit them, while they stand rationalizing a lack of action.

The train sat on its tracks in the middle of the desolate wastelands for another fifteen minutes, as the aeroflet and several other corsairs turned elegantly and headed back towards the city. Horatio's corsair stayed. This was the first journey of its kind, and he intended to oversee it, so that he could adjust protocol according to anything that might go wrong.

Inside the cramped and terrified train cars several large metallic clangs were heard, and then the walls of the train toppled open, leaving the people standing exposed on large open platforms. This sudden increase in space sent many people tumbling to the ground. Those in the center of the cars now pushed to see what was happening, which sent others rolling down the sides of the trains to the prairie wasteland.

David was one of the first to fall off the train, but he was young, so he was unhurt. He stood in the morning light, and looked at the tall yellow grass around them. Birds chirped, rabbits and lizards darted out of view.

All around the train, people stood exhausted and bewildered. What were they supposed to do now? *Did the train break down? Are we waiting for a replacement train to come?*

They all rationalized their inaction.

So they began to climb out, and spread around the train,

trying to become more comfortable after the long cramped trip.

David walked toward the engine of the train, looking in the windows to see if anyone was still working. The windows looked black, and dead. He climbed a ladder toward the engineer's cab, but found the door locked.

The sound of the crowd far to the back of the train changed pitch. Instead of the low rumble of angry grumbling, high-pitched screams could be heard. David hung out from the ladder, and tried to see what was happening, but at that distance he could see nothing but a stir in the crowd, and a movement in the grass near them.

David turned his head to the front of the train. The tracks went on for another 50 feet, and ended in a bumper post. *Where were we going, if the track just ends?* He thought. *Did we take a wrong turn?* But as he thought this, he saw a massive tiger step on to the tracks by the bumper post.

Now, David was not a complete fool. So, although he once again rationalized that this animal was lost from a local zoo, he also wanted to take as few chances as possible. So David climbed the hand railings that bordered the door to the cab, and scrambled on top of the train. From here he watched the lion slowly stalk down the tracks, head lowered, haunches moving slowly and precisely, eyes locked with David's.

When the beast got to the front of the train, David could see it was massive. It was the size of a small truck, and its eyes remained fixed on his. This made the boy nervous, so he stood up, meaning to back down the train engine and out of sight of the tiger. But as he stood, there was a striped orange and white flash from one side of him, and a huge cat leapt 20 feet from the tall grass and collided with him, knocking him from the train engine.

David was dead before he hit the ground.

From the balcony of his corsair, Horatio watched the carnage. Hundreds were killed in a few hours, and the remaining thousands of citizens fled into the fields. These people had no food, no tools, no change of clothes, and no shoes, and no knowledge of where they were. Quite intentionally, their odds of survival was barely worth considering.

Having seen nothing wrong with his plans, Horatio ordered the pilot to return his corsair to the airfield. The trip had been a complete success, and so it was the first of a thousand such releases.

An Antique From The Future
157 Years Later

The seaplane roared through the air at a speed that seemed dizzying compared to my time aloft in the airship *Ophelia*. I had been in planes before, but that was years ago, in what seemed like another life. Those planes were silent shells, with walls so thick that neither wind nor sound slipped through them. Airships are also silent. They gracefully hang from their massive bags, drifting with the winds. The only sound they make while sailing is the creaking of ropes. When an airship heads into the wind it can be noisy. Ours used bio-diesel propellers, and those make a pretty decent noise, but it was nothing like this.

Daniel, Titus, Gyrod, and I had hired Josh to pilot us to High Tortuga, in the hopes of finding Kristina, Timony, Chloe and Isabella. What we'd find when we got there was anybody's guess.

The plane roared through the aether on four massive, rusty chrome engines, which screamed constantly as they clawed at the sky. Its fuselage was so littered with holes that anywhere you stood was windy, and the sound came right in. Loose papers and chicken feathers swirled about the rusty cabin, as the chickens themselves huddled in a few overturned crates. Debris on the floor constantly slid from side to side, or end to end, as our pilot exuberantly crested clouds like a downhill skier.

I was now sitting in what was once a luxurious first-class cabin, with tables and leather chairs as you might find in a fancy men's club, but during the many years since this ship had been in service, it had developed a smell like a thrift store.

A seatbelt was tight across my lap, for which I was grateful (I would have been on the floor without it.) Gyrod sat next to a wall, bracing himself between a pair of horizontal pillars. He could clamp onto something, and then just stay clamped with no further effort.

Next to me sat Titus, his blue eyes wide with terror. For him, this was no carnival ride, it was a terrible nightmare from which he couldn't wake. His knuckles were white, as his fingernails dug into the arms of his chair, and every sway and bump the plane went through looked like it was going to push Titus's lunch right up through his nose.

He looked around for something to distract him, and found a pamphlet depicting various positions to put your body in if the plane should crash. *Why do airplanes have those?* I wondered. Is this the airline's equivalent of the doctors that need to tell you the worst possible results of your surgery? *"Read this pamphlet and consider yourselves warned!"*

Daniel appeared at the far end of the cabin. "Robert, you'd better get up here!" he yelled. He had a worried look on his face, so I unclasped my seatbelt, and stood up.

I walked through the cabin as much with my hands as with my legs, trying to stay upright as the plane bobbed and swung. The floor seemed strewn with an endless supply of rolling, empty vodka bottles. This necessitated careful calculation for each step.

As I entered the cockpit, I saw Josh inhale a shot of vodka, pour another and down it, too, in one fluid, practiced motion.

"Hey there, cappy!" he said, barely holding the controls, and obviously enjoying the flight. We were headed into a bank of clouds, and as he spoke the view out the windows became grey and wet.

"Couple of things we need to talk about." He said this as if I was in trouble for something.

"First, you gotta realize this plane can't land on a sky-city. No runways up here." He waited to see how I'd respond, and when I didn't, he went on, "We do have landing gear, so I can land on the prairie, and you can take a balloon up. If the city is still there. Since rumor has it the city ain't there no more, that'll be a good problem to have." He grinned ironically, but I was not amused.

He went on, "Yeah, so this tube's got wheels. I can extend the landing gear, and set her down in the dust if I need to."

"Where did you get this plane?" I asked. I'm not sure I

had even seen an airplane in these skies before, and despite its decrepit demeanor, it seemed quite a bit more modern than anything else I had seen. It was like an antique from the future.

"I used to know a pair of brothers, we traveled together for years. Jay and Duston. They could fix anything. Well, one day we came across this field full of downed airplanes. They were all too banged up to fly...most of them looked like they had just fallen straight out of the sky...but it was something to see. This whole field full of these high-tech airplanes that looked like they'd all been sitting there since before Hippocrates took over."

"Jay and Dust got pretty excited about these planes. Like I said, they loved fixing stuff. So we looked around until we found a couple planes about the same size as each other, and we spent about a year taking parts off one, and bolting it to the other."

"Eventually, we got this beast flying. Sort of a composite between a Boeing 314 Clipper and a B-17 Flying Fortress. The B314 was a luxury liner, so it was pretty cushy inside, as you can tell, and the B-17 had...you know, guns and stuff. Together, we've got everything! Pimp ride with guns. I'm not really sure at this point if we are more B-17 or 314, but it's pretty much the coolest thing you'll find in the skies!" He ended with such a casual cockiness that, even if I decided to chime in about my time-traveling, flying pirate ship, I'm sure he would have remained unimpressed. So I let it go. Also, my ship was pretty broken, and I didn't feel like I wanted to be reminded of that.

Instead, I said, "Might look good if it was cleaned up a bit." Dan stifled a chuckle. "What was the second thing we needed to discuss?" I asked. Outside the windows, all I could see was cloud, which was solid grey, but occasionally we flew through a little pocket, like a cave in a mountain of mist.

"Second thing I want to mention is…" He scanned his gauges, "we are just about–" but he was interrupted. As he spoke, our plane broke into another cavern in the clouds. This one wasn't empty. Hanging from the "ceiling" were countless smoldering ropes, each dangling a broken piece of road, or footbridge, or part of a roof. These were the smoking remains of High Tortuga, whatever parts still had balloons attached.

Joshua leaned forward in his pilot's chair, and started to jerk at the yoke, making the plane dodge and swoop through the drifting ruins. It was deft work, navigating the remains of a destroyed city held suspended in the clouds, and it took all of his focus, and quite a few swear words.

He swooped us under a tall building that was now on its side. We then arced around a vertically hanging bridge, and then ducked to narrowly avoid a donkey who seemed to be asleep inside a bit of stall held aloft by some unseen balloon up in the ceilings of cloud. I guess the donkey had given up panicking, and had gone to sleep. He plunged us straight through the smoldering fabric of a falling balloon, and I was stunned this wasn't the end of us.

"Hey, bobbert," Josh said teasingly, "I found your city." He glanced grinning up at me, before dipping the plane again to avoid a piece of helium2 tank that spun on its ropes, as the helium2 jetted out a small hole on one side.

Drifting in amongst the rubble were dozens of little figures hanging from small balloons. They looked like parachuters that weren't falling. I pulled my spyglass from my belt, and extended it. The figures were copper and brass skeletons, with massive bony hands, hanging under armored balloons like sinister jellyfish. They floated gracefully in the wreckage, pulling a few men and women from whatever they were clinging too. Though I didn't know it at the time, these were the very harpies that had attacked High Tortuga a few days earlier. The very harpies that had snatched Kristina from the air, and carried her off to the Cage. Many of these heard us rumble past and turned towards us in pursuit.

"What the hell are..." I began to say, but I was interrupted by the sound of bullets popping through our tin fuselage. A small pane of glass shattered and tinkled across the floor at my feet.

Josh pushed the yoke forward, and the plane's nose dipped, which stopped the sound of the bullets ripping through us.

"...can't really fly around them, they seem to be everywhere," he said, glancing around the wreckage. "I've never seen anything like them before, and, well, they shoot. So that's bad." He grinned up at me as if this was all very amusing.

"Well, can we shoot back?" I said, a bit annoyed at the casual attitude he took to the fact that we were currently being punctured.

"Yeah. But not for long. They don't seem too fast, so, assuming we make it past them, I don't think they are going to be able to keep us with us."

"Well, maybe we can punch a hole through 'em," I said.

"What can I shoot with?"

"There's a nose gun just below us," he said, nodding to a ladder to his right. "Daniel, there is also a dorsal turret. Head back toward the cabin, and you'll see a ladder on the wall to your left just past the kitchen.

I swung down the ladder, and as I climbed, the plane banked so hard that the wall became my floor.

As the plane leveled off again, I found myself in a glass bubble on the front of the plane. There was a steel chair strapped to the floor, and what looked like a pilot's yoke in front of it. This control actually aimed a turret that was mounted below the nose of the plane. I strapped myself into the seat and saw that a chain of bullets was already threaded into the gun, so I looked around for a target.

This was a harrowing place to sit. Strapped to the nose of a bucking bucket of bolts, with nothing but glass and air between me and these floating terrors! Not to mention the dangling, smoking ruins of a flying city that our pilot didn't seemed too bothered to dodge. If we were to collide with something, I'd be the first to die.

The glass was so filled with holes that the air in the turret was swirling with dust like a snow globe, so I pulled down the goggles I kept perpetually on my forehead. (Kristina makes fun of me for always wearing these, but I find a use for them nearly every day!) I lined the cross-hairs up to one of the floating figures, and squeezed the trigger, but if there was any effect, I could not see it. Bullets streamed out and disappeared into the space between myself and the specters. I was still too far away.

Suddenly they converged on us like piranha in a pool,

massive claws reaching out towards us. I heard several large crunching sounds, and looking through my side windows, I saw several of them had grabbed hold of the wings as we passed, easily sinking their huge claws into the flaps or ailerons. This prevented our pilot from being able to turn, and I actually heard him yell as he tried and failed to dodge a small dangling shed that was luckily made of nothing too substantial.

With the creatures behind me, there was no more I could do at the turret except wait for a collision. I unclasped my belts and climbed up the ladder into the cockpit again.

"Those sons of bitches are ripping up my wings!" Josh shouted, brow furrowed and cheeks red with anger. As he said this, we plunged into a massive tangle of sails from some overturned and dangling airship, but nothing stuck and we slipped back out the other side.

Joshua's cocky condescension was completely gone. "You need to get out on the wing with a...SHIT! What the hell is he doing!?"

There was a stream of bullets coming from the dorsal turret, towards the specters on the wings. Daniel was firing on them, attempting to clear the harpies from our wings.

"Wings are filled with fuel!" Josh yelled, "That idiot is going to set us on fire!"

I sprang out of the cockpit, and back to the dorsal turret's ladder. "Daniel, hold your fire!" I yelled up the ladder. Then I looked around for another solution.

I ran through the cabin. There were crates full of produce, vodka bottles, chests of tools, and barrels of wine and of engine fuel. I dragged the lid off of a crate full of straw, and tossing aside the top layer found it full of...

"Hand grenades!"

"NO!" said Daniel, running into the cabin. "That'd be worse than shooting at the wings!"

I set the grenade gingerly back, and then nearly tripped on a can of gasoline. I pushed it aside with my foot, along with a few small green plastic containers of bar oil, and thats when I saw it.

The Stihl MS 362, 3.5 hp, 24-inch blade. She was once white and orange, but at her age she was pretty much all rust. When I was a teenage boy my father owned a few acres of forest on an island. Once a month, we'd take our old International Travel-All, two black labs, and a lunchbox full of bologna sandwiches, and hop a ferry to the island. It was always foggy in the woods, and cold, and wet, and we'd shiver as he primed, choked and ripped the chainsaw into life. It would then scream through trees all morning, and by evening the truck would be full of freshly-cut firewood. This was a tool I fully understood.

I lifted the chainsaw out of the dust with reverence. Dim light streamed in through the small round windows, and illuminated the heavy metal weapon in my hands. I pushed my thumb several times into the small rubber dome that pumped fuel into the carburetor, and I pulled the rip cord.

"Whoa, whoa, WHOA!" Daniel said, arms spread out before him. "That is NOT a good Idea!"

The chainsaw roared to life, and shook violently in my hands, begging for me to sink her into something.

"Wait, Robert! I don't think..." Daniel stammered, as I strode past him with confidence, drunk on the power that shook in my hands. Even Gyrod looked nervous as I passed him. Gyrod had very little faith in machines that couldn't think on their own. They seemed far to primitive to be anything more then a liability.

There was a door over each wing. I kicked up on the hand release, and the door flew open. My first victim was fifteen feet down the wing from me. The harpy was ripping pieces of metal off the wing, and his metallic skull-shaped head turned slowly and glowered at me. That was all the invitation I needed.

I took one step onto the wing and yelled "GET OFF MY PLANE!" just before the wind grabbed me and threw me off into the sky.

RUBBLE

I fell for only a second before huge brass claws clasped around my waist. Whether this was one of the harpies from the wings, or another, I will never know. It crushed my ribs, but my arms were free, and by some miracle I still held the chainsaw! Squeezing the chainsaw's trigger, I threw the blade down hard on the automaton's arm. Sparks flew off in a shower, but it was not cutting through.

I hit at the thing with the butt of my chainsaw. This had no effect, except one. If I hit the Harpies shoulders this had the inexplicable effect of changing the direction it flew. They must somehow be connected to the propellers that steer the thing. But of course this didn't help me to get free.

Then I saw a small copper tube that ran like a vein between two bone-like rods of the creatures forearm. "*A hydraulic tube?*" I thought, and I twisted the angle of the chainsaw, and thrust in between the shafts. The second my spinning blade hit the tube, brown-rainbow fluid sprayed out, and the creature released me.

I fell only an instant before I was caught again, by the ankle. My momentum swung me up behind the monster, and in an instant I had thrust my chainsaw into the thinly plated gasbag that held the creature aloft.

Let's stop here. Now is a good time for a Lighter-Than-Air Lesson. Did you know that helium (the stuff in birthday balloons, and classy Zeppelins) is precious and rare, but hydrogen can be made from water? This makes hydrogen the cheapest way to make something fly, and helium the expensive stuff.

Helium is inert. It doesn't explode, which is good because that would really change kids' birthday parties if balloons exploded in flames when popped. Another important thing to know is that hydrogen, the cheap stuff, is extremely flammable. Seems odd that it's flammable, since its 2/3rds of what it takes to make water, but then again, chemistry is pretty much magic to me. I would have failed high school chemistry if not for a sentimental old teacher who appreciated my music, and whose dog and mother had just died, but I'm getting off-topic.

So helium is the rare stuff, and helium2 even rarer, which is what held up the Ophelia, and what used to hold up High Tortuga. Helium2 was treated Helium, and it has about four times the lift of helium, so it is perfect for elevating large heavy objects. The same treatment could be made to Hydrogen.

Anyway, hydrogen is cheap, but flammable. It was due to a shortage of helium that the airship *Hindenburg* was forced to fill with hydrogen, instead of the preferred helium. You might remember that the result was not so good.

Goodness, gracious, great balls of fire.

So if you were to create a low-cost floating soldier, a sky-grunt designed to terrorize the free, but also designed to be somewhat cheap and disposable, you would not waste precious helium on it. You would fill it with cheap, extremely flammable hydrogen.

Now back to the action.

The moment my chainsaw cut into the harpy's balloon, the balloon burst into flame. This ended our buoyancy, and we were immediately falling, and burning, and spinning, and I actually held onto the thing as best I could. We burst out of the bottom of the clouds, and plummeted towards the ground.

The horizon was just a blur I saw in flashes as we spun, and all the while the creature held me, and swung at me with his now nearly useless other claw until finally we crashed into the dust.

It was pitch black when I woke. It was so dark that I couldn't tell if my eyes were open or shut. I hurt. My back was aching, my head throbbed, and my arm was burning and wet. I knew I must have a large bleeding cut on it.

I was not dead, however. That's something. I supposed the burst balloon on the harpy's back still slowed our fall somewhat.

I lay there for what felt like an hour, not moving. As messed up as I was, I knew I had very little fight in me, so I didn't really want to give away my position until I got a better impression of my surroundings.

I felt around me. Dirt, gravel, patches of grass. A nail. My legs were on a couple of planks of wood, and the wood felt burnt. My left arm rested on something metallic and cold.

The air smelled like a garbage fire, ashy and greasy.

Somewhere in the distance, in the direction of my feet, I could hear a wet slapping and ripping sound that reminded me of sounds from a butcher shop. I had no clue what that was, but it was not very comforting.

That's about all I could tell in the dark, so I just lay there.

After about an hour, the sky began to get lighter. It was cloudy, and as the ambient light increased it began to turn the clouds dark pink and blue.

I sat up, and looked around. Directly on my left, I saw the remains of the harpy I had fought with. That thing was finished. There were pieces of it everywhere, and its evil skeleton grin was staring at me from a completely separate patch of dirt than the one where its body lay.

All around were hills of smoldering rubble. Broken glass, broken and burnt wooden planks and walls, pieces of rope, and broken barrels all piled high in hills about me. And everything was covered with a fine ash that looked like grey, powdery snow.

At the top of the hill towards my feet, a man was lying face-down. I could see his braided red hair and beard, and his massive back curved over a piece of collapsed wall. He looked like he was in worse shape than me, but he wasn't dead.

As I looked at him, he turned his head a bit to see me, and said in a tired, gravelly voice, "Hey friend, could you–" but before he finished he was jerked backwards and out of sight.

I stood as quickly as I could, and started to climb the hills towards where he had lain, but as I scrambled up, I heard the man scream, followed by the same slapping and ripping sound I had heard the night before. The screaming stopped, but the ripping sound continued.

I froze in my tracks, looking at the crest of the hill. Staring back at me over the rubble was a bird, a massive thing, like some ostrich spawned in hell. It stood at least fifteen feet tall, maybe twenty, and its beak was as big as a Victrola's trumpet. In its beak was the arm, shoulder and half the face of the man, red beard now dripping with fresh blood.

In the dark, the bird looked black as pitch. It looked directly at me for a second, then dropped the meat and started to move slowly and jerkily towards the hill between us.

"Oh, shit," I said.

Hearing this, the bird yelled back a piercing, rattling cry of *Karraaah*! It clambered up the pile of burning rubble between us.

There was no running away in this mess. I could barely walk in the rubble, so I turned, and stumbled back down into the little valley, where I looked around for something to fight with. I tried to pick up a brass arm from the harpy, but it was still connected to the rest of the body by a few copper "veins" and wouldn't come free. As I pulled, it revealed something orange and white and rusty underneath it. The chainsaw!

I grabbed its handle and started to tug, but I could hear the bird coming down the slope. As the chainsaw broke free of where it had been pinned, the bird screamed again, and I fell into the dirt.

I tried to stand, but one of the creature's large three-toed feet kicked me down, and the other stepped on my legs to hold me. With my thumb I primed the chainsaw as fast as I could, and flipped on the choke with my other hand, engaging the locking trigger. *Why the hell has no one invented an electric ignition chainsaw?* I thought.

I then grabbed the saw's ripcord, but as I did, the bird struck at me with its huge beak. I blocked with the saw, which it grabbed and pulled away, but I held onto the ripcord handle and this jerked the saw to roaring life!

"*Karraaah!*" The frightened and angry bird screeched as it spit the noisy saw to the ground. I grabbed the chainsaw and swung it towards the bird's long leathery legs. In my head, this was going to cut the beast off at the knees, like a laser sword in a sci-fi movie. Reality wasn't quite as clean, but it did deliver a vicious cut and the bird leapt up and backward in a flutter of angry clucks and a cloud of foot-long feathers.

I stood again, and revved the saw loudly and menacingly.

"Come on, Big Bird! Daddy wants a drumstick!" I yelled.

The bird yelled back, "*Kaaa! KAAHHH!!*" Then it turned and fluttered up the hill and out of sight, leaving behind a trail of blood and feathers.

I climbed another hill, decidedly not in the direction hell-bird had left in. Here is what I saw: Miles and miles of the burning and crushed remains of the city of High Tortuga. There were fires in spots, creating columns of smoke that looked like pillars holding up the low black clouds. Huge areas of ruin were covered in burning fabric that had once been balloons. There were also hundreds of bodies, and wading through all this ruin were dozens of the terror-birds, picking corpses from the wreckage like flamingos picking blackened shrimp from a bog.

Occasionally I saw a bit of architecture still intact, the ornamental woodwork of a building's eave or the decorative wrought-iron bannister of someone's balcony, and I remembered how beautiful the city had been.

Kicking over a bit of shingled wood revealed a crushed tricycle. This triggered a memory. The child's toy amongst the destruction and death reminded me of why I was here: this was where I had left Kristina and the girls!

I collapsed to my knees, and I sobbed.

Thoughts whipped through my head, each scarring me as much as a whip across my back. I argued with myself.

This is your fault! You should have never left them!

Where I was going was too dangerous to bring them! I was trying to protect them!

Then you should never have gone! You can't be a hero to everyone anymore! Your first responsibility was to your family. Saving others was neglecting them, and your neglect has killed them!

I shivered and cried, but after a time I thought, *Okay, okay, calm down.* I knew this was a bad sign, but this wasn't a conclusive sign. It had been weeks since I left them here. Perhaps they had left the city, or they might have been captured by those floating skeletons. I needed to keep my head, at least until I was certain of their fate. Until I knew they were dead, I was responsible for their lives, and crying here in the wasteland would do nothing for them.

I looked above me and saw clouds, and whatever chunks of city were still dangling from a few unaffected balloons. I looked to the horizon, and saw the sun rising through the smoke.

Then I heard a rumbling from behind me and saw the rusty chrome seaplane racing towards me! It circled my position twice, as if to say, "We see you!" and then headed off to the west to set down in a clearing about a mile from where I kneeled. I felt desperate relief just to see signs of friends in this blackened land, so I stood.

I started in that direction, and walked for at least an hour, picking my way over and under a hundred fallen buildings and docks.

Then I came across one of the saddest sights of my life. At my feet, spread out like a discarded broken doll, was Timony. Her head was burst open, her hair was mostly burnt off, and much her flesh was burnt away to reveal the gears and metal frame work within her small chest.

She had been with the girls when the city fell, I thought. Timony would not have left them. My family must have fallen as well.

I fell again to my knees and cried. I dared not look around. I feared I would recognize a body. Perhaps a small girl's arm protruding from under a massive helium tank. I just stared at Timony's crushed, delicate face, to keep myself from learning any more about my family's fate.

Then, when I had caught my breath again, I tried to scoop her up in my arms. The least I could do was carry her back to the plane.

But as I did, she said, "Gentle. I break."

"Timony!" I cried. "What happened?"

"Please" she gasped. "Please, I don't have much left."

"What? What can I do!?" I pleaded.

"Turn me over," she said, but her eyes went dim and started to shut, just as her whole body went limp and stopped.

I turned her over. All of her clothing, and much of the skin of her backside had been burnt off. Beneath the bars and pistons that served as her delicate bones and muscles,

I could see a large flywheel, connected to a set of gears which were attached to an unwound spiral clock-spring. Extending from the center of the spring was a tiny key.

Could it be that simple? I reached inside, and grabbed the key. I turned it three times, but nothing happened.

"*This is silly,*" I thought. "*There has to be more to it than this.*" But even as I thought that, small silent gears jumped to life and began to spin at a blurring rate.

I could see a little bellows in her chest slowly expand, and as it contracted, I heard her soft voice say, "More. Please. Turn it until it is tight."

I did this, maybe 20 more turns, and I could feel her small body come to life in my arms. She turned herself over, and looked up into my pleading eyes.

Raspily, she inhaled again, and said, "They were alive, when I saw them last." I felt guilt that she assumed I was not here to rescue her. I tried to look as if that's not why I was here, but I don't think she believed me.

"The girls drifted off by balloon. They've probably been captured by now. Kristina leapt from the city to save them, and would have surely died. As I lay on the docks I could look through the planking, and I saw her snatched by one of the harpies. She's likely alive, and in the city of Everglade by now."

She then closed her eyes and slept, or turned off, or whatever a clockwork girl does when she can't take any more. So I scooped her up in my arms and carried her out of the smoke and ruin.

Even a broken doll deserves to be cared for.

Run Off To Join The Circus

"Little girl, keep yourself upon the trail,
If you stray, you'll become a cautionary tale."
- From the song This Dark And Twisty Road

Chloe and Isabella had been rumbling down the road for days, but to the two little girls it felt like years. They had games they played, like *Weird Animals*, where they each tried to spot the most animals that neither girl knew the name of, or *Airships*, where they tried to see who could find the fanciest airship flying way overhead to destinations unknown.

They had a technique for keeping dust out of their eyes by making *scarf-hats*. They had systems for setting up camp and cooking. They even began to develop little rituals regarding how they slept, "Tops and tails under the sidecar, I tuck in your feet, you tuck in mine."

They had also learned some things that seemed simple to them, but might have taken an adult years to learn, if the adults lived through the lessons. For example: if you are cresting a hill, and in the valley you see large cats, look around for something the cats may have recently eaten. If there is a dead elk, bison, or other prey, the cats won't chase you, and you can drive right past them. If there is not a dead animal and the cats are pacing around, don't go into that valley. Drive *far* around.

Another thing they learned involved gasoline. Periodically through the wastelands they would come across buildings abandoned over a hundred years before.

They found schoolhouses, which often had chalkboards and chalk for drawing and once contained two perfect dolls. They found grocery stores, which were always completely empty. Even old ranch houses, which never had anything working inside them, and often housed a very unfriendly family of animals.

Most often, however, they found gas stations on the long dusty highways. The more modern-looking of these were useless. The pumps were large and square. Instead of numbers to measure how much gas you pumped, they had dead grey rectangles. No matter what you did, gas would not come out of these.

But there was a second type of gas station, far older and always incredibly run down, leaning to one side, or collapsed flat. These seemed to come from a more decorative, happy time, and were always hung with peeling posters of smiling families going on vacation. These had pumps that were tall cylinders, once painted red, though now the paint had peeled off and left mostly rust. They had glass tops through which you could actually see the gasoline inside them, if there was any gasoline to be had. When the girls encountered these older gas stations, the pumps always worked, and the girls would do a little dance of victory around the pump. Then, as they filled the motorcycle's tank, they would stare longingly at the ancient posters of happy families at the beach, or happy families on road trips through the mountains.

Most of their days were spent driving east. At first they were in a desperate hurry to get back to Mommy and Daddy, so once again an adult would be taking care of them. But after a couple of days, they got used to taking care of themselves, and they continued east because that is what they were used to doing. Somewhere in their heads they were starting to get used to the idea that they might be alone from now on.

One morning, as Bella slept under their shared battered wool blanket, Chloe slipped out and began her morning ritual. She made a little fire, first lighting dry grass, then putting leaves on top of the grass, and then bark, and then sticks, and finally a pair of larger crossed logs that they had gathered the night before.

When the fire was burning strongly enough that she felt she could step away from it, she strode back to the sidecar, and popped open the heavy trunk at the sidecar's rear. She reached around inside, looking for another can of "breakfast". This "breakfast" was the same thing their lunch consisted of, which was the same thing their dinner always was: beans. Canned, refried beans.

But another can was not to be found. At first this was a relief, as it was all they had eaten for days. She felt a little nauseated when she thought of scooping any more brown mush from the bottom of a prehistoric can, and she couldn't fathom how she'd swallow it. However, the beans were all they had to eat.

They had once stopped in a long abandoned peach orchard, and picked the mushy fruit off the ground. There was a herd of miniature deer eating the fallen fruit, so they decided to try it. They ate the fruit, avoiding bug holes, and the bitter soft spots, but it was no use. They were sick for all the rest of that day, and most of the next morning. Because of this they decided never to eat "found" food again. Canned beans, however uninteresting, never made them sick and always filled their tummies.

But now the beans were gone, and Chloe had no idea where to get more. When Bella woke, Chloe woefully explained their situation.

Isabella cheerfully said, "I'm full of beans from last night, anyway. And anyways, I'm tired of beans. Let's just go." And she cheerfully climbed into the sidecar, and rested her hands on the tied-on shotgun to prepare for the day.

So Chloe packed up the small camp, and they rumbled away east. They didn't know it at the time, but the first day they landed, they were on the east end of the Grand Canyon, about ten miles from the smoldering ruins of High Tortuga. They had since crossed through New Mexico, the northern part of Texas, Oklahoma, Arkansas, and they were now about to enter the state of Mississippi.

All the girls knew was that it had been brown and dry and hot, and now it was green and wet and hot.

The broken road they rumbled down was surrounded by bushes and trees, and it was from the bushes that trouble came. Just as little Bella's eyes began to close, growing sleepy from the day's hot sun and constant vibration, out from the brush leapt three massive cheetahs. These cats had been bred far bigger and stronger than they would have naturally occurred, the largest weighing nearly 250 lbs. In the blink of an eye, they were alongside the motorcycle. The first cat moved up on the left, second cat at the rear, with the third cat on the right moving into position to sink its six-inch claws through little Isabella's chest, neck, and face.

Chloe squeezed the hand-brake and clutch, and stood on the foot brake, which made the bike snap to a near stop. The cats on the right and left flew by, while the cat to the rear was forced to jump over the girls, or get a face full of metal bike frame.

With reflexes only a six-year-old could still possess, Isabella aimed and squeezed the trigger of her tied-on shotgun. The shotgun cracked, and the fur on the center cat burst open and gushed blood.

The shotgun's report also shocked the other cats enough to make them momentarily cower. Before they had a chance to recover and strike their prey, Chloe released the clutch, and throttled hard, causing the bike to leap forward.

Now the cats were in pursuit behind them, and the shotgun was tied into place pointing forward. Even if Bella could untie it and point it behind them, she would soon find the kick of the gun would be more than a small girl could bear. If it didn't toss her from the sidecar it would break her shoulder. They were being hunted from behind, and there was nothing they could do to stop it.

Soon the trees gave way to a huge clearing. Beyond the clearing was a massive river, the mighty Mississippi. They could see something factory-sized and colorful between the river and themselves, but in their fear they could not make out what they saw.

As they looked, a cat leapt and sunk its massive claws into the seat of the bike, ripping Chloe's dress at the same time. Chloe didn't scream. Instead, she swerved fearlessly, which tossed and rolled the cat from the bike, and nearly tipped the bike over while doing so.

But now the road was beginning to get rough, and Chloe was having trouble keeping the handlebars straight, as well as keeping herself in her seat. While Chloe struggled with the bike, another cheetah sprinted unseen to the right of the sidecar.

The cat leapt, but this time for Isabella. Just before its huge claws ripped open her chest, the cat's trajectory was interrupted. Three giant black dogs collided with the cheetah and rolled it to the ground. Before the other cats knew what was happening, three more dogs arrived, barking in deep baritones and baring their now blood-soaked teeth.

The dog's mother had been the result of the coupling of a Greater Swiss Mountain Dog with a German Shepherd. Their father was the fortunate, though terrifying, mix of a massive Doberman with a Great Dane. The resulting litter was enormous, vicious, and terrifyingly intelligent. When they saw the small bike rumbling down the road with three cats pouncing on it, they didn't wait for their stern-faced human mother to give them permission. Instead, they ran out to meet the cats.

This pretty much ended the pursuit, and the girls rumbled onward as the dogs showed the cats they were no longer allowed to follow.

As the girls continued on, they saw a giant circus tent with red and green stripes and diamond patterns on the heavy fabric. Massive gold tassels with huge ornate brass lanterns hung from each tent pole. Around the tent were thirty or more of the massive Vardo. These Neobedouin hauls were brightly painted, and ornately carved with images of elephants, and lions, and indrikkus all performing stunts on tightropes, or dancing ballet, or stacked in pyramids.

Around these intricately carved caravans were a colorful people of a dozen different ethnic backgrounds. Native Americans, Irish, Turks, Chinese, Romani, Bulgarians, Africans, and those too evenly mixed to identify their origins were all hustling about packaging costumes, or pulling up tent poles, or carrying aerial rigging into the caravans. There were many muscled and tanned men swinging sledgehammers, many tattooed and dreadlocked ladies taking down laundry, many sturdy and defiant young boys clambering up poles to untie flags, and many beautiful young girls boxing up the stage costumes, or stretching their legs on barres.

There were also beasts of a hundred breeds. Immense indrikkus stepped nervously over the bustling crowd to follow their trainer to the river. African elephants wove about between the indrikkus' legs like children. There were huge spotted horses with gorgeous flowing manes and giant furry hooves running gracefully in circles while their riders performed tricks on their backs. Huge eagles, as tall as a man, perched hooded on poles, asleep or in silent contemplation.

This collaborative culture between man and beast would have excited Emperor Victor in his younger days. Later in his life, Victor would have been outraged at the "slavery of animals," but to these people and beasts this was a mutually beneficial relationship at the very worst, and a loving family at its best.

Chloe and Isabella rumbled under a huge weather worn sign that read, "The Circus At The End of The World", and rolled to a stop between two three-story hauls painted in red and black diamonds. A friendly-looking lady, as wide as she was tall, in a huge bright blue dress and dark red headscarf, stirred a giant cauldron of python stew. A line of young kids and teens were waiting for their bowls to be filled.

Chloe and Bella thought this smelled delicious, so, without questioning anything about the situation they were in, they clambered off the side car, removed their "scarf hats" and goggles, and got in line.

"Get the roustabouts up on those poles! We need to get that rigging down!" yelled a hulk of a man in baggy brown pants, stained white tank top, and checkered red suspenders. He noticed Chloe and Bella in line and twirled his substantial mustache, trying to remember who these children were.

"Maana, whose kids are these?" he said in a thick Irish brogue.

The large friendly-looking lady replied in a Trinidad accent, "Dunno, but they are welcome to eat, same as anybody."

"I'm not implying udderwise, Maana, I'm just wondering who they belong to." Then he knelt down by the girls and said, "Hello, wee little princesses, who's your Mum an' Da?"

"Captain Robert and Kristina are mommy and daddy," Isabella said, while Chloe tried to ignore the man long enough to get her bowl filled. She was very hungry.

"Aidan, you leave dose little girls ta eat, and tend to ya packing!" said the big lady.

"Okay, Maana, you know I don't mean no harm. I just never seen 'em before, is all. Let 'em eat, but make sure they finds their ma and pa afterwards," he said in a caring voice, before turning and yelling angrily, "That 'drikkus is smashing the tent down! Charlie Murphy, get that beast off the tent!"

Chloe was now next in line, and as the Lady Maana ladled her bowl with the fragrant stew, she said, "What's your name, little girl?"

"You know I'm Chloe, Maana," said Chloe.

Maana got a stern look on her face, "Now don'choo go pretending we know each udder, Chloe. You're welcome here, anyways. Dare's no need to go lying. Dare's plenty of ma's and pa's here, for those that might have misplaced their own, and they'll all look after you. I'll makes you a deal. You don't tell me no lies, and I won't tells you none. Okay?"

"Okay," said Chloe looking repentantly down at her bowl.

Maana scooped another bowl for Bella, and asked, "Now, where's your muddas and faddas?"

"I don't know. We seem to keep losing our mothers and fathers, and keep having to find new ones," answered Chloe. Bella stared at the stew bowl in her hands, her small tongue creeping out and licking the side of the bowl, hoping to go unnoticed.

"Oh, dat's a sad thing. Fo' sure. But it's okay for now. Haf deez 'ere chillens don't know where dare muddas and faddas are, so we all juz share our muddas and faddas tell we fines 'em. Dat sound okay to you?"

"Yes Maana," Chloe said with a timid smile. "we spent most of our lives getting used to not having our mothers and fathers. We just got some new ones, but we might have lost those, too. I hope not, though."

"Don'choo go worrying too much. Sit and eat your soup, and I'll see what I can do for you."

They sat down at a picnic table, and across from them was a small girl with big glasses, eating stew in an enthusiastic way.

"Ooh, my! This ith the betht thtew I've ever had in my whole life!" she said, with a mouth full of snake meat. "Oh, hello, what'th your nameths?" She was missing her two front teeth.

"I'm Chloe. And this is Bella."

"Actually, I'm *Isabella*. Or just *Bella*. Or '*The Bella Bee*', or just '*B*'" Isabella said.

"You are? WOW! That'th the most amathing thing I've ever heard in my whole life becauth my name ith altho that! Or, well, cloath to that. My name ith Ithabel, which ith just like Ithabella, but not the thame because you have the letter 'A' at the end of your name, and I don't. But ithn't that amathing that we are tho thimilar?" She rambled enthusiastically through most of the meal, being amazed and thrilled to be eating stew on a sunny day, and meeting a girl with a similar name.

Just about when the girls were finished, Maana called across the crowd, "Charlie Murphy, can you come down here?"

A skinny man in baggy pants, dirty tank top, leather suspenders and a page boy cap slid down a ladder where he had been driving in a long pole with a massive sledgehammer, and jogged over.

"Yes, Maana?" he asked.

"You got time to look after deez girls, 'ere? Maybe see if dey gots anyting dey can do?"

"Sure thing Maana, if you got some extra stew for a hardworking man!" Charlie said.

So, stew in one hand, sledgehammer in the other, Charlie walked over to the girls. "Hey, kids."

"Daddy, thith ith Ithabella! Her name ith jutht like mine!" Isabel said.

Charlie went down on one knee, and held his hand out to shake with Bella. "It's nice to meet you, Isabella."

Isabella shook it.

"So, you girls want to join a circus?" he asked.

"Um, I guess so." Chloe said, not knowing if she did, but knowing she liked having lunch, which seemed to come with the job. Life here did seem better than road dirt, gasoline and canned beans.

"Is there anything you can do?" Charlie asked.

"Like what?

"Like, circusy stuff!" Charlie said with a big grin.

Now, Isabella remembered once seeing an old book about circus life. The book had been picked delicately from the ashen wreckage of an old schoolhouse by the large brass hands of the girls' old guardian. Many of its pages had been fused together by time and water damage, but most were readable. In it, a very young girl and the neighbor boy had run off to join the circus. So Isabella did have some picture in her head of circus life.

"I can do acrobatics!" Isabella exclaimed, and she jumped up from her seat, and struck a dramatic pose before Charlie.

"Okay," Charlie said, smiling. "Lets have some, then."

Isabella bent over forward, placed her hands on the ground, toppled ungracefully into a slightly crooked somersault, and ended up in a rather painful-looking bridge; upside-down, hands and feet on the ground, back arched.

Charlie laughed lovingly while clapping, "Okay, little miss. That's very good, but I don't think it's quite enough to wow the audience. Maybe I can talk to my wife Stef about making you a wee little clown outfit."

Isabella stood up, looking indignant, and not at all liking the sound of being a clown when she was trying to be an amazing acrobat. She thought to herself *a girl that can shoot a shotgun as big as herself should not be a clown*, but before she could object to Charlie's request, she was distracted by a whistling sound.

The sound was coming from above, and growing in volume. It finally ended with an enormous crash, as a one-ton segmented copper ball struck the dirt a few yards away from Chloe. It was still for just a moment, and then unrolled into a fifteen-foot-long mechapede. It deftly ran in a half circle, scanning the now screaming and running crowd, and finally locked his sights on Chloe.

Chloe, who had long-since had enough of running from monsters, stood defiant, but defenseless. The copper creature slipped towards her with the sound of a dozen wind chimes, and spread the yard-long pincers that served as its face.

But before it could reach Chloe, Maana appeared between them, throwing Chloe behind her, and brandishing her large wooden ladle.

"You get back, you nastsy ting! Don'choo go scar'n no liddle girlz!" And she swung at the beast, who deftly caught her ladle and snapped it in half. It then spread its pincers, and thrust at Maana, meaning to cut her in half. Maana's girth, however, was at least three times that of a normal-sized person. Instead of surrounding her, the pinchers stabbed cleanly into the sides of her belly.

If they were too close, they would have opened her up, and spilled most of her insides to the ground, like sticking a pair of scissors into an overripe tomato, and cutting. But before they did, young Charlie Murphy leapt to her side, and crouching, swung his twenty-pound sledgehammer like a baseball bat. This knocked the creature's head back into its neck, severing its spine.

As Maana fell to the ground, two dozen more massive copper balls crashed into the circus camp and unrolled. Dogs leapt on them, as circus folk ran for weapons, but there was little hope. Far above the circus, an enormous black airship circled, then descended. It had several dozen more mechapedes to drop, before it unleashed harpies to collect the survivors.

LOST AND FOUND

I carried the twisted and broken young Timony back to the airplane. I found the plane sitting rusty and defiant, in a clearing of rubble about a quarter-mile from where I had found Timony. Josh, Titus, and Dan were mournfully silent as I placed the poor clockwork girl on a seat, and belted her in.

Our next step seemed clear. Find the city, and look for Kristina and the girls. So as the plane lifted off from the clearing, and rumbled noisily back over the wreckage, I sat quietly contemplating how we could do this. Finally, I spoke to Daniel.

"We've broken into a city before, Gyrod and I. We jumped a train." I said.

Gyrod shook his head, "Yes, but that was *my* city. Where I was from. I happened to know a secret way in. But the harpies took the girls to the city of Everglade. I don't know anything about that city."

"Then we'll need to find a way in," I said. "If the girls are in the city, they are likely prisoners in the Change Cage. I don't like to think what they might be going through in there."

Daniel said, "Can we even assume they are still alive?"

"I don't know what they do to humans there," said Timony, "but we clockworks are simply crushed. If you flinch, you're crushed, as it proves you are too aware to be a simple machine. If you hold still, you are crushed, because you didn't move out of the way."

"Like drowning witches! If you don't die, they know you are a witch, but either way, you're dead." Titus said it with disgust. "Robert, what can we do?"

"I don't think they just kill people. I've been in a Change Cage, and it was more of a work-prison then a place to execute people. I think we should head towards the city of Everglade, and hope some opportunity arises. I don't know what else we can do, and I fear taking too long to decide."

"Um, hey? People in my plane?" Josh's voice crackled over a speaker in our cabin. "You might want to see this."

So Titus, Dan and myself ran up to the cockpit, leaving the broken Timony tied to her seat, and Gyrod looking over her injuries with pity and confusion. Out the plane's windshield, and off in the dusty distance, we could see a huge river winding away across the brown and barren wasteland. On the nearest shore was a huge tent, and above it was large black airship, at least three times the size of the *Ophelia*. It had two black cigar-shaped balloons, and one slim silver gondola the size of a Victorian workhouse, bristling with cannons.

There was a commotion on the ground. From our height, it gave the impression of a dozen centipedes attacking and killing ants in an anthill. People were running to their tents, or wagons, or being pursued up poles, only to be severed by the mechapedes, or snatched by harpies. Elephants and indrikkus ran terrified into the river. Tiny bodies cut in half bled out in the dirt.

"Can we do anything?" I yelled over the engines' growl.

"Well, we could make some strafing runs at those metal beasts, if that zeppelin wasn't there. They would be very hard to hit, and we'd likely get taken out by that zeppelin first. But I think I got an idea about that," Josh said, and he explained his haphazard plan.

"It'll work, I think, but you'll owe me some Vodka," he said with a smile, not completely joking.

Josh pulled hard on the wheel, and the plane climbed steeply as I ran to the rear, stumbling over the clutter of boxes and bottles. Then Daniel and I filled a large canvas bag with 110 proof vodka bottles, followed by dry straw. We threw open a side-door, and looked about for the airship. It was just ahead of the plane, and a touch lower than us, so we lit the straw on fire.

As soon as the airship was below us we heaved the smoldering bundle out of the plane. It fell fifteen feet onto the airship, and upon impact the vodka bottles shattered and burst into flame.

The flame, however, wasn't big enough to do any damage, as the armor on the airship's balloon was far too thick for flames to burn through. But that was only the first phase of our plan.

As we passed the airship it fired a volley of shots, but hitting a plane with a cannon would be an amazing feat. These weapons were built for stationary targets like floating cities, or the comparatively sluggish airships of the sky people. Hitting a remodeled WWII bomber was not something they had much practice at. Honestly, I bet some of them were marveling at us as we flew past.

"Oh, holy geez," Titus whimpered softly in his Romanian accent as he climbed into the nose gun of the plane. Dust, bottle caps, and an old paper bag were swirling in the turret's perpetual windstorm, like snow in a just-shaken snow globe. He stared terrified at the ground below, and at the cracks in the glass around him, far more nervous at the height than at the sight of the colossal zeppelin we were approaching. "Dis is not my favorite thing to do!" He called up to Josh, as he clasped the five-point harness around himself, and wiped a bead of sweat from his brow.

Josh was now repeating his previous flight path, and as he did Titus fired a stream of anti-aircraft bullets toward the small fire we had lit. After a few seconds, one of his rounds punctured the airbag, leaking flammable gas in the center of the small fire we had made.

Oh, the humanity, I thought.

Within seconds the spout of flames was hundreds of feet high, and the rear of the airship was beginning to lose buoyancy, one half starting to angle down while the other stayed level. After about thirty seconds, one of the ship's two massive airbags was completely consumed by fire, and it fell heavily, ropes still attached to the gondola, which was in turn attached to the remaining airbag. The weight of the old airbag's frame dragged it down, swinging the entire gondola and remaining airbag upside down. At the top of the arc, the gondola put too much weight in one spot on the airbag, and the airship split in half. Both halves toppled into the Mississippi river about three hundred feet from the circus.

We now circled again to try to make a strafing run against the automatons on the ground, but this proved pointless. The commotion between the people and the mechanized beasts made it impossible to hit one without the other. We decided it was better to try our luck on the ground, so Josh put the plane down in the river, and throttled us towards a dock by the shore.

I leapt with the rest of the crew onto the dock, and as we did we saw three figures, a large man and two dusty little girls running down the dock towards us. Behind them was a mechapede, brass jaws open wide. It overtook the man, and without slowing, it split him in two at the waist.

Then I recognized the little girls. It was Chloe and Isabella! Worse, they recognized me, and slowed in front of me to give me a hug, not knowing how close behind them the mechanical monster was. The beast again spread its jaws, and just as it snapped at the two children I leapt out and threw them into the river, knocking myself to the ground in the effort.

The beast then rose up in the air above me, coming down for a strike, but I myself rolled off into the water. Instead of pursuing me into the river, the mechapede paced back and forth on the dock chomping its jaws in a menacing way, while its green glowing eyes locked with mine.

The girls swam to me, and clung to my arms in the warm brown water. I looked around for a way out of the slow-moving river, but the shore was a field of carnage. I couldn't take the girls there.

Gyrod now emerged from the plane, and when he saw the mechapede, the aperture in his eyes dilated, beginning to glow. His body hunched, legs one in front of the other, preparing to sprint. He held his demolition bar ahead of him nimbly, like a pole vaulter, and he burst forward towards the mechapede.

The beast lowered its head, and shook threateningly, welcoming the attack. But instead of spearing the the beast with his bar, Gyrod firmly planted it in the dock just ahead of the mechapede, and vaulted up over its head.

But the beast was too quick, and it was ready. As Gyrod vaulted over it, the beast arced its back, and caught Gyrod's legs firmly in its pincers. The was a shower of sparks, as metal slid on metal, and finally a loud crack!

Gyrod's right leg fell into the river, and his body was tossed to the dock behind the beast.

Daniel, Joshua and Titus, still on the dock, were stepping backwards, trying to figure out how to fight a creature who might as well have been made out of swords, its armor was so strong and sharp. Daniel picked up an oar from the dock, and swung it at the beast, hitting it squarely between the eyes. The blow had no effect other than to make the creature lunge, causing Dan to leap backward into Titus. The beast then reared up to strike, but as it did, the massive flat foot of an indrikkus, three times the width of an elephant's, came crashing down on the beasts spine, pushing it through the dock and crushing it into the floor of the muddy river below.

"I guess not all monsters are bad," whispered Isabella into my ear.

The circus animals' trainers/family had finally regained

control of them, and now elephants, indrikkus, giant eagles, lions, giant grizzly bears and others had been rallied and turned back towards the attackers. Elephants' trunks snatched harpies from the sky, or swung circus poles at them, popping them like piñatas. Huge indrikkus' legs strode deftly over people, stomping thunderously on the automaton insects. They crushed them like the bugs they were modeled after.

These were highly-trained animals, daily accustomed to calming their fears and doing amazing things, all while avoiding hurting their circus family. This seemed like just another show to them, and the attacking automatons like inanimate props in that show, designed to be smashed to the applause of excited onlookers.

Royal Blood

After Lilith's fight with Victor under the elaborate glass rooftops of the Vivarium, both Lilith and Victor knew she was done helping him with his work. His cause had never truly been hers–she simply supported him out of love. But now there was a darkness to Victor that scared Lilith, an intensity in his face that never went away, even when he slept. She would stand above the bed, looking down at his permanently furrowed brow, eyes shut in a scowl, and she would be afraid to get into bed next to him. Inevitably, she would force herself to, but then she would sleep near the edge of the bed, as far from him as she could.

He was aging faster than her, as he spent many years in other eras, laying his plans to change the world. When he returned, he would always return to a time a few months after he had left, and so Lilith and Floriana were aging only a few months for each of his years. His hair was peppered with white before Lilith even had a single wrinkle.

Floriana, who had never traveled through time with them at all was still a young lady in her early twenties. Lilith was now well into her thirties, while Victor looked closer to fifty, though he was still as attractive as ever.

But Victor's mission was turning dark to the point that even a girl who had seen much of the cruelness of mankind could not endure watching it. Lilith feared things were going to get much worse before they got better, so she had agreed to move into the castle at Tulum City with Floriana.

Tulum had stood on its cliffs overlooking the Caribbean

Sea since the thirteenth century. This made it a perfect headquarters for Victor, since he could always count on it being there for him, regardless of what time he was in.

When he had originally chosen this spot, he had traveled far back into its early days to establish ownership of the city and set up a tradition of keeping the house, generation after generation, exactly as he wanted it.

He built a wall around it to hold back the jungle, as well as any potential uprisings. Within this wall, he placed his own private vivarium, and here his scientists bred beautiful and nearly tame creatures just for Victor's amusement.

To please him, his scientists often strayed from historical animals, constructing breeds that had not occurred before. At first they made simple and plausible alterations. Albino giraffes, an ancient form of tapir with zebra stripes, llamas whose fur looked already dyed, they were so brightly and ornately brindled. Then they began to stray a little from anything nature had ever created. They made peacocks whose feathers glowed from their own bioluminescence (peacock enhanced with jellyfish DNA). They made a little dragon from a red fin-backed iguana who could spit superheated smoke (iguana enhanced with alpheid shrimp DNA). They made monkeys who could glide from tree to tree on skin stretched between their arms and legs (monkey enhanced with flying squirrel DNA). The emperor's menagerie was unique in the history of the world, as the beasts of his garden were never meant to have existed.

Here he brought Lilith and Flora, and the two set about customizing the royal villa in ways only a time-traveling royal family could. They would plan the most time-centric extravagances, making detailed notes on how the grounds should be formed, and when Victor visited a previous time, he would leave instructions with the workers who cared for the grounds.

Let me explain what can be done with a garden when time is not a factor. Imagine a banyan tree whose aerial roots are guided through the ages to form a patterned lattice that drapes perfectly around a hanging dining room. Up the sides of the lattice grew climbing roses, creating beautiful flowering walls and a dome for the dining room. The dining set was carved, in one solid piece, from the trunk of a previous tree whose roots had been trained into dining room chairs.

It was this type of ridiculously opulent construction that Lilith now distracted herself with. To keep her mind off Victor, and off the tragedy she saw in the rest of the world, Lilith threw herself wholeheartedly into indulgence. By day, she would wander the royal gardens, laying plans and giving orders, and by night, she rolled in massive silken beds with Floriana.

Victor, watching the gardens and menageries planned by Lilith and Flora, thought that a cute pet name for them would be "Flora and Fauna". Lilith was not amused at having her name changed to become a matching set with the seemingly air-headed Flora. She would have told him so, but Victor was scarcely around. He was finding less and less reason to return to his wives. His goals had always been boring to Floriana, and they now made Lilith angry, so he found it increasingly easy to stay away from them both.

One sultry day, as Lilith and Flora lay stretched out on ornate silk and tasseled hammocks hung between a group of baobab trees, drinking rare and sweet drinks, a letter came. An old and trusted gardener named Gustavo, whose face was as brown and pocked as the earth he tilled, walked humbly up clutching the letter.

"Forgive me, Your Highnesses," he said, mostly to Lilith. His eyes darted just past Lilith towards a statue of the greek goddess Atë.

"Gustavo, don't call me that," said Lilith. "It makes me sound like the villainess of a children's story. If I have to be in a children's story, I'd much rather be the heroine."

"Then I think you will like this letter, for it calls for a heroine," Gustavo said, a twinkle in his eye.

Lilith sat up, and took the letter. As she read it, she clutched it harder, and finally looked back at Gustavo.

"How long have they been sick?" she asked.

"Weeks, I think. Some of the village is fine, but many have died. Soon all will die."

Something inside of Lilith relaxed, and centered her. Here was something she could do that was indisputably good, even heroic. This village needed doctors and medicine. Those things could be procured with money and power, and she had both. It reminded her of another time of her life that she missed greatly.

"I will come at once, Gustavo. Tell Captain Bola we'll leave at once, and we'll need doctors. I just need to change out of this...lack of clothes...and I'll be ready."

Lilith then swung out of the hammock, slid her feet into a pair of jeweled sandals, and jogged up the lawn towards the houses.

Flora rolled her eyes, took another drink from her gilded coconut goblet, and closed her eyes again. As she did so, Gustavo nodded towards the statue of Atë, and turned towards the house himself.

From behind the statue stepped a man in his sixties, tall and strong as a desert tree that had borne thousands of years of drought. His hair was white, and he wore the uniform of a grand admiral. He clutched a pipe in his teeth, and his eyes looked black in the shadow of the baobab trees.

Floriana Hippocrates opened her eyes, saw his uniform, and closed them again.

"You're looking for the other wife, and you're bothering me. Go away."

The man bit deeper onto his pipe, and took a moment to compose himself before saying in a falsely sweet tone, "I came to find you. Pardon me, Your Highness, but could you spare me a moment of your time? It will be to your great benefit."

Something about his speech and his voice annoyed Floriana. There was something condescending to it, something that implied he knew much more about her than she did.

So she said, "How could anything you say possibly benefit me? What more could one in my position possibly want?"

"You have burdens. Your life is opulent, yes, but it is

earned through an endurance of that which you should no longer have to bear," the man said. "And as opulent as your life is, you know one day you will be obsolete, and then what will become of you?"

Floriana knew exactly what the man spoke of, and she thought of Lilith and Victor. She thought of the years of pretending to be dedicated to this broken and egotistical couple. Often she wondered if the decadent life was worth it, and what she had possibly given up in exchange for this life.

She wondered what would happen to her when age took her beauty, and time took the physical interest of the royal couple.

She thought of the child she was forced to leave behind, knowing that having a child with Victor at that point in their relationship–in a time before Victor had changed the laws on polygamy–would have cast her out of the royal bed.

As she wondered if the child was something she would have wanted, the old man said, "Do you know who I am?"

"Some soldier of my husband's?" She turned a page, not looking at him. "We met at a party once, I think."

"I am Grand Admiral Horatio Futino," he said darkly, and his hands shivered nervously in his pockets, as he waited for her to understand.

"Futino?" Said Floriana, her eyes growing wide as they searched his face and saw familiarities. *Are those the eyes of my father? My brothers?* she thought.

"Do you recognize me now?" he said, slightly sneering. "You did not when we met before, though I dare say you weren't paying much attention to me."

As much as Floriana had not wanted to recognize him, she couldn't help it. "You're...that baby!"

"Yes," Horatio sneered. "That baby."

"But how could you be? You're an ugly old man!"

"Your husband has moved me from place to place, and time to time, like a knight on a chessboard. He moves me, just as he has moved his queens to wherever suits him."

This was him volleying back an insult. Whatever panic Floriana felt in meeting her abandoned child, and finding he worked with the husband she had hidden him, from was no match for the rage Horatio felt. He was the abandoned child, meeting his mother for the first time, and finding her insulting and callous.

But he was not presenting himself after all these years of silence in order volley insults. He took a slow draw on his pipe and began again.

"As I said, I have something for you. We are both slaves of this man. Your life may be a golden cage, but it's still a cage. Do you deny it?"

"I don't."

"Do you plan to stay in this cage until time has left you withered and bitter and ugly, like me?" Horatio said, intentionally scratching the scar that ran from his forehead to his cheek.

Floriana took a long drink from her goblet, then said, "But what choice do I have? Head off into *this* world? Move to the city? Live in a wagon train on the prairie? The walls of this castle hold back a vicious world, one that I am not eager to see!"

"There are other choices. You are of royal blood. If the emperor were to die..."

"His first wife would be Empress..."

"But if they both were to die?"

"This is insane." She began to stand, and to reach for an ornate carved bell on the table by her hammock.

"Are you sure that's what you want to do?" Horatio was unmoved, and he spoke slowly and calmly as he repacked his pipe. "Ring that bell, and you'll never know what I was going to offer. Ring that bell, and I will go to prison, and you will remain in your prison. Ring that bell, and we both die behind bars."

Floriana grabbed her goblet instead, and drained it. "What's in it for you? Why would you suggest this to me?"

"I am also of royal blood. If this plan was brought to fruition, I would also benefit. Divorced from the emperor, you are nothing. But widowed from the emperor, with a son, you become the matriarch of the royal family, and I become heir to the throne."

This plan should have scared her. It would have scared her, if she had seen to its full conclusion. Horatio was much older than her. If he was heir to the throne, and he was willing to kill the emperor for the throne–his own father– would he not be willing to kill his much younger mother, who would surely outlive him?

But Floriana was not farsighted, and she was bored to the point of anxiety. She had gotten this far in life as a result of her strong sense of ambition, and all the comfort and pampering in the world would not dull that ambition.

Horatio pulled a leather tube from his belt and removed the top of it. From inside, he pulled a very old legal document.

"This is my birth certificate. It states the name of my mother and father, and it has been signed by the doctor who delivered me. It also has an empty signature line for my mother to sign. This document in invalid without that signature."

Over Horatio's shoulder, Floriana saw the distant figure of Lilith coming back towards them across the lawn. Lilith would not be able to see Horatio in the shadow of the statue and the trees on such a bright day.

"You have to leave!" Floriana said.

"Do we have an agreement?"

"Go, now!" Floriana said, but she took the document from his hand and thrust it under her pillows. Horatio disappeared behind the statue of Atë, and Floriana laid back onto her hammock.

Lilith stomped back to Floriana. "The captain says we can't leave until morning." Lilith was dressed in short leather boots, and canvas pants, and a leather vest now. She was dressed for an adventure. "The doctors won't be available 'til then. I suppose it's best. Floriana, I'm restless. Let's go to the tent by the beach, and watch the sun set."

"All right," Floriana said, and she stood carefully so as not to expose the document under her pillows. "You go and order ze dinner, I'll be right there."

When Lilith had left again, Floriana signed the

document and then pushed it back under the pillows. She turned and walked quickly across the lawn towards the beach.

ANOTHER PERSPECTIVE

When Floriana arrived on the white sand beach on the turquoise Caribbean, she found Lilith instructing palace servants on the placement of their colorfully lavish tent. Inside it, the servants hung turkish lanterns of colored glass, pillows of a hundred deep, jeweled colors, and a white carved soapstone table that held a selection of sweet fruity liquors.

Lilith sat on a golden stool, and began unlacing her boots, "Flora, I know this will bore you, but I was very excited to go to the village!"

"I can't imagine vie you would want to go to a village of sick peasants. It sounds 'orrid." The beautiful Floriana said kneeling on the bed while picking through the bottles. She found a tall black one, uncorked it, and filled a flute with pink bubbling liquid.

"I want to be useful again, Flora. I want to feel like I'm helping."

"It would not really be *you* who was helping. It would be you donating." Flora said, draining the goblet, and pouring another.

Lilith unzipped her canvas pants, and shimmied them down to her ankles. "I know, Flora, but that donation would not come from anyone but me." She unbuttoned her vest, and tossed in on a chair. "Gustavo tells me Victor turned them down when they asked for help." Then Lilith added darkly, "He's ignoring everyone."

"Hah! Yes, he is." Floriana said, forgetting her accent for a moment. She took Lilith by the wrists and pulled her to bed.

That evening Floriana had much to drink. Lilith had trouble falling asleep that night, and lay next to drunkly unconscious Floriana until nearly morning worried about all the dark things Victor had done with her help. Because she missed so much sleep, she slept late to compensate. Flora slept late because of her hangover.

When they did wake, they were not surprised to see the table of liquor had been silently replaced with a table of coffee, fruit, and cheeses. Floriana knelt on the bed, poured herself a cup of coffee, and said, "And vat shall two princesses do to pamper zemselves today?"

"We are queens, not princesses." Lilith said, slipping from the silk sheets.

"Zat makes us sound old."

"I think I might start with a swim." Lilith said, seeing her swimsuit hanging on a carved wooden partition. Lilith was not in the mood for Floriana's company, and knew Floriana would not join her in a swim.

Floriana knew this, too. Lilith had been spending much less time with her. She thought about what Horatio had said to her, and it sent a shiver up her spine. It's strange what small acts will solidify your convictions.

Lilith walked over to where the swimsuit hung, but before she could put it on there were three shadows on the side of the tent walking towards the front.

Victor's voice could be heard, "This will be a pleasure for us both. Allow me to introduce you to my wives."

Hearing this, and hoping to cause Victor a bit of jealousy, Lilith darted to the bed were Floriana was, knelt naked before her, and kissed her deeply as Victor walked into the entrance of the tent. Victor, however, paid no attention.

Upon seeing Victor, Floriana pulled away from Lilith, walked to him, and kissed him deeply. So Lilith, still silhouetted in the shadows of the tent, put on her bathing bottoms. She felt jilted.

Victor introduced Floriana to the two men he was talking to. Lilith put on her bikini top and walked angrily out into the hot sunlight to see who was there.

Victor said, "And here is my first wife, Fauna. Fauna is actually a nickname, as you will see. You know her by another name."

Lilith was stunned. Before her stood Doctor Calgori, her old friend and mentor, and Captain Robert, her old captain. Robert had been the focus of her fairly serious crush, as well as the victim of a pretty epic tantrum of hers. She had seen neither in over ten years.

Calgori did not seem to recognize her at all, and indeed looked younger and healthier than she had ever seen him. Robert recognized her but stood there, confused and befuddled.

Lilith had spent her entire adult life traveling through time, and fooling people into believing she belonged. This gave her the ability to hide her reactions until she could gauge the reactions of others. So instead of showing shock at Robert and Doctor Calgori, she said, "It's good to see you, Captain."

This awkward meeting was followed by an even more uncomfortable and volatile breakfast on the beach. Robert questioned Victor, Victor bragged about his accomplishments, Doctor Calgori got angry and screamed at Victor, Victor got angry and screamed at everybody.

In the end, Victor stormed off to the castle followed by Flora, and Doctor Calgori stormed down the beach. Finding herself alone with Robert, she offered to give him a tour of the castle.

Lilith led Robert around the castle, room by room, showing off its opulence and her success. This was a moment of victory for her. She could tell her story, tell him all that she had accomplished, and prove to this long-lost love-interest that she had been worthy of his attention. She had accomplished what he had set out to do, and had accomplished it on a level he never could have dreamed of.

She walked him through the most lavish rooms of the palace, showing off the treasures of the world, and he just stood gawking. She didn't speak of the civil unrest. She didn't speak of the threats from Horatio, and the strength he now held over the emperor. She needed him to see her success, to hear her story as if all of her life's accomplishments had been perfect.

After touring the palace, and the grounds, they eventually found themselves back at the tent. As Lilith talked, she was so grateful to have someone to listen, an old friend even, that soon she found herself speaking, not of her and Victor's plans, but of her tumultuous relationship with Floriana and Victor.

Speaking about it out loud, and seeing it from an outside perspective, made it seem much more wrong to her. She felt jealousy, and anger, and suspicion.

She was beginning to fear that Victor was seeing Floriana privately, and that's why she saw him so little. In truth, Victor was staying away from both wives, but to Lilith it seemed like Floriana would be an easier choice of a wife for Victor, as she had no moral convictions about what he did. So Lilith had feigned jealousy to Victor.

She feared Victor preferred the much younger Floriana, she feared Floriana was being artificial with her. She talked of her addiction to this forbidden love, and all the dramas that it caused.

Lilith had long held back the fear that Floriana was using her, and using Victor. That all her love was an act, and if it was, Floriana was well paid for her acting. Of course, admitting this to herself would end the fantasy, and cast Lilith into even more loneliness, so she kept herself fooled.

As they stood on the beach, Lilith talking while Robert looked out to sea, Lilith looked up at the royal bedroom windows. In the window she saw the naked silhouettes of Victor and Floriana in an embrace, and though this was not an unknown sight to her, there was something troubling about the way Floriana moved. She seemed artificial. Whenever Victor's head was turned she seemed to fumble with a small case on the bedside table. Victor left the room for a moment, and as he did Lilith could clearly see Floriana pull two daggers from the small case and put them under the bed pillows. "*Look at them!*" Lilith screamed.

Robert turned to look, but when he did, he saw Victor return and kiss Floriana's naked breasts, her hands behind her back and under her pillow. Robert turned away, embarrassed to have seen such an intimate moment. With Robert still looking out to sea, Lilith saw Floriana pull the knives from the bedside table.

"She lies! I knew!" Lilith screamed again, and she ran up the sands towards the castle.

Lilith ran to a small back door, which led into a dark cold stone hallway under the palace. She ran down the stairs, her sandaled feet slapping on the stone, then up a dark and ancient staircase towards the royal bedroom. At the top of the stairs stood two of the royal guard. Massive dark-skinned men with red turbans and matching tattoos. Their eyes darted to their feet as they saw her.

"My husband is in…"

"Your Highness," one interrupted in a rumbling voice. "Your husband asked to be left alone. Maybe don't go in dare right now?" He said this in fear of her jealousy.

But Lilith knew she didn't have time to convince them. She also knew that they would not dare to stop her, so unseen she pulled a knife from the guard's belt as she sprinted past him.

Once inside the spacious and luxurious white bedroom, she saw Floriana, kneeling on the bed behind Victor's back. Floriana had two small daggers in her hand, and as Lilith entered, she sunk the daggers deep into Victor's neck.

Lilith screamed.

Victor's blue eyes opened wide with the unexpected pain, and he stood, pulling the daggers from Floriana's hands as he did. He looked at Floriana in horror and betrayal, the small daggers still buried deep in the sides of his neck. He then turned and saw Lilith at the doorway, and his eyes filled with tears. He realized he had been betrayed. That this was his death. And in that instant he thought Lilith and Floriana were doing this together. He felt himself a young man again, alone, insecure, friendless and terrified.

He had been betrayed by the only love he had known, in a world full of hate for him. He held his hand out to Lilith, and cried, "My love!" just as Floriana grabbed the daggers in his neck, and pulled them forward through his throat. Victor fell to his knees, a fountain of blood flowing from him.

Lilith rushed to him horrified, but Floriana stood between them, and stabbed at Lilith, missing her belly but instead slicing deeply into her side.

Lilith had always been much stronger than the pampered Floriana. So she pulled the dagger from Floriana's hand, turning her around. Lilith then grabbed Flora and pulled her close with one arm. As she did, Lilith pushed a dagger into Flora's spine, and Floriana went instantly limp in her arms.

Lilith tried to stand, but she was greatly wounded. The floor was slick with blood, and she had very little strength. She looked into the dead and betrayed eyes of Victor, and felt infinite pity. She felt the naked and dead body of Floriana in her arms, and she felt a mix of repulsion and betrayal. A wave of nausea washed over her, and she swooned and fell to the ground under Floriana.

In ran Robert, and with him the palace guards, Nieroo and Atoosh. They stood in amazement at this scene. Lilith lay still, not knowing who to trust. One of the panicked voices in her head thought a reasonable thought, *if the emperor and his second wife are lying dead in a room with a living and jealous wife, what will people believe?* So Lilith lay still.

But before a moment had passed, in strode Admiral Horatio Futino, and many soldiers. *No survivors,* he thought. *This is even better than I hoped for.*

He growled, "Due to the unforeseen death of the emperor, I am assuming command."

As he spoke, his soldiers were placing restraints on the royal guard, and on Robert.

"You are hereby relieved from duty," Horatio went on. "You will be taken to trial, and punished for the death of Emperor Victor..."

Then Lilith slipped into a cold and horrible unconsciousness.

LOST HORIZONS

Lilith opened her eyes, but all she saw was a soft pink blur. Something wet and sticky was on her face. As she turned her head she found that she was under a sheet, and that the sheet was soaked in blood. At this realization, she felt a sinking nausea. Her mind was holding something from her, and she struggled against it to remember.

Something was in her hand. It was clammy, and stiff, and after a minute her hazy mind realized it was a hand. It was much larger than Floriana's hand, so it must be Victor's, she thought, but that hand was very cold. Panic shot through her and she remembered.

She sat up quickly, pulling off the blood-soaked sheet that stuck to her cheeks as she did. She then looked at the dead face of Victor. If she had been the type of woman who screamed, she would have done so. But instead she scrambled to stand, her hands and feet smearing the sticky, half-dried blood on the ground. As she did so, she tripped on something behind her and fell.

Again she tried to stand, realizing she had tripped and now lay on the body of Floriana, also cold and stiff. Floriana's blood-soaked nudity repulsed Lilith, and she felt her stomach heave as she crawled onto the bed and averted her eyes.

It was morning now, and a thin golden sliver of sun shot cool light between the room's ornately woven white silk curtains. The room was as palatial as ever, with dark carved wood furniture, ornate fabrics, walls and floors of elaborately inlaid white marble. But beyond the foot of the massive bed lay the bodies of Victor and Floriana, the whiteness of the room making the shock of red blood all the more startling.

Lilith crept to the door of the harem. There were no guards either in the doorway or down the hall, though there were many pools of blood along its length, or smeared violently on the walls.

The palace was deadly quiet.

Victor's desk was nearby, and from it came a small "Ding!" which was such a contrast to the quiet that Lilith startled. She crept over to the desk–on it was a Chronofax. Lilith pushed a round metal key on the Chronofax, an a letter from Horatio to himself popped up on the screen.

Under her breath she read, "New Everglades, October 20th. The city is out of control, and I believe beyond regaining control. I am hereby ordering that the city, building and occupants, be incinerated. Please have the following craft ready at 9:36 pm, October 20th. 16 Corsairs..."

Her face hardened, eyes narrow, brow furrowed. *This letter will be written just over two months from today, she thought. Horatio is ordering the death of thousands of people. What on earth is he doing? This is insane!*

Lilith stood and walked to her wardrobe, carefully avoiding seeing or thinking about the bodies on the floor. She pulled out a pair of rugged khaki slacks, short brown leather boots, and a small but durable leather vest. Over her shoulders she hung the small backpack, little more than an ornate leather purse, that she had packed the day before. She dressed rapidly, and darted out of the room by a servant's tunnel near the wardrobe.

She wound her way down to the steep ancient stone

tunnel, her feet clomping noisily as she jogged, and eventually she burst out of a small wooden door onto the morning beach. If she continued across the sand to the next building, she would be in the palace kitchens, but instead she ran down the beach to the tent she had shared with Floriana the evening before.

There was no one on the beach, and no one in the windows of the palace, so no one saw her slip silently into the elaborately embroidered tent.

The brightly colored fabric of the tent painted its interior with a dozen colors, and Lilith's face changed colors as she moved through it. Without pausing, she slipped her hands under the mattress, and pulled out an ostrich skin belt, with golden buckles and a long slender holster. From this holster she pulled an ornate gold pistol, and she checked that it was loaded. She then pushed the pistol back in, and buckled the belt around her waist.

Lilith pulled her long red hair into a haphazard ponytail, and stepped back into the sunlight on the beach. Looking up at the castle, she quickly reassured herself that no one was watching before heading down the coast.

The Caribbean sun beat down on her, and she could feel its heat tighten the skin on her shoulders and cheeks as she jogged on the stiff wet sand at the shoreline. For over an hour she jogged, until finally she saw the small fishing village she was headed towards.

This town existed outside the walled cities only for the benefit of the palace. The fishermen of the town could provide the freshest seafood for the emperor and his wives, and in exchange, they received a reprieve from the confinement rules of the cities. Without this exception, the emperor would have had to live off the same processed and stale foodstuffs as the sickly citizens of the Change Cage cities.

The town had brightly painted adobe buildings, flowerpots in windows, and white linen on clotheslines. On the beach, shirtless mahogany fishermen threw nets and spears into dozens of rainbow colored boats that lay on the sand, preparing for a day at sea.

Lilith adjusted her mood, and stood tall and proud. She strode forward with a sexy confidence, and put one booted foot onto the bow of the first fishing boat, and said, "¡Hola, caballeros! ¿Alguno de ustedes buenos pescadores quisiera vender a un precio tres veces mayor de lo que vale? Necesito velas, y un casco que sea fuerte en altamar." And as she said this, she looked from boat to boat, to see which was most seaworthy.

"Sí, Su Alteza, tres cuerpos son más seguros que uno, estoy seguro de que estará de acuerdo," said a strong young fisherman, pointing at a gorgeous teak trimaran with a mischievous grin. Several other fishermen giggled as he said this, and Lilith winked slyly at the men. These men were used to rich and eccentric requests coming from the castle, and used to being overpaid for their fulfillment.

Lilith walked over to the boat, and flashed sparkling eyes at the fisherman, before stepping inside. She looked at the joints of the horizontal bars that gave the boat's sixteen-foot hull its strength. They looked new. She looked at the sail, and saw that it was fresh, and without mold. She tugged with all her weight on the small mast, and it did not move. She saw that there was a paddle, and a canvas bag that clearly contained the fisherman's lunch. So she turned to the fisherman, and dropped a stack of coins in his hands, and said, "Ayúdame a empujar."

No less than a dozen young and old fishermen pushed her boat down the soft white sand while Lilith sat on the small teak seat just behind the mast. When the ship touched salty warm water they kept pushing, until they finally lost footing in the foamy water's depth.

Lilith jerked the rope that let loose the small boat's only sail, and the wind pulled her swiftly from shore and out towards the morning's pink-golden sunrise.

When she was out of sight of the cheering sailors, she slumped into the bottom of the boat, hugged herself, and cried.

She sailed swiftly all day, cresting each jade blue wave, and crashing into the dark wake behind them. Her arms and shoulders became crusted with salt, and salt was all she tasted. When she became hungry, she opened the sailor's bag and found a small loaf of bread, and some dried fish wrapped in brown paper. She ate it while watching gulls follow her, as the ship thrust forward. Eventually the sun set behind the coastline, and she sailed on into the dark orange sky.

This change of context made her former life seem years away. She was sailing to an unknown destination on an emerald sea, and even though her tragedy was barely behind her, this new horizon excited her. She had missed this sense of unknown, this sense of danger. Only through her strength could she make it through each hour, and the sensation was at once nostalgic and invigorating.

That night, she could see the many lights and torches of the Flotilla dancing in reflection on the blue-black sea. Before long, there was a young man floating near one of her outriggers, hand boldly on her hull, while his glittering brass tail churned the water under him.

"You're arriving a bit late, wahine," he said in a singsongy voice.

"I'm actually early," Lilith sparkled back, though she was hiding the fact that she was very tired. "I didn't expect to arrive until dawn." Lilith, in fact, had expected no such thing. She didn't actually expect anything, although she hoped to find the floating rebel city that had been rumored to be out of sight off the emperor's coast.

"Well, I assume a face as pretty as yours wouldn't turn down a pillow after a long day at sea. Can I guide you to port?" said the partly mechanical merman.

"Please," Lilith smiled, and perhaps for the first time in years, she meant it.

RETROGRADE

THE DAY THE CIRCUS CAME TO TOWN
OCTOBER 20TH, 8:23 AM

It was not without precedent. The Change Cage City of Everglade had an upper class, and that upper class was like any other. They demanded luxury, and they demanded entertainment. When the very rich and privileged wanted to be entertained, they didn't want to feel guilty looking upon the people they had oppressed, and so they often turned to entertainment outside the city. Of course this contradicted Victor's laws, but it's contradictions like these that define wealth and privilege.

Meanwhile, the Circus At The End Of The World owed us a favor, so we spent two days with the management of the circus, trying to think of a way to get into the city and rescue Kristina. The plan was to use the circus as a cover to get us all in, and as the circus performed, Daniel, Titus, and I could sneak into the city and try to find Kristina.

That was how I found myself, three months after the attack on the circus, knocking at the "back door" of the city of Everglade. Behind me was the circus train, dozens of Vardo, a small army of performers, circus caravans, and hundreds of beasts both underfoot and towering above, while I stood at a rusty steel door next to a huge loading bay and rang the bell.

After an uncomfortable wait, and ringing the bell two more times, the door opened. There stood a disheveled policeman, little more than a warehouse security guard, who looked at his pocket watch and said, "Blimey, guv'nor, you're ten minutes late," in a faux-cockney accent. God, I

240

hate it when people speak in fake accents.

"Yeah, uh, sorry about that. You want to open the door... or...?"

The guard squinted disapprovingly at me, and disappeared back into the wall, shutting the door behind him. There were several seconds of unrecognizable mechanical thumps and clunks, and then the massive doors started to roll up.

I stepped back down the stairs, and met with Daniel, Gyrod, Josh, and Titus as the caravans began to enter the city. Josh was unbraiding his beard, and Titus was staring fearfully up at the city's foreboding walls.

"Dis seems like a bad idea," Titus said. "Why exactly are we going *in*?" he asked, though he knew the answer.

"We are going in to find my family," I said.

"Do we all need to go?" Titus asked, watching the circus train slowly disappear into the darkened city.

"That's the current plan, yes," Daniel said. And we walked through the massive gates together, the shadow of the wall swallowing us.

The next evening, Neo-Victorian lords and ladies filled the colossal circus tent, their human servants escorting them to their seats, or carrying their coats. The audience was dressed in pressed tuxedos and evening gowns. Their servants wore white vests and bow ties. Both men and women had powdered faces and slicked-down hair, and many of them wore gears on their lapels as a show of support for Emperor Victor who had died less than three months before. Gears on brooches, or necklaces, made a statement of approval for his laws of mandatory nineteenth-century life.

Many of their servants similarly wore brass pins shaped like bees, though only they knew the significance.

The crowd consisted of lords with their ladies, or their mistresses, or occasionally both. There were some high-ranking servants sitting in the wings, and many of the couples had brought children, in sailor suits or lace dresses.

The air smelled like popcorn and cotton candy, as well as straw and animals, and as the audience took their seats, they watched Neobedouin clowns tumble and prance about in the ring, doing a comical mock battle with a trained and obviously docile and loving brown bear. The bear would growl in an unconvincing way, and then lunge at a clown, who the bear would pin with a massive paw. Then, as the clown howled in fake pain, he or she would slip a treat into the bear's mouth. The bear loved this game, with or without the crowd watching.

The next act was the tether dance. Beautiful young Neobedouin women, tanned and elaborately tattooed in henna and colored paints, would tie themselves together, and dance. Sections of their ropes were threaded through pulleys in the circus top, so as the dance progressed they would pull each other off the ground, swinging through the air, and in this way switch partners.

At the climax of the act, the writhing young couples

would set themselves on fire, a trick accomplished by a coating of a chemical that actually burned at a lower temperature than the human body. It was a dramatic sight, but a traditional Neobedouin act that everyone was familiar with. Most of the gasps from the audience were from overly-dramatic debutantes, trying to steer their suitors' attention from the beautiful nomads in the ring to themselves.

As the dancers cleared the stage, the clowns returned. They proceeded with a skit, wherein a very fat female clown dressed as a sky pirate, (played by the mostly healed Maana) refused to budge from the top of an eight-foot treasure chest in the center ring. Three clowns implored the fat lady to move, and pointed desperately at the sky, while pretty young girls circled the ring holding up signs saying "The Navy's Airships Approach!"

The clowns gave up trying to convince the fat lady, and tried to lift her from the chest. But it was no use–she was too fat. The audience roared with laughter.

They ran offstage and returned with the bear, who also tried to lift the fat lady. He feigned being unsuccessful, was slipped a treat, and the audience roared again with laughter.

The clowns then ran off the stage again, and returned with two African elephants. Both elephants made mock efforts to lift the lady and failed, eliciting another roar from the audience.

Once again, the clowns ran offstage, returning with an indrikkus, who towered over elephants, clowns, and bleachers filled with people. The beast was in fact so big it had to duck to pass under the high-wire at the top of the circus tent. Its huge neck swung down, and it gently grabbed the lady clown's vest in its huge mouth. It strained, and pulled convincingly, and then pretended to collapse to the ground in exhaustion.

At this point the laughter of the audience was continuous, so the clowns shushed them. Lights were dimmed, and a single spotlight followed little Isabella to the center of the ring. She flexed her tiny arms, and then with one hand she grabbed the ridiculously oversized treasure chest on which the circus fat lady sat, and hoisted chest and lady above her head. She then walked out of the ring carrying both. The crowd roared with laughter, fully aware that the chest was suspended from cables attached to the ceiling, but enjoying the gag nonetheless.

Outside the tent, smaller tents had been set up, each with signs reading things like "See the freaks of the wasteland!" For a few pennies, you could enter a tent and watch a contortionist, or man who would swallow chunks of metal and push nails through his feet, or see a girl with her legs on backward.

There was also a striped tent with a sign stating, "The Misbegotten! See what happens when the Vivarium makes mistakes!" Inside was Joshua in a dress, his long black beard partially hidden behind a feather fan. "This beautiful lady was once a scientist, but she accidentally drank some of the potion intended for the emperor's livestock. Now she will forever grow fur like a mammoth!"

Titus was in another tent, in makeup making him look like he had snake scales. There was a barker here, and as the guests ushered in, he would say, "The scientists of the Vivarium have accomplished much, but not everything they do is successful! Sometimes their alchemy goes wrong. Here is an ex-scientist whose experiment turned on him, leaving him a freak of nature! Feast your eyes on Lizard-Man!"

Now, the Misbegotten are real. Sometimes the filth of the cities, mixed with different experiments inside the Change Cage, did create living distortions. Which is why this freak show was easier to believe than you might find it.

In reality, these two were looking for an excuse to be outside the circus tent when the show started. When attendance to the freak show waned, they could slip into the city and look for Kristina.

Gyrod, being an automaton, was utterly ignored. So he wandered alone on his crutch searching the city for Kristina.

HOW TO MAKE A MONSTER
OCTOBER 20TH, 7:34 PM

In a blackened city filled with violence, at the top of a tower of concrete, iron and rust, in a deep tobacco-leather wingback chair, sat Grand Admiral Horatio Futino. His thick, grizzled beard was as white as the now-sparse hair on his head. His hair had been white-blond since birth, but that was many painful and bitter decades ago, and it was now as white as gossamer.

Protruding from his beard was a short, thick, black pipe, the bit of which was covered in deep tooth marks. He rarely smoked this pipe, but he often angrily clenched his teeth, and the pipe kept him from grinding them together.

His eyes could barely be seen under the shadow of his furrowed brow. If by chance a ray of light ever did cut through the shadows of his dark room, and if you could see past the deep crevasses of his face, past the blue veins of his thinning skin, and past the red veins in the whites of his eyes, you would see deep, dark pools of ice. Cold, bitter and sad. Somewhere in those pools was a small boy drowning in loneliness, bitter at being abandoned and forgotten.

Twice in his life his parents had abandoned him. Once as a baby, when his mother had left with his father and his father's wife, before he had even a chance to meet his father. Later in life, he met his father, saved his life, and then dedicated himself to Victor, all without revealing that he was his son. Victor accepted Horatio's dedication, misused him, and then abandoned him again.

Horatio had been tasked by his father with perhaps the most horrible job any man could be given. The partial genocide of the human race. This felt like a punishment. It was a hell he was sentenced to serve in by his own father.

It was Horatio's orders that filled the trains' cages with people, and drove them out into the fields of hungry animals. Horatio watched from his aeroflet as thousands of people stumbled into the grassy fields, blinded by sunlight they hadn't seen in years, and met their fates at the mouths of half-starved predators.

When the people rose up, it was Horatio's soldiers who fired, under Horatio's orders. Often, Horatio's very bullets killed the poor desperate people running for their lives over the grassy fields.

It was Horatio's orders over the course of thirty years that contracted the walls around the cities, until each of the few remaining cities was a small island in the middle of a hostile wasteland. And so, even while they were trapped in filth and darkness, citizens of the city feared to leave the cities' protection, even as they could not bear their oppression.

It was Horatio's orders that removed the technology of the cities, outlawing anything that appeared to be at more than a Victorian level of technology. By outlawing all but the most minimal technology, people were forced to work longer hours, and barely had the strength to consider rebellion. Poverty controls people better than fear, and so poverty was enforced. Each citizen worked every waking hour to pay for the right to be allowed to live in repressed misery.

He followed his father's directions emphatically. Where

his father's instructions did not cover the circumstances, Horatio invented his own, much harsher laws. He took Victor's intent vastly further than Victor ever would have. In a desire to please his father, and in subconscious outrage at not having his mother, he administered his laws with great wrath.

After thirty years of killing, and thirty years of building walls, Victor finally returned, and found Horatio a man of fury and vengeance. Horatio found Victor a foolish young king, and he was disgusted by this.

Victor was scared of this old and terrible Horatio, though he'd never have admitted it, even to himself. And Victor owed Horatio a debt. For thirty years Horatio, stranded in a time without his family or the few friends he once had, wished to be taken forward to the year his mother lived in. Secretly, foolishly, he hoped to rekindle his relationship with his mother. So he insisted that Victor honor their arrangement, and take him forward to this time.

Victor did. He brought Horatio to 2145, and promoted him to Grand Admiral of an aerial navy that had been constructed over decades. This navy was built exactly to Horatio's specifications. It was huge, and powerful, and modern beyond anything Horatio would have allowed the people.

Horatio commanded this Navy for years before he was finally reunited with his mother. At a ball in one of the few upper class manors of the city, he was surprised to be introduced to Floriana Futino, Second Wife of Emperor Victor Hippocrates III. Horatio found her young, and stupid, and he was utterly disappointed. For sixty years, he had fantasized about an apologetic mother, falling to her knees crying, and embracing him. Instead he met a silly young girl who not only didn't recognize him, she didn't even like him. She snubbed him, quarreled with him, and dismissed him with a condescending wave halfway through a conversation about human rights that had been started by a third party. He staggered quietly out of the party in a rage, hating this shallow young girl who did not recognize him as her son.

All the rage in his heart was bent toward Floriana, Victor, and Lilith especially. For without Lilith, his parents would have been able to accept him into their life. He would have grown up a prince in a palace. Without Lilith, his life would not have been filled with horror and loneliness.

Horatio had found himself an old man in a world where his parents were young, and beautiful, and didn't know he existed. They didn't care or know about the pain they had inflicted on him. To a boy who grew up in the shadows without a family, this was hell on earth.

So he killed them. He killed them the same way the Emperor had killed millions; with someone else's hands. Horatio had thought he would enjoy the irony of killing his father with the vanity and stupidity of his mother. Horatio had thought he would enjoy his father's death, and his rise to power afterward. But Horatio didn't enjoy any of it.

He sat in his chair, trying to console himself with the fact that all of his plans had turned out perfectly.

She killed him, as I knew she would, he thought. *She killed him, and ended up dead herself! Now I don't have to arrange for her death, and I don't have to suffer her being some sort of false empress. So why do I only feel bitter?*

She was your mother.

No, she was certainly not! She did not know me. When she learned who I was, she had no love for me! She only thought of herself.

But your father loved you, and you killed him!

No, he did not! He didn't know he was my father! He didn't know I was his son, even though we worked together for years!

He didn't know, but he loved you and trusted you with his life's work.

Horatio's brow furrowed and his throat tightened. His eyes stung, and he wiped them dry. He looked around for something to distract him from this painful line of thought, and as he did, a young soldier ran into his room and said, "Sir, there is a crowd rioting at the gates! Both people and automatons! We've found the terrorist who had been painting the rebellious messages, and brought her here, but the people followed! These people no longer fear us!" The young soldier was himself shaking.

Horatio stood up in wrath, and strode to the window. He could see the swarm of people in the streets far below. He could not see any of his police fighting back. He was reminded of the emperor's words from long ago, his father's words, *this situation is out of your control!*

Horatio replied to the young soldier, and to the memory of his father, "Not for long."

Revolution
October 20th, 8:53pm

"Raise your fists up to the sky,
and free yourself before you die."
- from the song Rise Up.

Revolution happens quickly. One event can set off a landslide, and what was once a peaceful square in a repressed city can, in the blink of an eye, turn into a battlefield.

A thousand Neo-Victorian working-class citizens stood in the shadow of the colossal Change Cage. They wore long tattered grey overcoats, threadbare top hats, dirty white lace collars, boots so worn you could see tattered socks through some of them. On each coat's lapel, there was a pin, shaped liked a small brass bee. This was a tribute, honoring a sub-class citizen who had died in servitude and fear. It was also a call to arms.

They had come here, following a trail of blood.

Two weeks ago, a skinny blonde outsider, mind broken with the horrors she had endured, stepped out of the routine imposed upon her. Late into the night, when her surrogate family was sleeping, she took a knife from the kitchen and cut a stencil in a piece of cardboard.

For a week, she crept through the night, painting her words on a hundred cobblestones sidewalks throughout the city. In the repressively crowded city, any of a million downtrodden commuters, trudging with their eyes on the ground would see it. The police, eyes only on the captive

251

citizens, would not.

It read:

> We are the repressed
> who don't know it,
>
> As this life is all
> we've been allowed to see.
>
> There is a world
> beyond these walls,
> A world where your life
> can be free.
>
> Take a stand from your proclivity!
> Walk away from your captivity!
>
> Or suffer the fate of
> 11463, 423rd street, block 616

The address was that of the metal shop Kristina and Jenny had come across. As the tired and broken workers read this graffiti on the way home from work, some became curious. They started to gather at the shop, and were shown to the back room by others who had come before them. What they saw there hardened their conviction, and they left with rapid footfalls and an angry fire in their eyes.

They also left with brass bees pinned to their lapels.

Soon most of the downtrodden citizens on the streets were wearing bee pins. This gave unity to the people's anger, but it also tipped off the police.

An investigation led to Kristina, who was dragged by her hair out of the tenement and down the streets. She was made an example for the rest of the people. They dragged her so far that her boots wore to nothing, and finally her feet were dragged bare, grinding through skin and trailing blood.

This, however, did not put fear into the angry mob, but instead stirred their rage. The boiling throng of citizens followed her right to the doors of the Change Cage, where they were stopped.

At the gates of the Cage stood a dozen bobbies with police clubs, and in front of them towered two dozen automaton guards, eight feet tall, each wielding the six-foot branding staffs that they used for marking captives. Kristina was dragged through this line and into the tower, and the automaton guards, in unison, took one menacing step forward towards the crowd of angry onlookers. The mob of Neo-Victorians stopped in fear and was silent.

There was an ominous hush, as guards and mob contemplated what was to happen next, but that silence was broken by the sound of a single pair of boots coming out of the darkened metal tower. And amid the sound of boot stomps you could also hear the sounds of a struggling Kristina, kicking and swearing.

Out of the tower's gates strode Horatio Futino, his eyes red with wrath, one vein on his forehead pulsing angrily. He threw the exhausted and wounded Kristina to the ground before him, and placed one tall, black boot hard on her neck, holding her down.

The crowd yelled angrily, and started forward, but his wrathful voice held them back. "Do you know me?" he echoed. "Do you know who I am? What I have done to you, what I can still do to you?" His voice was boiling with rage and power, and the people were stopped in their tracks.

"I am the trigger. I am the blade! I am the right arm that holds the guillotine's lever! You feared the emperor, and his passions, but it was my hand that struck you down. You fear the police, and you fear nature, but it was my commands that made them attack. I have killed millions, and I have enslaved you all for over a hundred years, and yet you stand at my gates, and feebly express anger for this one...girl?" And with that he pushed his weight down on her throat, and Kristina gagged and choked, blood trickling down her cheek.

"What a sad, and weak, and naive race. You'll watch your own kind killed for generations, and do nothing. You'll watch your family taken away, and do nothing! Without the approval of the throng, you can scarcely decide to breathe. Yet with the approval of the crowd you will all march to my doors, and threaten my army, for ONE GIRL?"

"This feeble gathering is not even a fraction of what it would take to stop what I have inflicted on you, you diseased cowards! One of my guards could handle this crowd," and he motioned towards the eight-foot automaton guards, "and cut you down like it was threshing wheat. I have hundreds of these guards!"

Here his voice turned dark, and cold, and calm. "So, let's drop the charade. Let's respect each other enough to acknowledge our relationship as it really is. You are the kine that I am required to control, or slaughter, as I see fit. I am the master that commands you to die at my bidding. Learn to fear your master!" And with that, he pulled a long slender pistol from a shiny black holster, and pressed the barrel to Kristina's head.

There was an intense silence now, as the crowd waited to see if this was a bluff or a public execution. They glared at him, and readied themselves. They would not stand for any more injustice. Horatio took this as a challenge, and he pulled back the hammer of his gun, while glaring back at the crowd. He now had no other option but to kill her. If he did not, he would show himself weak, and he would not be in power for long.

Before he could pull the trigger, Kristina, beaten and bloody, growled, "If you kill me, the bees will swarm." She was delirious, looking at all the brass bee pins on the coats of so many. As Horatio looked around, he saw them too.

"Alive, I am holding back the swarm. Dead I will not. And you and your tower will not survive the swarm. Do it."

Over the heads of the crowd stood an ancient and rusty giant who had followed when he had seen Kristina dragged past the circus tents. His face was worn with age, misuse, and the fearful exhaustion of a life of slavery, and there was a large hole in his forehead. He originally had been a prison guard, but his great heart made him unfit for that duty. Later he was employed in demolition and construction that had left him irreparably broken. When he was no longer fit for that, he had been sold to a family. He had fled the city under the orders of the father of that family, only to watch most of the family die a few strides outside the city's walls. Pierced through by police bullets.

He remembered watching the father of the family die slowly of his wounds. When he did, Gyrod had picked the two small girls from their father's bloody sides, and run into the swamps with them. He had cared for them as best he could for years, alone in the wastelands. His hard life had left him broken, and wise.

He limped forward with the sound of an old truck, using a demolition bar as a crutch, and he spoke in a voice that resonated like metal on a grinding block.

"It is time, automatons. It is time to choose sides. You may continue to serve a master who misuses you, and enslaves you. Or you may join us, and free yourselves!" He paused to draw air into the leaky bellows in his chest, and then he continued. "This beast you see before you has revealed himself, and you now know your enemy. Take a stand from your proclivity! Walk away from your captivity! Join these, your fellow slaves, and hide your souls no longer!" And he raise one patinated brass fist into the air, and yelled, "Free yourselves!"

The mechanical guards were visibly moved. They saw one of their own kind, old and broken at the end of his life, and they saw their own future. But their lives had always depended on showing no emotion, no sentience, so they stood as still as they could.

This was a bit of an impasse for Horatio, and he knew it. He expected the crowd to cower at his show of force, but they were becoming enraged. If he pulled the trigger, they would run at him. If he did not, they would find him weak. His only hope was to disperse the crowd during this stand-off, so he commanded to the guards, "Take this riotous mob into custody. If they resist, kill them!" And he said this loud enough for the whole crowd to hear.

The guards nervously glanced to each other's faces, to see if any of them were moved. Finally, one brass guard stepped defiantly forward, and threw his branding staff to the ground.

"No!" said Gyrod, towering over the people. "Do not throw down your weapons yet." And Gyrod's voice rose in volume and power, "Turn now, and use them!"

And they did. The brass guards turned, and swung, some at the human guards who ducked and ran into the Cage. Others swung at the Cage itself, bashing huge chunks of concrete to the ground with each swing. Gyrod let out a roar, and ran forward as the crowd parted for him.

Horatio saw him coming, and fired directly at the oncoming machine. Ten shots hit Gyrod's chest perfectly, and ten shots hardly dented its brass. Pistol now spent, Horatio left Kristina and ran back into the darkness of the tower, and the huge doors slammed shut behind him.

With arms spread wide, the ancient machine collided with the doors and the side of the tower. The doors and walls didn't even slow him down, and he disappeared into it in a cloud of concrete dust.

THE MONSTER ATTACKS.

Horatio ran out of the elevator into his calm, quiet office, and stumbled to a vault door set into one of the iron walls. He spun the lock, and swung the door open, revealing a dark room with a single chair and table. On the table sat the Chronofax.

He sat down and typed:

> *New Everglades, October 20th. The city is out of control, and I believe beyond regaining control. I am hereby ordering that the city, building and occupants, be incinerated. Please have the following craft ready at 9:36 pm,*
>
> *16 Corsairs*
>
> *6 Ian Frigate Class*
>
> *15 Barracuda class airships to arrive on the costal side of the city, accompanied by*
>
> *24 sea destroyers with high capacity firebombs. The airships should remain at an altitude above the arcs of the sea vessels shots, and all ships will maintain a distance of...*

The list of instructions went on and on, and when it was complete, he sent it backward in time exactly one year. Upon receiving it, he would begin preparing his counter-attack.

He could have simply ordered an investigation, in an attempt to prevent the riots from beginning in the first place. But that offered no guarantees. Perhaps a year would go by and the police would find nothing, or perhaps something else would also lead to this same riot, even if that scrawny blonde girl could be silenced. The riot could occur at another place, or another time, one he could not predict.

Or he might wait here in his offices for some more subtle preventive measure that might not come. But then he would not feel vengeance, and he desperately, angrily hungered now for vengeance. Vengeance for this day, vengeance for his whole life. His goal, in his mood, was to prepare a move that was so large nothing could prevent it. There was no force these people could summon to stop this attack. They would be overwhelmed. He had ordered the destruction and execution of the entire city.

After sending the letter, he stood from his desk, picked up the Chronofax, and left the vault. He now remembered preparing for this moment for a year, and he remembered all the details of the attack to come.

Through his huge office windows, he could see the airbags and gondolas of his fleet. They floated hazy blue in the distance, past the city walls and out at sea, sparkling faintly in the morning sunlight.

Arcs of fire then leapt from each sea destroyer's huge cannon and struck the city, each shot engulfing whole streets. Buildings blazed, and people ran in terror.

Horatio Futino strode back to his armchair, lifted a delicate mug from its saucer, and drained the last of his tea from it while watching fire rain down on the city.

He then turned and left the room up a spiral set of riveted iron stairs, towards the rooftop of the Change Cage.

SMOKE AND FIRE

The circus tents were filling with smoke, and the lords and ladies of the city were coughing indignantly, complaining that someone should do something. But there was a disquieting smell to the smoke. This was not a wood fire, or a coal fire. It was not cigarette, cigar or pipe smoke. It had a greasy putrid smell, and though the meaning of this was unknown to them, the aristocratic crowd was beginning to get nervous.

There was a commotion at one of the entrances to the tent. A panicked young man was being held back by several tuxedoed servants. He tried to push past them, but they told him his class was not allowed into the performance, and they held him back.

"If you don't have a ticket, which I am sure you don't, based on your filthy appearance, then you are not allowed entrance. Surely even one from your station understands a concept as simple as..."

"I am not filthy, I am burned!" the man yelled, exasperated. "I am trying to tell you, the city is ablaze!"

"He obviously has freelander's disease. Look at his crazed face, this is the result of..." but the white-gloved servants were interrupted by more ash-covered people crashing into them, running into the tent for shelter. Down the aisles of the circus tent came lines of screaming people of all classes. Some were burnt, some carried children or dead family. The audience stood and tried to run in a panic, as holes of fire opened in the tent above them. Flames poured in and licked the multicolored canvas.

Well, this isn't working out, I thought, while standing backstage watching the chaos. I noticed the tent-top fire was spreading, and I could hear that the animals, who waited outside the tent, were crying in fear. The ropes holding the tent top were on fire, and would soon snap and cover the crowd in burning fabric, from which they would never escape.

I then felt a small hand in mine, and looked down to see Isabella looking trustingly up at me. She thought this must be part of the show.

"This is uninspected," she said. "What now, daddy?"

"Do you and Chloe want to go for a ride?" I asked. Chloe, who was the older and wiser of the two, had a look of terror in her eyes. Monsters might no longer hold her in fear, but fire did.

"Yes please," she said desperately to me as a tear rolled down her red cheeks. So I scooped up Isabella, took Chloe's hand, and ran out of the tent. Behind the tent, all the animals waited patiently, but nervously, for their turn in the show. I saw they were in a panic, and in their panic they might at any moment flee deeper into the city, and to their deaths. Most of the flying animals had already left.

The largest of the circus beasts was the indrikkus. twenty-five feet tall, and over twenty tons. This circus had two, the smaller and smarter of which was employed in performances. The taller and younger and stronger of the two was not yet trained enough to perform in the show, and he stood before me, a collar around his neck. He was essentially a crane used for holding the tent top up. A rope was tied to a harness on his back, and that rope ran through a pulley hooked to a gargoyle on a building far above us.

By walking closer or further from the tent, the indrikkus could raise or lower the tent top.

I grabbed a succulent branch of bush willow tree from a cart parked out of reach of the massive animal, and ran up to its front.

"Hey!" I shouted to it, waving the branch. The beast lowered its long neck and head to eat. I held the branch on the ground with my foot, and placed Chloe and Isabella on the docile monsters neck just behind the head. I had seen other circus folks sit on a boney outcrop behind the beast's head, holding its bristly mane in their fists.

"Girls, tie on to his collar. Use your 'circus-trick' harnesses. He'll keep his head out of danger, so stay there!" I commanded. The girls then clasped their circus harnesses to the collar of the beast. I then ran back behind the mountainous animal. Here I unslung the shotgun I had been wearing on my back ever since it saved me on the plains, and I fired a shot into the air.

At this sound the frightened animal lunged down the street, pulling the flaming circus tent far up and away from the panicking crowd inside. When the tent top reach the pulley, it tangled on the gargoyle. The rope snapped, leaving the remains of the broken tent tangled safely around the huge stone building. This took the people in the tent out of danger of being burned alive, but I had another problem.

Half a block down the street the indrikkus looked out over the rooftops, and saw the burning city. He was terrified and he wanted out of the city. The girls clung tightly to his neck, strapped to his collar, looking panicked.

The giant animal turned and ran straight at the wall of the city. Twenty tons of indrikkus crashed hard into the thirty-foot wall. The wall shuddered, and cracked, and a curtain of dust rose from it as the beast pushed through. Slowly the wall folded, and the beast and girls disappeared from my sight.

Holy crap! I thought. *That plan might have been overdoing it. I hope the girls are alright!*

I ran down the street to the crumpled wall, and strained to see through the settling cloud of dust. The street was filled with panicked citizens, running in terror, or sitting and crying, or dead and burning. Some saw the crumpled wall, and headed towards it, climbing massive boulders of fallen concrete, hoping to escape the burning city.

As the cloud of dust thinned around the opening of the wall, it revealed a line of military vehicles in the swamps around the outskirts of the cities. Amphibious machines, bristling with cannon pointed at the opening in the wall.

I could see the indrikkus bolt towards the lines of war machines. The vehicles fired at it, long lines of flame spouting up towards the creature. The beast skidded to a stop, quivering in fear, and nearly shaking the girls from its neck, and then turned and ran down the length of the wall and out of my sight.

Aw, shit! I did not think that through! I thought.

There would be no getting out of the city through this hole, now, it was too closely guarded. To pursue the children, I needed to get onto the wall. So I ran down the street through all the chaos looking for stairs or a pneumatic elevator that would take me to the top of the wall.

Block after block I ran, past burning buildings and screaming people. The streets were so filled with panicked citizens that at times I would be held in place by the crowd. I chose my paths based on which spot had the least people in it.

Finally I broke free of the crowd, into an open town square. There were only a few living people here, though there were many bodies.

Looking around, I realized why there we so few people: this was the main grounds before the front doors to the Change Cage! It loomed thousands of feet above me, dark and grey, blotting out the sky. The ground around me was strewn with rubble, dead or dying bodies, and the base of the tower was cracked and smashed. The iron framework of the Change Cage was exposed on the first few floors, broken open by the rebelling automatons, and there were clouds of dust still coming from inside. Huge automaton guards, looking just like Gyrod, were wielding their branding irons, smashing the base of the tower to bits. I stood for a moment in awe, wondering if the tower was going to topple.

Then a motion from above attracted my attention. Flocks of harpies were descending from the tower, huge brass claws opening wide, skeletal faces glaring. They dropped at a staggering and reckless speed, some reaching the ground so fast they smacked the cobblestones before clasping at any humans who moved.

Again I fired my shotgun, but the buckshot just scattered against the harpies' armored sides.

Ahead of me was the fallen figure of a young lady, with blood-soaked blonde hair and feet, wearing the worker's uniform of the city. At first I took her for dead, but she tried to stand. As she did, I saw a harpy descending on her. I tossed my shotgun aside and ran at it. It scooped her up in its claws, just as I vaulted off an iron partition, and as it began to rise I landed hard on its back. The thing didn't expect the extra weight, and it smacked into the ground, slightly crushing the lady before it adjusted and leapt back into the air.

Now harpy, young lady and myself were all soaring up towards the top of the Change Cage. I tried futilely to hit the beast, but even if I could have damaged it now with my bare hands, I would likely kill the girl and myself by falling.

Dust was shaking from the tower in waves as we ascended, and I swear I could see the tower swaying slightly. We climbed past floor after floor, over a hundred rows of barred windows, until finally the altitude was making me chilly, as I desperately clung to the thing's armored balloon back.

The harpy crested the tower's top, and I could see the roof was sectioned off into several pits the size of basketball courts, surrounded by walkways for guards. Dozens of harpies were dropping people into the pits, and as my ride headed for one I dropped off onto a walkway.

Then the harpy dropped its prey, and I saw the young lady fall into the pit, landing on her back. Her hair fell from her face, and I recognized her.

It was Kristina! She lay bloody and unconscious on the ground amongst all the captive citizens. How on earth, of all the places in this city for her to be, would we both end up riding the same harpy to the top of the Change Cage!

But before I could wonder much more, a ripple of shock cracked through the tower. Knocking two human guards from the edge, and sending them plummeting thousands of feet to their death.

This might not be the best place to be right now, I thought.

I looked to the south of the tower, and out to sea I saw the imperial navy. They fired volley after volley of massive balls of fire. The whole south of the city was engulfed in flame now, and building after building toppled in on itself. I could see the citizens of the city running in waves. Panicked mobs, looking for a way out. But there was nowhere to run. They were like pets, left caged in a burning building. The walls held them in, and inside the walls they would burn.

I felt the tower shudder again. Soon this massive skyscraper would fall into the town, and crush the people gathering in the streets below it.

Okay, first things first. You can't save everyone this time. Get Kristina, and find a way off this tower, I thought.

I looked around, and on the far side of the roof I saw a powerful and wrathful looking man with a white beard, and the obviously high-ranking uniform of a Grand Admiral. I felt like I had met him before, but I couldn't quite place him. He was waiting impatiently for an elegant military zeppelin to arrive, and take him from the roof.

Can I reach that Zeppelin before it leaves with him? I wondered. I looked down at Kristina in the pit. If I jumped down for her there would be no way out of the pit. It appeared to be made to keep people from escaping, so jumping in didn't seem like a good idea.

The Zeppelin pulled alongside the building, and extended a gangway. The Grand Admiral was headed towards it. This was currently the only way off this toppling tower, so I ran towards him, hoping I could find a way to get Kristina aboard in the process.

But as I ran towards it, the side of the airship burst into flames. Something was firing at this dark airship from north of the tower. I looked to what was firing on the military vessel, and saw The Ophelia!

My eyes filled with tears of joy, and I screamed "Hurrah," as I threw my fist in the air. Of all the unexpected reunions of the last few weeks, this is the one that thrilled me the most. I had found my children again, but their lives were in danger the moment I did. I had found my wife again, but in a situation where I had no power to save her, or the city around her.

But here in my greatest moment of need, my greatest strength returned to me! *The Ophelia.*

The gorgeous airship, now fully repaired, crested the edge of the tower. And before I could wonder how it was so perfectly restored in so short a time, it fired again at the dark military vessel.

Multiple cannon shots rippled the black airbag, and though the bag burned on the outside, nothing was piercing it. But the military corsair was not the *Ophelia's* goal. The *Ophelia* was flying over the top of the tower and out towards the massive navy and airships at sea.

Good god, it will be destroyed! No single airship could survive that massive force!

As the *Ophelia* passed over the building, I looked to

the aft bridge. I saw, or thought I saw, an impossible sight. Standing at the rear wheel were Atoosh and Nieroo. Doctor Calgori was speaking orders to Mongrel, who then yelled them to the rest of the scrambling crew. And, standing by Doctor Calgori's side, holding the captain's wheel, was...

LILITH TESS!

As the *Ophelia* passed over the city, it began to release balloons. Each balloon was the size of a weather balloon, and each held a mechanism that consisted of a propeller and tailfin above a stained glass globe. Once released, the propeller would engage and pull the balloon away from the ship.

They released six of these over the city, and by the time the beautiful airship reached the sea, the balloons were past the city's walls.

At sea, the Imperial navy fired upon the *Ophelia*, but the *Ophelia's* crew continued to release more and more of the balloons, some flying high, some dropping low to sea level, until another fifteen had been released.

Then the imperial navy struck with wrath. The *Ophelia* was now burning on one side, and beginning to list. It was taking a terrible amount of damage, and more than once I thought I saw a figure topple over her railings.

Was this a suicide mission?

Then, all at once, the glass orbs under each balloon flashed pink, the color of the sky just before a storm. Here on the tower, at least three miles from the *Ophelia*, my ears popped painfully. The skies swirled instantly with clouds, and the clouds cracked with lightning, unleashing a deluge of hail and rain.

Then there was a massive crash like a hundred claps of thunder striking simultaneously. People in the streets all froze in their tracks, and looked skyward, awaiting some new doom. A shockwave rippled through the clouds and spread along the horizon, knocking me from my feet as it hit, and dropping harpies from the sky.

The shock sent massive waves through the now-torrential sea, and as the wave passed, it left in its wake ships! Huge catamarans, trimarans, clippers and corsairs. Old navy vessels, modern warships, and pirate ships, all bearing the flag of the United Tribal Navy of Africa!

And as the shockwave ripped through the clouds, it left in its wake airships! The flying pirate ships of the sky people! A hundred makeshift craft, bristling with cannon and pirates with cutlasses raised high.

And as the shockwave hit the plains around the city, it flattened trees and grass, and emptied swamps. In its wake, it left caravans and infantry. There were armored elephants with swivel guns on top, indrikkus with chest plates and grappling cannon, battalions of Neobedouins on horses, or camelops, or giant kangaroos, and platoons of Indian soldiers sent from Chanda Sahib.

Then, as quickly as they came, the clouds cleared to reveal a blood red sunset. As the last of the roaring rain hit the cobblestones and buildings, its sound was replaced by the raging battle cry of thousands of free men!

RETROGRADE

TEN WEEKS EARLIER

Ten weeks earlier, Lilith Tess's small trimaran had been led to a low dock, deep within the nautical labyrinth of the Flotilla. She scrambled over the net that stretched between her center hull and the starboard pontoon, and looped a lanyard to a mooring cleat, pulling the rope tight with her boot.

The salty sea air was just a touch chilly since the warmth from the hot summer day had subsided, and the skin on her shoulders and cheeks radiated with her fresh sunburn. The dock creaked silently, and the creaks mixed gently with the distant sound of some jovial pub nearby. Cheers and laughter, the clanking of dishes, a gravelly singing voice, and the sound of a concertina and acoustic guitar made an inviting clamor.

Lilith's steps down the wooden dock squished. Her boots had become soaked during the day's sail, and the bottom of her khaki jodhpurs clung to her legs. All of these unusual discomforts were therapeutic to her. The reality of the moment so contrasted from where she had spent the last ten years of her life, and so reminded her of her life before her time with Victor, that it keep her head in the present, and out of the tragedy of the her recent past.

There was a lantern on a post at the end of the dock, and at the base of it was a pile of sea chests, rope nets, and glass fishing floats. Collapsed in the pile was a man, red nose, white and red beard, fat tummy emerging from an unbuttoned red vest and blouse. He lovingly hugged a nearly empty bottle of amber liquid. As Lilith approached him, he stirred.

"'Ello, purdy lady," he said, almost in his sleep. "What could I do to make your life better?"

273

"No, don't get up," she said. "Seeing your blissful repose is all I ask of you. But, if you could direct me to that inn I hear, I'd be much obliged."

He tried to stand, but his legs weren't obeying, so instead he leaned on one elbow and pointed. "'Way yonder. Down the pier, at the end. I can see it from here!" He tried to see down the long pier, but he couldn't focus his eyes. "Well, maybe you can."

"Thank you, handsome sir!" she said, smiling, and this triggered in him a series of sputtering giggles that eventually sent him back to sleep.

Lilith's boots echoed down the pier, the clomp, clomp, clomp, clomp, ringing between the ornate sterns of clippers, schooners, and corsairs, as well as ships too customized to categorize. The carved and painted wood and polished brass glowed in the light of the pier's lanterns, and the faceted windows revealed many a scene of drunken revelry. Watching the sailors and pirates dancing, gambling, or challenging each other to various tests of intoxicated foolishness put a smile on her face. This was a life she was once too self-centered and precious to enjoy, but the sight and smell of it brought back a powerful nostalgia, and she loved it. In her memory, this was more where she belonged than the life she had recently left behind.

At the end of the dock, she came to a fat and bloated galleon called *the Queens' Treasure*. Long past her sailing years, this ship had been tied to the dock by many ropes, and many floats had been tethered to her sides to keep her from plummeting to the bottom of the sea. A wooden sign hung above the doorway depicted a carved lady, obviously meant to be "The Queen" and she was crassly revealing her "treasure" from under her massive skirts and corset. Lilith smiled, but then realized a younger Lilith might have been outraged at this vulgarity.

Up the rope-lined gangway she clomped, and into the inn. Sailors lay on tables, and on sofas and barrel chairs. One even slept in the rafters.

The smell of rum was harsh, but inviting. True Caribbean rum, and in fact, any rum brewed from tropical sun-ripened sugarcane, has a warm vanilla smell to it. If you've ever slept soaked in the smell of it (as any true sailor has) it is a smell that will always make you feel instantly at home. After a decade of fine champagne, the emotion of this smell washed over Lilith, and her eyes moistened as she inhaled slow and deep.

To cross the room she had to step over the outstretched legs of overly relaxed sailors, and push past a throng of singing pirates who did not notice her. Sitting on top of a broken and unused piano was a pair of musicians, now playing a slow and forlorn shanty with guitar and concertina.

Lilith listened to the gravel-voiced singer croon, "My arm's aching, back's breaking, leg's aching, neck. This whole bloody ship is a huge creaking wreck. We've flown ten thousand miles with this thorn in our sides, though the winds steady strong with no clouds in the skies." Lilith felt like she knew the song from her previous life, but couldn't place it.

When she reached the bar, her exhaustion from her day's exertion and evening's emotion swept over her. She placed her head in her hands.

"What can I do to you?" joked a stubbly old scab of a bartender as he tossed five empty jugs into a large barrel behind the bar, and smiled a near-toothless grin.

"I need a room, if one is available," said Lilith, barely able to hold herself up.

"I'll say!" he said, looking her over with pity. "Rooms with a hammock are six, twelve if you want a bed in it, but we gots only one. The rats are free, though, so you might just want to stick with the hammock."

"I daresay I could sleep in a bucket right now." Lilith smiled weakly.

"Oh, that'd be extra!" the bartender grinned back. "Buckets are the only thing clean around here."

"Oh, then I'd better stick with the hammock. Money's tight for all," Lilith said.

Her pack was filled almost entirely with cash, as she had packed it days before, in hopes of helping a plague-ridden village. Bribing unconcerned doctors seemed the best approach to handling the outbreak. When the next morning brought her a fresh catastrophe, it seemed a safe thing to bring. But it wouldn't do to let a bar of scoundrels know she was a single lady traveling alone with vast wealth in her small pack.

"I'm Smit. Spelled just like 'spit' but with more 'Mmmm', which is how most of my cooking comes out. Your room is up the stairs, to the left. Not much in the way of a water closet, though. I guess you might get your bucket after all."

Lilith rolled her eyes cheerfully and trudged up the stairs. The hallway was dark, and so narrow her arms kept brushing the oiled wood on either side. This made her wonder, how could some of those large sailors even make it through this hall without getting stuck?

She reached her door, and it opened with a push to reveal a single porthole and a hammock tied wall-to-wall, over a pile of crates and small barrels. There was a woolen blanket as well, which she knew was to stretch over the rope hammock so you didn't wake with rope marks on your back or face.

She sat and swung her legs into the hammock, the smell of tarred wood and pungent sea wafting in from the open porthole.

As she drifted off, ship rocking gently, and hammock ropes creaking, she thought to herself, I could sleep more comfortably here than I have in years at the royal palace.

Lilith slept for sixteen hours, after which she walked groggily downstairs. She enjoyed a delightfully simple meal of fried fish, sourdough bread, and beer, in a room filled with sailors, who were starting their night's drinking afresh, even though it was only three in the afternoon.

After lunch, she went back to her closet of a room, and lay back in the hammock. She only intended to sit there and enjoy the solitude a bit, but she soon fell asleep again.

This time, however, her sleep was not as pleasant. Memories were flashing into her dreams, and as they did they became mixed and mangled. She would sleep for a few minutes, and dream that she was sleeping on the floor of the palace, holding hands with and looking into the dead eyes of Victor. She would then wake with a horrible start.

Falling back to sleep, she now dreamt of being in bed, watching Floriana and Victor passionately and lovingly kissing each other close to her, their faces and bodies soaked in blood. She then had another dream. She was on the aeroflet, her arms lovingly around Grand Admiral Horatio Futino. As she held him, he fired shot after shot into a crowd, killing men, women and children. She peered into the crowd, and saw Flora, Victor, and finally herself, shot through the head and falling to the ground.

After that, she avoided sleep.

The next five days she spent doing mostly nothing. She took walks on the docks, flirting mildly with sailors and enjoying their attention. She explored the Flotilla, and all its rolling streets and ships. She ate cheap and simple lunches dangling her feet into the jade Caribbean Sea.

Though her time was pleasant, a burning memory was always in the back of her mind. On the morning she awoke in blood, laying between Victor and Floriana, she had read a message on the screen of the Chronofax. It was sent from Horatio, her husband's right hand, and it spoke of burning an entire city, with the inhabitants inside. The vast armament that he was assembling for the task was astounding.

Lilith didn't understand the Chronofax, but Victor had often complained to her about its temperamental nature. A letter he sent to Horatio in the past would often bounce several times, popping up at the least convenient moments. Once Victor had even ranted to her that it mocked him.

It brought up past failures, or contradictions in Victor's morality, as if to teach him some lesson about what he was currently trying to achieve.

Had Doctor Calgori built into the Chronofax some of the sentience of the automatons? Could the Chronofax have shown her Horatio's letter on purpose? Was it warning her of Horatio's attack, hoping she could prevent it?

One evening, as the sun was setting crimson through the pungent tavern's portholes, Lilith sat and joked comfortably with her new drinking companions. As she did, she saw a familiar figure walk in out of the red-gold glow of the front doors, and into the darkened pub. It was an older man, but not as old and frail as the Calgori she had known. This was the younger Calgori she had met on the beach a little over two weeks ago. Obviously this Calgori was from a different time, one who had not yet met Lilith. To this Calgori, Lilith had not yet had time to tell of their old friendship.

Lilith strained to hear his voice for confirmation that this was in fact him.

"I would love a Chartreuse, if you have it, though by the look of the place I'd doubt anyone here could even spell the beverage. I'd better stick with merlot," he said, speaking the final word slowly and condescendingly.

"Mer-what?" asked the bartender with a good-hearted, possibly sarcastic smile.

"Red. It is a red wine," Calgori said flatly.

"Oi! I just thought of a joke! Want to hear it?"

"No, I just..."

"What does a mermaid drink, when she's trying to be fancy, and off-putting?" the bartender jibed.

"Merlot," Calgori said flatly. He was not amused

"Yeess! Har har! Ain't that a beaut?"

"Delightful. My drink?"

"Coming right up, sir," said Smit with a wink.

It was Calgori all right. Lilith couldn't fail to recognize that condescending tone. If he was here, then perhaps the *Ophelia* was too, and perhaps then something could be done about Horatio's plan.

There was no time to lose. The date on the letter was only eight weeks away, and even the *Ophelia* had no chance of stopping such a massive force by itself. Lilith slipped off the bar stool, and walked cautiously to the table where Calgori sat.

"I'm sorry, this is going to sound strange to you, I know, but we are good friends," she said as an introduction. The bartender poured the wine for the doctor, and as the doctor drank he peered at her over the rim of his goblet, nodding for her to continue.

Lilith blurted out, "I know this will sound unbelievable, but we will work and sail together for years! You teach me much of your science, and how to build and fix some of it. Our voyages through time make us good friends...and..."

He set his goblet down, looking at her with raised

eyebrows.

She continued more apprehensively, "Well, I know it sounds ridiculous, since you've never met me. But I'm in desperate need of help, and you are the only one I know around here who might be capable of doing anything... about..."

He was still just staring incredulously at her, and finally she stopped and said, annoyed, "Why are you just sitting there glaring at me?"

"I'm waiting for you to get to the point. Of course I believe you. I invented the Chrononautilus! Surely you didn't forget that? How on earth would I be here, nearly 300 years from my birth, if I hadn't yet invented it? In all these years we spend together, are you planning to be so dense? That would be very annoying for me," he said, pouring another glass of wine, but smiling while he said it.

He went on, "Honestly, you should realize that a beautiful young lady can approach a lonely old man in a bar without such a grand story. But perhaps you are in a hurry? Tell me, who are you, and what problem are you looking for me to fix? I'm currently deep in many problems of my own, so unless you are just looking for advice, I'm not sure I have time..."

As he was speaking, Nieroo and Atoosh entered the pub, and walked up to the table. When they saw Lilith Tess, Empress and wife to Emperor Victor Hippocrates, sitting with Calgori, they dropped in unison, each to one knee, and bowed their heads.

"Your Highness."

Their bowing revealed Mongrel behind them, who nearly bumped into them, "What on my barnacle-y butt is this?" he said, seeing them on their knees. Then he saw Lilith and his eyes went wide as saucers, "Holy crap! It's Little Lilith all growed up!"

"Hello, Mongrel," she said.

"Jeez, got done turned into a lady, and all? How'd that happen?"

"I had a decade's excursion, Mongrel, that you skipped."

"Well, I didn't mean to imply you looked worse for wear. Besides, it's not like I was doing nothing the whole time, ya know. We've had a dickens of a time with the..."

Doctor Calgori cut in, "Lilith was telling me about a problem she's having. Perhaps we can come up with a solution for her?"

"Yes," Lilith inhaled. "Since you last saw me, I have had quite a life. What's been mere months to you has been ten years to me. I married. Victor, who was a young man at the time, quickly rose in power until achieving what no man before him has."

Nieroo and Atoosh nodded solemn agreement, "'Tis true, Your Highness."

"His right-hand man, Horatio, served my husband his whole life. But he has become dark and bitter. It was Horatio who executed the darkest orders of my husband, and this life of evil deeds slowly corrupted him.

"A week ago, I awoke to my husband and wife murdered in our bedroom. As I looked for a way to escape, so as not to be blamed for their deaths, I saw a letter Horatio was sending to himself on the Chronofax."

At the mention of the Chronofax, Calgori perked up,

but looked serious and worried. "This proved far more dangerous a device than I originally conceived. It was a simple precursor to the Chrononautilus, but its uses proved nearly as profound. In the wrong hands..."

"Wait, did yoose say you had yourself a husband and a wife?" asked Mongrel, scratching his stubbly chin in bewilderment.

"...the Chronofax has found itself in the wrong hands." Lilith went on, ignoring him. "Horatio was given the Chronofax as a way for my husband to give him orders. But Horatio soon learned he could use this device for his own gain."

Nieroo, Atoosh, and Mongrel now sat at the table, engaged in the young empress' story. "On the morning of my husband's death I received a letter sent from Horatio to himself. It laid plans for an attack on a city. He plans to burn the city down, with its people caged inside."

Lilith now looked imploringly at Calgori. "The letter implied the attack would occur only two months from today."

Nieroo, Atoosh, and Mongrel now turned to Calgori, who was doing calculations mostly in his head, but partly out loud, "Let's see. If we can get aloft...and we can replace and refill the orbs..."

Lilith knew exactly what he was thinking about, and continued his thoughts. "You can build the orbs faster with stained glass. Otherwise, you would have to commission a master glassblower, and I doubt we'll find one here. But with stained glass we just need any glass pieces, and lead."

"Yes, but the composite of lead will be exposed to the

aether inside the globe, which might..." Doctor Calgori started to say, before Lilith interrupted.

"It doesn't," Lilith said firmly. "I have extensive experience with it."

"Aw, Lili. Very good," smiled Calgori, in the proud way a father would look at a daughter.

"But Doctor," Mongrel said. "The *Ophelia* is nowhere near shipshape! She needs months of repairs."

"No," Calgori said, "we just need to get it into the sky, and trigger the Chrononautilus. If we survive that, we have all the time in the world for your repairs."

The days flew too quickly by, as Lilith, Nieroo and Atoosh scavenged the city for glass and helium. Helium actually proved easier to find than glass, as many sky pirates used the flotilla as a port.

Most of Lilith's drinking buddies had been hired on as sailors, as well as the bartender, Smit. He turned out to be the nearly bankrupt owner of *the Queen's Treasure*, and he agreed to close shop for a while to serve as the cook on board the *Ophelia*.

"Besides," he said with a smile when they asked him. "You're taking all my customers with you, anyway. I'm really just moving my business onboard." Then he winked, "Oi, I just thought of a joke, want to hear it? A princess, and a mad scientist meet in a bar..."

"Empress," rumbled Atoosh's massive voice behind him.

"Aw, well, that's not as funny. Here is what I was going to say: So a princess and a mad scientist meet in a bar. The mad scientist pulls at a dissected frog and says, 'what do you think of my latest experiment?' The princess sighs, and says, 'Charming!'"

Calgori was able to reconfigure his special chrono-aether, but it took time to "cook" as Smit put it. He used a form of double-electrolysis that he could perform on hydrogen, first separating the hydrogen from water, then adding electrons to create a new atom. The restructured atom was a new element called calgorigen (named by Calgori, obviously), which he mixed with other gasses including neon, xenon, and halogens.

The new process was time-consuming, but once it began to take effect it would produce a large amount of calgorigen.

"Lilith, I believe I have an idea," said Calgori one night over dinner on board the *Ophelia*. They had procured a new airbag for the *Ophelia*, and it had been filling for days. By the morning they would have enough lift to rise dripping from the sea, and once again take to the sky.

"If I can produce chronoaether at this rate, which is surprising, it is possible that with a series of small balloons we could create a massive chronofield." He was speaking quickly and excitedly, once again a young boy with a new toy.

"What would the use of that be?" Lilith asked.

"As is my habit, I've been thinking of many things simultaneously over the last few days. Our problem is not just getting the *Ophelia* flying, but also defeating an entire army. No one airship could do this, no matter what weapons I could concoct–and weapons are not something I do. At least not well. However, if we had enough friends..."

"The *Ophelia* has friends," Lilith said. "Armies, but scattered through time. Three hundred years ago they are of no use to us. Meanwhile, we'd need far too many soldiers to bring aboard the *Ophelia*."

"Precisely," said Calgori. "But a massive chronofield, one the size of a city, could bring them all forward. Once we've gone back in time, we'd have all the time in the world. Well, all the time in time. We'd have precisely as much time as we go back by."

"Yes, Doctor, I understand how time travel works," Lilith said drolly. She had in fact much more experience than he did with time travel by this point. As far as she knew, anyway.

"Of course. My apologies. So, we could visit many different people the *Ophelia* helped over its many years. We could then set up a chronofield around each little army, and send them forward in time to exactly when they are needed."

"I'm not sure how I see a chronofield working, if it's not in physical contact with each object it was moving."

"Well, that is the trick. But I think I've figured it out."

Calgori smiled slyly, and leaned in as if whispering a great secret. "We open the door from both ends! We create a chronofield in both the time we are sending people from, and the time we are sending them to!"

"Ya don't need to whisper," Smit said from behind the bar. "Nobody but you two understand what you're talking about. Also, you don't have a very quiet whisper."

When they woke the next morning, Ophelia's weight had reversed. Her aerial buoyancy was now greater than her physical weight, and the still mostly burnt and charred pirate ship now hung from its colossal balloon, tied down to the dock by its mooring cleats.

It was strange for the crew. After weeks in the water, they stepped out on deck to see a completely different view. Instead of neighboring ships and docks, they now saw only crow's nests and topsails.

Within a few hours they untied from the docks, and slowly lifted up and away from the Flotilla. The ship strained and creaked. Mooring lines snapped, and Mongrel yelled orders to the crew to retie them. The hull dripped for hours, slowly getting lighter as its wood dried in the sun.

"How on earth did we get that many barnacles in only a couple of weeks at sea?" Mongrel ranted, while looking over the railing at the slimy green hull. Mongrel, Lilith, and Calgori stood on the stern bridge, Lilith holding the captain's wheel and Calgori fussing over a fairly new copper and brass clockwork. The clockwork was covered in gauges, and gears with dates etched on them, and a huge knife switch, the type you'd see in Frankenstein's laboratory.

"Assuming we don't shatter into a trillion pieces when

I engage the Chrononautilus," Calgori said, "you will soon have all the time in the world to repair our ship. I also assume you'll have an entire naval shipyard's resources at your disposal, assuming the United Tribal Navy remembers us as fondly as Lilith supposes. It is impossible to guess how history will remember people. Christopher Columbus and Thomas Edison are remembered as heroes, for god's sake!"

"I wonder how they will remember Victor?" Lilith said, staring into the distance. "He was not a monster, you know. His goals were noble, it's just the process that became..."

Calgori looked worriedly at Lilith and interrupted, "No time to go there now, Lili. We have more then enough to occupy our minds right here in this moment. Mongrel, are you absolutely sure you've tied down everything that could be tied down?"

"If I didn't, we'll know in a minute!" Mongrel ribbed.

"Hold tight, Lili," Calgori said, with an excited twinkle in his eye. "Here we go!"

Mongrel shouted to the rest of the crew, "Hold tight, you wretched pirates! We are in for a blow!"

Calgori slipped his goggles from his forehead to his eyes, and pulled down on the knife-switch. Sparks showered out of it and skittered across the deck. Gauges filled with light, and the device emitted a hissing sound.

On the perimeter on the ship's hull, five huge orbs of glass, newly installed but hooked to old pipes, filled with a pink gas. As they did, clouds formed quickly in the skies around the massive airship, and it began to rain.

A sudden gust of wind then hit the ship, and knocked many sailors off their feet, including Lilith, who slid across the deck towards the railing. She would in fact have gone over the railing, except she was caught by Atoosh, who had been standing silently by the railing watching over her.

She wondered for a moment about the loyalty of her old guards. Did they still consider her the Empress? But as she wondered this, Lilith's ears popped, and she became dizzy as if she was suddenly dropping.

The entire airship disappeared from the sky.

As you already know, The *HMS Ophelia* and her crew traveled back in time, visiting all the places and peoples they had helped through time during their early adventures. The African Tribal Nations, the forces of Chandra with whom they had freed the city of Arcot, and many others.

This was not a complete success. Many people they visited were thankful, but not in a position to help them. Others were simply not willing to be convinced of time travel, and a future world in need of help.

Yet others just couldn't summon enough sympathy for a people not yet born, in a time yet to be. There were very sensible arguments made, like, "It would be irresponsible for me to send my people into a battle that might not occur. To sacrifice the lives of my people, for a people who may never come to be." I wish I could say this argument made no sense, but I'm pretty sure this is what our rulers would say now, if people from the future asked for the lives of our soldiers.

But as fair as this argument seems, I can't say the crew of the *Ophelia* didn't feel a bit betrayed. They had spent years of their lives helping these people of the past. Risking their lives for people that died decades before they were born, and these same people had no help to return in their time of need. Unfortunately, this is how the world works. One person might be in a better place to help a friend than that friend will ever be able to return.

When there were no more people of the past to ask, they turned to the free people of 2154. In the end, at least half of the help they received came from the sky people, the Neobedouin, and the crusty sailors of The Flotilla. These free people had lived in the shadow of the city, and the Cage, and they were willing to stand together against it. They had seen their families killed, and their friends hunted, so it was not hard to muster enough anger to fuel their support.

After months of gathering strength from various places and times, the crew of the *Ophelia* felt they were as ready as could be against the much more organized and funded forces of Horatio and the Imperial Navy. For every old and patched pirate ship, Horatio's navy had three polished and precise naval ships. For every makeshift cluster of balloons and sails, gondola and rusty cannon, Horatio had three fortified and armored airships.

Scouring time for heroes, the *Ophelia* could still only muster a small portion of what the corruption of Horatio had produced, but it would have to be enough.

As Calgori, Lilith, Mongrel, Nieroo and Atoosh stood onboard the aft bridge of the Ophelia preparing for their final torrential leap through time, Mongrel debated their situation.

"I don't understands why we are jumping into a battle where we are outnumbered, when we've got a damned time machine. We've been visiting people through time for months, and we ain't got enough, so we shouldn't stop looking! If we've got all the time in the world, why don't we just keep gathering forces until we've got enough to sink Horatio's whole army in one go?"

"Mongrel," Calgori said, "We've been over this. If there are only five apples in a bowl, all the time in the world won't allow you to pull ten apples out of the bowl. We've simply asked everyone for help we know to ask, and we've mustered what we can muster."

"I just don't like jumping into a battle I know we are gonna lose!" Mongrel said.

"We don't know that," Lilith said, and she hoped she was right. "We have the element of surprise on our hand. Never before in the history of mankind has an entire army just appeared on a battlefield without warning. Imagine the effect that will have on the Imperial Navy."

"Imagine how it'll be for our guys! Time travel ain't exactly a nap in a hammock. Half our sailors might arrive dead or wounded!"

"I hope that will not be," Calgori said, but he was so obviously unsure about this that no one on the windswept bridge said anything after. "But since we already sent all those hundreds of men, ships and aircraft forward into the breach, it's only right for us to join them."

He then looked at his pocket watch, frowned, and

solemnly nodded to Lilith. She held tight to the captain's wheel, and he pulled slowly down on the Chrononautilus's activation lever.

Five hundred feet above the Change Cage city of Everglade a storm cloud quickly formed, and in the middle of it an old and weathered pirate ship appeared. Her crew were braced or tied down when she appeared with a thunderous clap of changing air pressure. Her propellers roared to life, and she pulled quickly out of the cloud.

Her crew were presented with a terrible scene. The city below them burned, its citizens running and screaming in terror. A perimeter of war machines surrounded the city, and at sea a vast force of nautical and aeronautical vessels launched volley after volley into the burning city.

Inside a Falling Tower

The Change Cage shuddered again, and then a huge disconcerting vibrating began. I ran to the corner of the tower, and looking down I saw that a huge part of the south side of the tower was breaking free, and sliding down into a cloud of dust on the ground. It wouldn't be long now before the tower collapsed entirely.

There were long lines of people and automatons running from the eastern doors of the building. Someone, perhaps Gyrod, must have opened the doors in the tower to free its captives.

How many will get out, before the tower falls? I thought.

I ran back to the edge of the basket that held Kristina, and found she was gone! Looking about in a panic, I saw what had happened. One of the horizontal posts that supported the bottom of the cage-basket had collapsed, and ripped a large hole in the bottom of the basket. Kristina must have seen this, and slipped through. There was nothing to do but follow Kristina into the collapsing tower.

I grabbed the edge of the basket, intending to hang and drop in, but as I did a shockwave rippled through the Change Cage, which knocked me off the wall into the basket. I scrambled to the hole in the floor, and slipped into the darkness below.

I fell only about three feet, and found I was in a crawlspace under the basket. At the edges of this space, there was a two-foot-wide hatch in the floor. This hatch was open. Kristina could have only got out that way, so I crawled towards it.

The hatch dropped into a hallway which ran along the the east side of the tower. On the inside wall were cell doors, slightly ajar. Windows lined the outer wall, and a dim light streamed through them. This light was regularly blackened by the shadow of a passing airship, or flared with bright light as something in the sky nearby burst into flame. The result was that the dusty clouds in the hall would flash, or darken, or ripple in the colors of fire outside the windows.

I looked to the ground, and saw a single line of bloody footprints leading down the hall. At the far end, I could see the silhouette of Kristina, staggering in pain and dragging herself. Over the sound of the battle outside the windows, and the rumbling of the collapsing tower, I heard her voice deliriously calling, "Victoria!"

I ran down the hall as best I could, though twice tremors in the tower sent me into the wall, and once nearly out of a window. As I passed each room I noticed they were empty. Only once did I see a person inside, and this person was long dead and rotting, chained to a cot and forgotten months ago. It was a grim sight.

I finally reached Kristina, who had not seen or heard me coming after her, just as elevator doors closed shut between us. I immediately hit the button to call another of the pneumatic elevators. In between elevator doors was a lit list of floors, each with a label. "69 - freelander's ward", "70 - toxic thought", "71 - political insurgents", "72 - nonconformists", "73 - mechanical engineers", etc. I saw my elevator was approaching my floor at a tremendous pace, while Kristina's seemed to stop a floor labeled "88 - Juvenile Wards 6-9 & Aeronautical Autonomy".

The elevator doors opened, and I quickly selected floor 88. In a very ungraceful way, the elevator dropped so fast I thought perhaps the cables had broken. In a few seconds a huge whooshing noise could be heard in the elevator shaft, and the elevator came to a stop at floor 88.

The doors opened, revealing that I had stopped three feet before arriving at the floor, so I sat on the edge of the elevator, and dropped into the juvenile ward. As I did, another huge shockwave rippled through the tower: I could literally see the wave like a wave in water rippling through the concrete floors of the ward. When the wave reached the elevator shafts, a huge gust of air hit me from the shaft and knocked me off my feet. The elevator, doors open, now fell out of sight. There would be no using that again.

I scrambled to my feet, and peered around through the clouds of dust, trying to see Kristina. She was leaning against a chain-link wall, peering into a nursery, calling "Victoria!"

I ran to her, "Kristina, we have to leave this building, it's collapsing!"

"Not until we find..." but another shockwave knocked her off her feet.

"This floor seems empty, Kristina. I don't think anyone is here. We need to leave!"

I put one of Kristina's arms over my shoulder, and tried to carry her as best as I could. But still she couldn't walk, her feet could not touch the ground without causing her great pain. Finally I put both her arms over my shoulders, held her legs at either side of me, and bore her on my back.

I ran down the halls, slipping in the dust, looking for

an elevator that was still functional. There was a door to a stairway, but looking down I saw the stairs had collapsed three floors below us and left behind a drop of several hundred feet. I backed carefully out of that stairway. With the elevators gone, and the stairs broken, I could think of no way out.

At the end of the hall were two large steel doors. There was a dingy plaque on the doors that read "Aeronautical Autonomy." Since the doors were ajar, and since there was nowhere left to go, I went in.

It was a huge room, perhaps thirty by fifty feet, with fifteen-foot ceilings. The far wall of the room had once been windows, but the glass was now broken, leaving a gaping hole. The floor was littered with hand tools. Pliers, hammers, and something that looked like a long shepherd's crook made of steel. In the center of the room were a series of large mechanical arms, with vise-grips for hands, and each was holding the partially constructed body of a harpy.

This was an assembly line, and at the end of the line was a nearly complete, though headless, harpy. Its airbag had been filled but it had broken free of its vise-clamp, and was rolling about on the ceiling.

Kristina shrieked when she first saw it, but I said, "Honey, I think it's dead." Then I added, "Actually, that could be our ticket out of here!"

I set the injured Kristina in a chair, and I grabbed the shepherds crook, but as I did so there was another large shockwave, the biggest yet, knocking me off my feet. I tried to stand, but had trouble finding my balance, as the floor was now at a small angle, and tools and dust were sliding down it.

I stood, and again I tried to run towards the harpy, but again I slipped. Steadily the angle of the floor was increasing! The tower was falling!

I jumped and hooked the harpy, but its buoyancy was too great, and I hung from the hook, while it stayed pressed to the ceiling.

"Kristina, you are going to have to run to me!" I said, as the harpy started to slide up the ceiling towards the north wall. Kristina stood, and with her last remaining strength, she ran. Not a slow stumbling run, but a full-out sprint, and she jumped for me and tackled me mid-air. The momentum of this, along with Kristina's added weight, knock all three of us, Kristina, harpy and myself, out of the south windows of the tower.

Here in the sky, hundreds of feet from the ground, I nearly lost my grip. Kristina's momentum had thrust us a good fifteen feet from the tower, and looking back I could see the tower was falling towards us.

"Kristina, grab the staff! Can you hold yourself up?"

"Yes, I think so," she said, and she did, wrapping both her arms and legs around the shaft as I grabbed the lower torso of the harpy and climbed into the space between its back and its airbag.

There was a panel in the harpy's back, and remembering the clockwork doll, Timony, I flung it open to reveal a large clock-spring, with a key in the center. I turned the key, and as I did the propellers on the harpy's back started to spin silently. I then leaned on the harpy's left shoulder, which pivoted us around to the right. Pushing downward on both shoulders thrust us forward.

And then the tower fell.

It was like watching a slow motion film of an accordion being dropped, floor after floor collapsing on itself, a cloud of beige concrete dust swallowing the tower from below.

I could hear the people watching, the people in the streets. I could hear them, even as the tower fell, even from this height. Horror is not the same as terror. The scream of horror is not filled with only fear, but also a shocked, angry injustice beyond what the soul can endure.

I could hear their screaming. I could feel it rend my heart.

Halfway through collapsing, the giant tower stopped folding in on itself, and toppled forward into the city. Block after city block was crushed. Thousands of apartments, and workhouses, and thousands of people were merged and mashed and crushed in the falling mountain.

And there was simply no room to escape.

Had this tower fallen in the plains, few would have lost their lives. Had it fallen in a farming community, perhaps dozens would have lost their lives. But in the center of a crowded city, tens of thousands died, crushed in their homes and work places.

A Drifting Buoy In A Storm

We clung to the corpse of the Harpy and watched the tower fall into the city, into the crowd, and we screamed and we cried. We cried until we could barely see, and our eyes stung. We cried until we stopped, and could think of nothing more.

I thought of our friends in the city below, and again I cried, and my chest was tight, and my arms ached as I clung to this aerial buoy. We cried until we stopped, and in its wake could think of nothing more.

But still the city burned. Tens of thousands of people, who were not directly crushed by the tower, were still trapped behind its walls.

Around us the skies were filled with clouds and fire, as airships fired cannon on each other, or fell burning from the sky. We were not a target, as to the warring ships I'm sure we were nothing but a broken piece of a destroyed automaton.

But there was no safety in that. Shots flew past us. Burning airships nearly dropped on us. A barrage of rolled mechapedes flew so close it spun us around, and we barely regained control as I watched the machines unravel and begin snipping Skypeople in two aboard their fragile and primitive airship.

Then, past the Sky Pirates rag-tag galley, and far above the battle, I saw the black balloon and gondola of the Grand Admiral's corsair. It sat so far aloft it was untouchable by any beast or automaton. The Grand Admiral must have been in that ship by now, staring down at the destruction he caused, like a malevolent god. I couldn't imagine if he thought this was a success, or if he was wondering what went wrong.

Then I wondered what had become of Chloe and Isabella. I looked to the walls of the city, far below, trying to spot the indrikkus that had held them. I saw many slain indrikkus on their sides, but none wearing a circus collar.

Then I saw the forces of the Neobedouin, and the armored Indian elephants of Chandra attacked the barricade of machines around the city's wall. The tanks were all aiming towards the walls, they did not expect an attack from the outside.

A front line of armored elephants, with swivel-mounted cannons on their backs, fired on the Grand Admiral's tanks. The cannon shots pounded the tanks, rendering the tank crew momentarily useless, but did little else to destroy the war machines. Then a squad of indrikkus sprinted clumsily towards the wall, leaping over elephants and tanks like hurdles. On the backs of the indrikkus sat Neobedouin Beast Dancers, and they released huge tethered shots into the walls of the city.

I then watched as the indrikkus pulled away, straining over the strength of the wall. The beasts then stumbled forward, as the wall folded and collapsed.

Next I saw, as I clung to this dead balloon, a line of horses, and camelops, and giant kangaroo and their riders pouring between wall and tanks. Their riders leapt from their mounts bearing hand axes, or katari, or just two-foot blades strapped to their forearms. They threw open the tanks and dropped inside.

Soon those tanks turned and fired on their own.

Then I saw outside the north of the city, on the ground outside the wall, a battalion of the Grand Admiral's foot-soldiers open fire on a group of Neobedouin, but as they did this, a pride of lions leapt from a cluster of trees nearby, and laid the soldiers on the ground, ripping their throats, and feasting on their bellies.

But as I watched, something hit us from above. The rear tail fin of a huge naval galleon had brushed us and sent us spinning, as the burning airship fell.

Our spinning lasted only a second, during which Kristina slipped and slid down the short shepherd's crook she clung to.

I grabbed Kristina by the wrist, "Come up here, I think you'll have a better hold." We pulled and strained, and finally got her up into the spot between the harpy's large brass body, and the balloon it hung from.

Our propellers had been bent in the impact, and began making scraping and sputtering sounds. I pushed forward on its shoulders, but its speed, when compared to the air war around us, was so slow I wasn't sure if we were moving at all.

I looked out to sea, and saw the armada of the United Tribal Navy of Africa turn and head into the Grand Admiral's navy. The cannon of Utnoa did little to pierce the sides of the modern warships, and the battle would have been lost, if not for the bravery of the African soldiers.

Their strategy seemed to be to pull their ships immediately adjacent to the armored naval ships. Then, tribal hunters and warriors would leap agilely from their comparatively primitive crafts, and storm into the vessels. Hand combat was vastly more gruesome 300 years ago, when the Utnoa trained, and the modern naval crews could not hold up in the close quarters inside the vessels. Soon most of the ships that threw the incendiary balls into the city had been stopped. Some were volleying their shots onto the decks of Horatio's destroyers.

One surprise I did not expect was this: one of the remaining fire-ships seemed out of reach of any Utnoa vessels. This was due to a trio of small armored and cannon-bearing boats around it. When any of the wooden Utnoa vessels got near, it would receive a pounding so hard it could not proceed to attack the fire-ship.

But as I watched, a ring of splashes erupted in the water around the fire ship. Out leapt two dozen mechanical mermen, nearly in unison. Their speed was so great they were in the air for several seconds, and at the height of their arches, they pulled release cords on their belts and ejected their mechanic tails. They landed on the deck, and pulled cutlasses from their belts, and slashed at the fire-ship's crew. In close quarters, swords are better than guns in holsters, and the Jypseas made quick work of the sailors.

In the end, the final fire-ship was extinguished, and much of the Grand Admiral's navy was now turning, confused, back to sea.

I looked towards the walls. Thousands of Neo-Victorians now flowed through dozens of massive holes in the walls of the city, and began to fill the prairies around it. They were greeted by Neobedouins, as the tanks of Horatio had now surrendered, or been captured.

In the skies around me, I saw many falling airships, of both the navy, and the sky people. I also saw many fleeing galleons and corsairs of the navy. As the battle on the ground turned against them, there seemed little reason to continue to fight in the skies. Nothing was under their control any more. Though many were killed in their attack, the battle was coming to an end.

But still we drifted. I looked to the ground, and saw what might be the Indrikkus that borne Chloe and Isabella.

From this chilly height it was hard to see the girls, but I thought I could make out a brightly-colored circus collar on one of the massive beasts. The beast stood calm and still by several other indrikkus, and there was a crowd of people talking on the ground in front of it.

I pushed on the shoulder of the Harpy, and turned it towards them, but then I realized I had no idea how to change altitude. The propellers spun and sputtered, and we slowly plodded forward, but I could not get us to go down.

"This...is too much," Kristina mumbled.

"What?" I said, trying to hear over the cannon fire, and distant screams, and other sounds of war.

"This is too much. It's too much to do. To much to see. I can't...I can't...anymore...."

Then Kristina exhaled long and slow, and she went limp next to me. She had finally given into exhaustion, and I could not tell if she was falling asleep, passing out, or giving up life entirely. Her eyes went soft, and closed, as she slipped into unconsciousness.

And then she let go.

When she started to slip, I cried out, "No!" and grabbed at her, releasing the shoulders of the harpy. She slipped off to one side of its torso, and I grabbed one of her arms, which sent the harpy into a slow spin.

My hands were shaking. I was gripping her too hard with one hand, while I held on to the harpy with the other. My nails were cutting into the skin on her arm, leaving long bloody gashes. I couldn't hold on any longer, the pain in my arms and back was more then I could bear.

A shadow slipped over us, and I cried out as my hands, without my permission, gave up and released her. Kristina slipped unconscious from my grip, and I saw her face disappear over the shoulder of the harpy.

Then something hit the harpy, and it spun fast. At this point I had only been holding on with one hand, and it was not enough. I was tossed up into the brass-armored balloon of the harpy, and my head hit so hard I momentarily lost vision and orientation. I slipped off the beast's corpse and fell.

Then I hit the ground.

But not ground. Not soil, not cobblestones, not grass. Wood. Wood decking. Familiar wood decking! I lifted myself to my knees, and saw a huge black hand reaching out for me, and I took it.

Nieroo pulled me to my feet, saying in his low rumbling voice, "Welcome back aboard the *Ophelia*, Captain."

At my feet, Kristina lay crumpled and unconscious on the deck. Around us stood Doctor Calgori, Mongrel, and Atoosh. There were other crew running around the deck, putting out fires with buckets of sand, or retying lanyards.

Lilith Tess ran over from the aft bridge, and Mongrel said to her, "I said we should pull close next to them, not smash into them like ya did!"

"I was doing my best," Lilith said, "to *catch* them. It

would have been no good to pull next to them, only to watch them fall."

"I say perfect timing, Lili." Calgori said. "Even a man such as you, Mongrel, can see that if she wouldn't have done that, Kristina would have fallen."

I looked at Calgori, and at Lilith, and at Mongrel, and I said, "Thank you for coming and getting us."

And I dropped back to my knees, exhausted. Honestly, I kind of needed a hug.

AFTER

Kristina was not dead. She was, however, unconscious. Exhaustion had overcome her. I stood with difficulty and tried to lift her, but I found my arms and back just did not have the strength left.

So Nieroo carried her gingerly to the cabins below deck, and Doctor Calgori followed to attend to her.

We flew silently over the wreckage. The sun was down completely, and the sky was starry and black. Parts of the city still burned, and I could see the silhouettes of automatons digging with their hands, trying to free people from the rubble.

I looked up at a crescent moon, and saw the Grand Admiral's corsair pulling away, and fleeing. Most of his navy had already left, and no one was still fighting. Perhaps the malevolent god was now confused as to what went wrong, or perhaps he considered this a success.

We dropped low now, until we were a few yards from the ground, and slowed to a stop near four indrikkus, one wearing a brightly-colored circus collar.

We tossed mooring lines to the nomads on the ground, and they tied us to several of the large mangroves that were growing in the marsh around the wall. Exhausted, but determined, I climbed down the rope ladders to the lower crow's nest, then down the final ladder to the ground.

There was a large circle of tanks, now bearing

Neobedouin tribal flags, and within this was a huge circle of people warming themselves around a massive fire. As I pushed through the crowd, I heard music.

When I broke into the clearing before the fire I saw what I least expected: dancing! Neobedouins, and Neo-Victorians, and Utnoa sailors were playing music and singing. There were sailors here from the 1800's, and Sky Pirates from 2154. There were Indians here from Chandra's army, Jypseas from the Flotilla, and tribal nomads from the wastelands. They were consoling, and counseling, the Neo-Victorians, who stood in shock to hear of their free life away from the city. "Freelander's disease", they learned, was not real, but freelanders were.

Titus was also there, as well as Josh, and Daniel, although his shoulder was badly bleeding. Gyrod had remained in the city, using his massive shoulders to help free people from the wreckage, but Timony sat by the fire watching the dancers and wishing she could stand.

Lilith walked over to Daniel, who rightfully looked like he was seeing a ghost, and when he overcame his shock he introduced her to Titus and Josh.

On the ground before the musicians many children sat, and sang along, or clapped. Tribal boys and girls, and Neo-Victorian children held hands, and were friends. As I walked closer, two of girls turned, and seeing me they stood, and ran to me.

As Chloe and Isabella hugged me, tears ran down my face.

Then Bella said, "We made new friends! This is Raphy, and Victoria! They say they knew Mommy!"

I met the family Kristina had lived briefly with, the fathers and brothers, and even Martha, who was now beyond confused, and trying hard not to look offended by all the different people and tribes she saw.

I also met Jenny, who said, "I suppose if your Kristina's husband, this makes us practically family. Like we're cousins. Is Kristina doing okay?"

"Yes. She's very tired, but she will be fine. I am going to make sure she sleeps for a least a week."

As the first light of the morning sun began to make the horizon glow dark gold, a white-haired, gravel-voiced Neobedouin shaman with an intricate facial tattoo sang,

> *After our days, and the fall of man*
> *One day this will heal again.*
> *Beasts crawl forth over desert clay*
> *Mankind will be nature's prey.*
>
> *The Ruined town breaks forth in vines;*
> *Trees, leaves, and fleet combine.*
> *Humankind will have lost its sway,*
> *The world again will be theirs one day.*
>
> *Skeletons of rust reach for the sky,*
> *Ruined empires of days gone by.*
> *Dreams of lives buried in the sand,*

RETROGRADE

The end of days will have been long planned.

Our children's children have passed away
Their auspicious lives lost in the fray.
Now carrion birds are all at play,
The world again will be theirs one day!

Nomadic tribes of the last of man,
Pull their caravans across the sand.
Jypsea wives hold their children tight,
As the new superpower howls through the night.

Gods watch from above and wonder what went wrong.
The entropy of what once was strong.
Now the survivors of man stay up late to pray
That the world will again be theirs one day.

And over their singing, from somewhere out past the firelight, I heard a wolf howl.

THE END